a

set

A High Sierra Mystery

TERRY GOOCH ROSS

outskirts press

A Twin Set
A High Sierra Mystery

v4.0

Outskirts Press, Inc.
http://www.outskirtspress.com

ISBN: 978-1-9772-5861-8

PRINTED IN THE UNITED STATES OF AMERICA

a twin falls
my heart grows by half again
Mary lives there

For my aunt
Violet Gerardi
who gave me my love of books

Acknowledgements

After my twin died, I found solace in writing fiction. It was a chance to spend time with her. *A Twin Set* is the last book in the series. It is preceded by *A Twin Falls*, *A Twin Pursuit*, and *A Twin Pique*. The support for this process was overwhelming. I will be forever grateful to those who have helped throughout this process for the generosity of time, patience, and willingness to share their knowledge. Without them, these books would not exist.

I begin with my friend and editor, Diane Eagle. Put simply, she taught me how to write. If you had read the first draft of the first book you would understand what an extraordinary achievement that was.

For this book I have consulted a few technical advisors, from explaining how to remotely blow up a house, to understanding how one is charged with a crime. They include: Ray & Karen Tupas, Judge Ed Forstenzer, my niece Lindsey Gooch, and my brother and sister-in-law Patrick Gooch and Roseann Scoloveno.

I was lucky to discover Jeff Mills, whose hobby is photography. While I was golfing at Mammoth's Sierra Star golf course, I took a picture with my iPhone of the Sherwin mountains. I thought it would be perfect for the cover. Unfortunately, it was a gray day; the picture turned out dreary. Jeff walked the golf course (I couldn't remember what hole I was on), replicated the photo, and gave it life and color. He also performed his magic with my iPhone pic of the author's picture.

Then there are the host of friends I ambushed with: "Would you just read this passage and tell me what you think?", to "It's a short book, it shouldn't take too long." They include my stepdaughter Erin Bulkley, my sister, Missy Stevens, my nieces Delaney Stevens and Anna Gooch, Denise Boucher, Sandi Forstenzer, Linda Delaney, Larry Todor, Susan Schaus, Jenny White, Kate McCormick, Maria Elisa Berenguer, my closest friend Pam Koslov, and, of course, my husband, Ross.

Finally, to the readers. Thank you.

DAY 1

J, the consultant

Through the fog of sleep, I heard Ross moving around our bedroom. It was early May, and thanks to a winter of atmospheric-river storms, the Eastern Sierra ski resort of Mammoth Mountain still had a snow base of 150 - 300 inches. Last night's storm brought with it a cruel reminder: winter wasn't over. And, of course, the storm meant that as a ski patroller, Ross had to be at work by dawn.

I moved deeper into our nest of quilts and pillows, anxious to keep hold of the threads of my dream, which seemed more important than morning. *My twin, Mary, and I were hiking on the eastern side of the Santa Cruz mountains, just minutes from Mary's home. Mary was talking like she always had when we hiked—nonstop. As we walked, I listened to the sound of her voice, paying little notice to content. It was comforting, like home. I smiled as a memory flashed of a time in our early twenties when I offered her twenty dollars if she would not utter a word for an hour. Of course she lost. Focusing my attention back on Mary, I realized she had quickened her stride—considerably. Soon I was in a dead run, struggling to keep up. In moments, she was out of sight—Mary's patter lost in wind and space. Gasping for breath, I croaked, "Mary! Mary, wait for me. Mary…"*

Rocking me in his arms, Ross made soothing sounds while I struggled to wake. My sobs turned to whimpers and soon quieted. It was *the* dream. My very real version of those stupid *Groundhog Day* movies, when the hero relives the same day over and over again until he gets it right. Though for me, there would never be a right.

A little over two years ago, my twin, Mary, her husband, Bob, and I had been in a plane crash. I was the only one to survive. The man who orchestrated the accident was now serving a life sentence in prison. Little consolation for his actions. But I did take solace in the gift Mary and Bob had given me. Occasionally they would visit—sometimes to rescue, often to warn or get me to do their bidding, and every once in a while, just to hang out. The downside of this miracle was that after the crash I never heard either of them utter a word again.

Following Ross into the kitchen, I sat half-asleep while he made me tea, and breakfast for himself. As he moved around the kitchen, I studied him. We had been a couple for a long time, but only moved in together ten months ago. We'd tried cohabitation early in our relationship with little success. But the events of the last few years had clarified our priorities, softened our edges, and deepened our bond. From the day he moved in, we knew it would work.

I never tired of watching him. Brown-haired, brown-eyed, he was built like a bodyguard and had the grace of a runner. This morning, however, his six-foot-two frame didn't move with its usual agility. He was winter-weary, as were most of those who lived in the Eastern Sierra town of Mammoth Lakes. Five months of nonstop snowstorms could have that effect. But those who worked outside on the mountain five days a week, ten hours a day, had taken the brunt of this endless winter.

"What's on your agenda today, J?" Ross asked, sitting down beside me.

"I'm having lunch with Brian at Couloir," I said without enthusiasm.

Ross's eyes widened. "Janet Westmore, you're having lunch with a good looking, charming, rich guy at his boutique hotel nestled in the Sherwin Mountains? A hotel, I might add, which has been nominated for several eco-awards… Oh, yeah. And the only thing to rival the views is the cuisine. Yet you sound like you're going to see your accountant?"

I glared at Ross for using my given name, even though I knew he was joking. I'd always hated my name and insisted everyone call me "J." He hugged me. I responded by burrowing into his embrace.

"From the way Brian framed his invitation, I suspect he has a job for me—of a sensitive nature."

"Your work is always sensitive. Don't you want to work for him?"

Ross was right. As a human resources consultant, I usually didn't get hired unless there was a messy conflict to be resolved. One of my more recent jobs involved a junior attorney who tried and almost succeeded in sabotaging his law firm.

"No, I like Brian. And I love my work. It's just this feeling I have."

Ross looked concerned.

I shook my head. "I sound pathetic. Ask me what's on my agenda again."

Ross complied.

"I'm having lunch with a hot dude in a romantic restaurant that happens to be located in a four-star hotel. And I may even have a glass of chardonnay with my meal." I raised my eyebrows up and down for effect.

Ross stood and left the room.

I was too stunned to move. Ross knew I was kidding. Didn't he?

Seconds that seemed like minutes passed before he returned. He found me as he had left me. I hadn't moved a muscle. He placed a small black velvet box in front of me. "Perhaps you should wear this to your lunch date."

I stared at the box.

When I didn't make a move Ross opened it, revealing the most beautiful ring I'd ever seen—a gold band inlaid with micro-pavé diamonds. "I bought this almost two years ago..." voice cracking, eyes filming over. "I've been waiting for the right moment." He broke into a wide grin. "And for some outrageous reason, this seemed like it."

Fifteen minutes later I was waving goodbye as he pulled out of the driveway on his way to work—the first rays of dawn glinting off the delicate ring on my left hand.

A trip to Couloir in the winter is always a bit of a production. I dressed in layers that included brown wool leggings, an ivory silk-wool turtleneck, and a thin gray cashmere crew-neck sweater. Downstairs in the mud room, I added brown leather gloves, an ivory wool scarf, my favorite black ski beanie, a silver down parka, and brown Ugg boots. I was prepared for the journey.

Exiting my garage, I found the sun and storm clouds battling for dominance. I hoped for a solar victory but wasn't holding my breath.

I drove the few miles to the base of the Sherwin Range of mountains that border the east side of town, and pulled into a small dirt parking lot surrounded by a thick forest of pine and fir trees. A valet magically stepped out from the trees, took my keys, and escorted me to a cozy looking sleigh towed by a snowmobile with a driver, rather than reindeer. All this happened as if the two valets had been standing in the forest waiting for me. In actuality, the garage and valet station—as well as the entire hotel complex— were housed in mirrored buildings nestled among the trees, which reflected the landscape, rendering them almost invisible. The roof of the building was tiered to match the slope of the mountain and was planted with flora native to the Sierra—currently covered in snow.

Once I was belted into the sleigh and draped with a blanket, the driver, who had been introduced as Frank, took off through the woods. It felt like Christmas. Moments later as we sped out of the trees, a collection of small and medium-sized mirrored dwellings came into view. Some of the smaller units seemed to be suspended from trees. It was hard to distinguish what was landscape and what was hardscape. Unbelievably beautiful. I'd been on this trip several times, and it still left me speechless.

We pulled up to the largest of the buildings. The storm clouds had temporarily won their battle with the sun, and snowflakes were starting to swirl in the wind. I hadn't overdressed.

Head down, I ran toward the lobby, only to collide with an angry woman exiting the building. She pushed me aside and ran toward the driver who'd brought me up the hill, screaming. "Frank! Don't you dare leave without me. I'm not staying here another minute." She was so angry, spittle flew from her mouth as she yelled.

I was struggling to regain my balance on the snowy stairs as they drove off, until strong arms grabbed me just as I was about to fall. "This wasn't exactly how I intended to start our meeting, J."

"I take it the angry woman is part of the reason you phoned?" I said to the tall, athletic, grinning man who was holding me upright.

"I'm afraid she is, but only a small part."

Inwardly I groaned my apprehension as Brian led me to Couloir's main entrance and through a giant wooden door. The landscape seemed to follow us inside. The expansive lobby décor was sparse yet inviting and could only be called mountain elegant. Tasteful wood furniture upholstered in forest greens and cobalt blues, glass and rock tables, bowls of fragrant spring flowers, and roaring fireplaces in every corner of the giant room highlighted the winter-spring Mammoth Lakes was experiencing.

I followed Brian through the lobby into a small dining room. A linen-cloaked table set for two was arranged in a corner. The table's centerpiece of red tulips and daffodils loosely arranged in a crystal vase contrasted with the snowy vista offered by the floor-to-ceiling windows.

"I thought it was best we meet in here. It provides some, er, privacy..." Brian hesitated, apparently seeking the right words.

His awkwardness was in conflict with my impression of him. He struck me as the quintessential business owner: professional, driven, and self-assured, almost to the point of being cocky. "Are you uncomfortable about meeting with me?"

His cheeks pinked. "It's not you. It's just that, well, I feel out of my element. I don't like losing control of a situation to the point I have to call in someone from the outside to ask for help. Ordinarily the management team deals with personnel issues. But I think the problem *is* the management team. Taylor, for example."

"Taylor?"

Brian gestured for me to sit down and took his own seat. "Taylor Hunter, our hotel services director, or should I say former director—the woman you encountered as..."

He was interrupted by a soft knock on the door. He whispered, "Our food & beverage director, she's delivering lunch. She seems to be at the core of the situation we'll be discussing this afternoon."

Before I could ask any questions, Brian opened the door to an attractive young woman pushing a large room-service cart.

"J, I'd like you to meet Aileen O'Toole. Aileen is responsible for all Couloir's food and beverage services."

She gave me a quick nod. Before me stood a woman in her mid-thirties, of average height clad in a white button-down, long-sleeved shirt and black pants. Jet black, shoulder-length hair was pulled back in a barrette at the nape of her neck.

Her skin was pale, yet flawless, her movements fluid. My first impression was professional, but something didn't jibe. Her back was straight, but her eyes were downcast. Once lunch was served, Aileen left without a word, never having established eye contact. *She is at the heart of whatever is making Brian so ill at ease?*

I started on the tomato-artichoke bisque, watching Brian order his thoughts as he stared at his soup.

Brian, the hotelier

My hands were sweating. What was wrong with me? I've built three successful hotels, led a board of directors, handled hundreds of management issues. Why was I so uptight about this particular problem? Sure, it was complicated, but what wasn't these days? Tackling staff problems wasn't my forte, but how hard could it be? I decided to start with the phone call that began this entire mess.

I took a deep breath. "When I was staffing Couloir, there were a couple of critical positions I had difficulty filling. One of them was the Food & Beverage Director. Don't get me wrong, there were several applicants, even our executive chef applied. But none felt right. My human resources manager was out of sorts with me because I couldn't describe what I was looking for. I just knew I'd recognize the person when I met him or her."

I watched J closely as I said, "I think an effective management team is more than just the experience or qualifications each brings to the table. It's about how they complement one another. Do you know what I mean, J?"

Nodding, J held my gaze. "I do, Brian. And I agree."

She passed the eye test. I believed her.

Swapping my barely touched soup for salad, I continued. "But we got down to the wire. Opening was a few weeks away and the position was still vacant. Just as I considered lowering my expectations, I got a call from Patrick, the general manager of my first hotel, Les Bosses. He told me he thought he had the perfect candidate. She'd started working for a reputable Colorado restaurant as a hostess, and in a little over three years worked her way through every position to become manager. A high-end restaurant in Aspen stole her away, where she'd been the operations manager for the last two years. Under her leadership the restaurant earned its first Michelin Star. When I asked why she would want to leave such an obviously successful posting, Patrick said she grew up in Mammoth and was anxious to return home. But Patrick got my full attention when he said, 'She's not only perfect for the position, she's also the best person I know...' I was excited until he added, 'But, there are just a couple of *issues* you need to be aware of before you decide whether you want to meet with her.'"

J and I were at the critical point. I re-established eye contact. "Patrick is the best person *I know.* He was with me from the beginning when Les Bosses was little more than a dream, and I've always relied on his input. He puts the best interests of the hotels and me first. I would trust him with my life."

I felt J's eyes on me as I dropped my head and stared at the table, remembering. My memory was loud, the room was silent. The only sound came from the ice melting in the water pitcher.

It could have been seconds or minutes before J asked,

"Brian… the couple of issues?"

Looking up at J, all I could think was how crazy the whole situation seemed. "In Patrick's words… 'She spent four years in prison for embezzlement, and she's my twin sister.'"

Her only reaction was a slight widening of the eyes. And I wasn't sure whether that was in response to the crime or the relationship.

"We're talking about Aileen O'Toole?"

"We are."

Instead of asking another question as I expected, J sat back in her chair, attentively waiting for me to continue.

"As I said, I trust Patrick. So, I asked for Aileen's cell number and gave her a call. She flew out two days later for an interview. Initially she appeared docile, almost meek. But as our conversation turned to how her restaurant experience made her a good candidate for director of food & beverage, she came alive. I hired her on the spot and have not been disappointed. Patrick was right. She's perfect for the job. When she arrived, she took charge. Opening day was a success, despite almost every unforeseeable thing going wrong…"

Pictures of opening day streamed before me. "I was on edge more than normal. I knew I had invited way too many people. Then just hours before the party was to start, power in the kitchen went out. By the time we found and solved the problem, there was no time to heat the hors d'oeuvres. The ovens were needed for dinner preparation. When I asked Aileen if we had enough cold appetizers to cover the loss, she motioned for me to follow her to the large deck encircling most of the hotel's lobby and dining areas. All the firepits had been converted to small open grills, with a staff member manning each—shrimp grilled at one station, quiche at another. There were seven in all. Aileen also restaged the bars to be more convenient to the grills. The combination of the views, crisp mountain air, and hospitality was a hit. Better yet, no one knew it wasn't planned.

"She's continued to excel at every other event we've held, as well as day-to-day operations. The changes she instituted in Food & Beverage have been implemented in the other two hotels with great results. What's even more amazing is that if any of her key staff are sick, she is able and willing to fill in for them, even our executive chef."

I sat back in my chair, mentally reviewing all of Aileen's successes. "J, next to her brother, Aileen is the best hire I've ever made."

J grinned at me. "And this is the *problem* you need help with?"

"Ahh," I sighed. "No, that would be the group of influential community members who have withdrawn their business as long as Aileen works here, not to mention the two sexual harassment claims filed against her—one by our bartender, and the other by Taylor, the woman who almost knocked you down when you arrived."

J responded, unflustered, "Sounds interesting. How do you want to proceed?"

J, the consultant

Customers boycotting? Sexual harassment? Sounded like a lot of drama for one employee, no matter how good she was. But he believed in her. I asked Brian how he wanted to proceed.

In response, he went to a side table in the room, pulling out two identical iPads from its single drawer. He handed me one. "You'll find all the relevant documentation: Aileen's personnel file, copies of letters from customers withdrawing support for Couloir, the employee complaints with investigation reports, and notes from meetings I had concerning these issues. In addition, I included the notes from the last six months of management team meetings. I thought we could hit the highlights then you could take the tablet with you to review."

Accepting the computer, I said, "I assume internet access has been disabled."

Brian beamed at me. "Besides no internet access, these tablets don't have copying or print-screen capabilities. We take employee confidentiality very seriously..." A knock at the door cut him off midsentence. Glancing at his watch, he said sheepishly, "It's already three o'clock." I scheduled a call for three. Do you mind reviewing Aileen's file while I take this call? I shouldn't be long, then we can outline our plan."

Before I could tell Brian to take his time, the door shut behind him.

With a deep sigh, I cleared my thoughts and prepared for the emotional incontinence that always seemed to accompany complaints and accusations.

Aileen's personnel file provided substance to Brian's brief outline. Aileen was sixteen when she began a part-time position at Reynolds Home Care. After graduating from high school, she moved to full time. A little over seven years later she was arrested and convicted for embezzlement. While in prison she took a variety of culinary and restaurant management classes. At twenty-nine, she was released, moved in with her brother, and went to work for a restaurant in Aspen. For the next five years she paid restitution for her crime, took more classes in restaurant management, and gained practical experience in every aspect of the business. References from both Aspen restaurant owners she worked for confirmed she was not just fluent in dining arts, she was gifted.

Next came Brian's press release announcing Aileen's appointment as Couloir's Food & Beverage Director. It was a glowing summary of her background—avoiding, of course, any mention of her incarceration.

This document was followed by a series of emails all sent within a twenty-four period—dated two days after the announcement was published. They were from Fred and Maureen Reynolds. After a summary of their mutual civic club memberships, mention of their shared relationships with Mammoth's "most influential," and a list of events they had held at Couloir, they wrote:

"It's clear to us, dear friend, you are unaware that Ms. O'Toole embezzled significant funds from our company while working as our office manager. It was particularly devastating because we treated Ms. O'Toole more like a member of the family than an employee. We are surprised she did not mention this on her application, or you did not learn of it during her background check. We can provide you with the details of her crime if you so wish.

Now that you are aware of her betrayal, and what it says about her character, we are certain you will rescind your employment offer."

Next came Brian's terse reply.

"Actually, I was aware of the incident long before I interviewed Aileen. While I appreciate your concern, the matter you refer to is in the past, and she has paid both in time and restitution. Given your previous relationship with Aileen, I am sure you will be pleased to know that she is a hardworking, multi-talented manager with a promising future."

The Reynolds' response came within minutes.

"Brian, you know we are only looking out for your best interests. Ms. O'Toole fooled us, too. For your own sake,

we think you should seriously consider getting rid of her before you pay the same price we did."

Again, Brian answered immediately.

"Thanks, but I am confident in my decision to hire Aileen, her ability to succeed, and the contribution she will make to Couloir's reputation."

It was several hours before the next email.

"You give us no choice. We will no longer patronize Couloir. We will also inform the numerous civic organizations we participate in of the situation to ensure that no events will be held at the hotel. We will send you a list of events already scheduled, so they may be canceled. We cannot believe you would sacrifice the good will of the community that has supported you since the opening of Couloir for a cheap embezzler."

Brian simply wrote back.

"I would rather support an individual whose integrity is evident by how she paid for her mistakes then built a career when the odds were stacked against her than priggish blackmailers."

Reeling from the email exchange, I slumped back in my chair. The electronic encounter had taken place last year, just after our Labor Day golf tournament. It was hard to believe in a town as small as Mammoth Lakes I'd never heard the slightest hint of this conflict, especially since it involved such prominent people. Brian was a hospitality star; Fred and his wife Maureen were on just about every board and committee in town. And despite the threats, to my knowledge the hotel and restaurant were almost always fully booked. What was I missing?

The door opened. A smiling Brian said, "Sorry the call took so long. How far have you gotten?"

When I looked up at him, mouth open, wide-eyed, he answered his own question. "Ah, I would guess you're reading the Reynolds and my emails."

"So, what happened?" I demanded. "They couldn't have acted on the threat, you're too successful. Besides I've seen lots of people from the Chamber, the Foundation, Lions Club dining here."

"Oh, they followed through. I received several calls during those first few weeks. Most, outraged that I would knowingly hire a felon, especially one who had violated the trust of important Mammoth citizens." Gazing trance-like out the window as lights began to twinkle on in town, he added with a smile, "But others like our police chief, the head of the ski area, restaurant owners in town, people who make Mammoth what it is, all communicated their support for my decision."

"So did the Reynoldses back down?"

"No, Fred and Maureen, their family, and some of their closer friends never come up to Couloir, regardless of who's hosting an event. Occasionally they try to make it an issue again, but no one pays attention."

"You and the Reynoldses must still be members of the same groups. That must be awkward."

"Actually, I'm on boards with both Fred and Maureen. Fred and I are able to work together quite well, as if the exchange never happened. But not Maureen. Anytime I participate she blocks, interrupts, and disagrees. It's something I should have dealt with early on, but I decided it wasn't worth the angst."

"Does Aileen know about the boycott?"

"Not from me, though she may have heard rumors around town." Brian paused then mumbled more to himself than to me, "I hope not. She's suffered enough."

Tearing his eyes from the window, he said, "But I kept you a lot longer than I was planning. I'm sorry. I suggest you finish reviewing the file at home, and call when you're ready to discuss a plan of action."

Standing, I felt the stiffness of sitting so long. "Good idea. But first, what are you hoping to achieve by engaging my services?"

Brian searched for an answer in the ceiling beams. I stretched as I waited for his response. Finally, he looked at me, melancholy etched in his features. "J, I want a management team that finishes each other's sentences, helps one another out, believes in each other, owns and solves problems as a team. Not one that files spurious complaints against one another."

Brian, the hotelier

I snuck a couple of miniature Armagnac bottles I keep for guests into J's bag as I helped her into the hotel sleigh and gave the snowmobile driver the signal to take off. It was a cold ride down the mountain, and I hoped she would discover the French brandy when she got home. The Armagnac and a warm fire would take the chill off. Besides, I'd thrown a lot at her in a few short hours, and she hadn't yet read the details of the sexual harassment complaints.

When I returned, I walked through the kitchen to my office. Aileen was deep in conversation with Missy Stewart, our executive chef. They both looked up as I approached. I apologized for the interruption and asked Aileen to come and see me when she was through.

I began to relax as soon as I entered my office. No decorator had been in this sparsely furnished room. With my father's old farmhouse desk and guest bench at its center, it felt like a little bit of home. I studied the single photo on my desk, as I did whenever I needed a reminder of why I was so driven: A couple stood with their arms around one another, smiles of anticipation on their faces. My mother and father in front of a well-worn, vacant country inn. Dad and Mom fulfilling a lifelong dream: to own and operate a small hotel in France. Halfway through the renovation, a leaky gas tank valve ended their dream and their lives. I was finishing my senior year of college when I learned of the tragedy. There and then I dedicated myself to finishing what they had started. The three pictures on the walls were *our* legacy—each of my hotels on opening day: Les Bosses, Les Pistes, and Couloir. French names, a further tribute to their dream.

My mood took a hit when I noticed a post-it stuck to the back of my desk chair. It was from Sierra, the human resources manager. "*Guess you're not listening to voice mail or reading texts. Taylor texted to say she quit. Do you have any idea what that's all about? Want to talk to you before I return her message. I hope this doesn't have anything to do with the investigation. You know I'm supposed to be in on all the meetings related to both complaints. I worked with our worker's compensation carrier all morning, and now I'm off to a Chamber of Commerce meeting. Hope you have time first thing in the morning to meet.*" It was signed, *S.T. 2 p.m.*

Tomorrow was going to be a long day. Sierra always became annoyed when I deviated from a plan of action. She was going to be one unhappy person in the morning.

Twenty minutes later there was a soft knock on the door. Aileen had arrived, and I was ready for the last and most awkward task of the day.

"Is it true Taylor quit today?" she asked tentatively.

"Yes. That was part of the reason I wanted to see you before you left for the evening."

She furrowed her brow as she absentmindedly sat on the bench. "Did you receive the harassment investigation results today?"

"Yes, the investigator phoned last night and asked if she could meet with me a couple of days early. Her reports were finished, and she wanted to get back to her office in Sacramento where another case is waiting for her. We reviewed the reports and her findings for both complaints. Somehow, Taylor found out about the meeting and demanded to hear the conclusions directly from the investigator. I saw no reason why not. Given how she reacted, it may not have been my best decision."

Aileen folded in on herself, placing her head in her hands. "I guess the investigation didn't turn out as she had hoped."

"Of course not. Clearly, I'm not having an affair with you, and you didn't receive preferential treatment when I gave you a bonus in January. You earned it and more after what you accomplished over the holidays. The praise is still pouring in from our guests, especially the four bridal parties, and from the New Year's Eve gala." I was about to add a smart-ass remark about the time, money, and disruption spent on hiring an independent professional investigator when I noticed Aileen was trembling.

I knew not to approach her—Aileen is a very private person and does not like her space invaded. I assume this is a remnant of her time in prison. I remained behind my desk and asked. "Are you all right?"

When she looked up at me, I could see tears in her eyes. She held up her hand as if to ask for a moment. I left the room and came back with bottles of cold water, placing one on the bench next to her.

A few minutes and sips of water later, she said, "Sorry."

My response came out of my mouth a bit too loudly before I could stop myself. "What do you have to apologize for? All you did was your job—an outstanding one at that—and the result was having your success demeaned by claims of favoritism. I, for one, am pissed. The investigator, a lawyer from Sacramento who specializes in harassment law, could find no evidence of the slightest impropriety. And, believe me, she spoke with a lot of people."

Aileen's posture straightened during my tirade, but she continued to look at her hands clasped tightly in her lap. In a voice that was low and betrayed little emotion, she said, "You shared the results with Taylor, she quit, and you did nothing to stop her."

I wasn't certain whether it was a question or statement but answered anyway. "That about sums it up. I'll get the management team together tomorrow so we can discuss coverage and replacement."

"I think you should call Taylor and ask her to reconsider her resignation," she suggested so softly, I had to ask her to repeat it.

"Why would I do that?"

Still looking at her hands, she answered. "Because she's very good at what she does. She will be almost impossible to replace. She cares about Couloir and the guests. And, from her perspective, she most likely saw you hire an unknown ex-con for a high-level position. Then, she somehow found out about the bonus you gave me, while she received none when she works just as hard, if not harder, than I do."

Without another word, Aileen stood up to leave.

"Don't you want to know about Matteo's complaint? The results? What he had to say after we met?"

She shook her head. "No, thank you. Good evening."

Aileen, the food & beverage director

Heading to the locker room, I felt the familiar weight of frustration. Whenever things were going well, something bad happened. And, just like every time before, the litany of life's disappointments dominated my thoughts.

My introduction to loss came when I was seven. About a week before Patrick's and my birthday, mom told me she and I were going someplace special to celebrate. Just the two of us. I asked about Patrick, because it was his birthday too, but mom said it was going to just be "us girls." It was supposed to be a secret, but I couldn't stop myself; I told Patrick, I was so excited. When the day arrived, I got up really early—it was still dark, put on my best dress, and quietly went to the kitchen to wait for her. After the sun was up for a while, daddy came into the kitchen. He wasn't smiling. He told me he was taking Patrick and me to the park, so I should change. I asked him where mom was. He said, "Your mother needed to take a timeout for a while." I tried to explain mom and I had a special day planned, but he got upset and told me to wake Patrick and get into my play clothes. Two weeks later we moved to Mammoth, without mom.

All the way to Mammoth, dad told Patrick and me how lucky we were to be moving to the mountains. It wasn't good to live in the city. Too many distractions. We would learn to ski, hike, fish, and camp. I started to ask when mom was coming, but Patrick squeezed my hand real hard to stop me. Dad didn't say another word for the rest of the trip.

For the first few weeks, the three of us had fun. Dad found a small condo near the elementary school, and he enrolled us for the fall, which was almost a month away. He would look for work once we started school. Then we went exploring. Dad was happy that summer, but as the days got shorter and the weather turned cold, he got quiet and sad. He'd go to work, come home, and sit in front of the TV. Patrick and I cleaned the house and made the meals—mostly cereal and peanut butter and jelly sandwiches—until we learned how to make other things. By the time we turned eight, dad had pretty much quit talking to us at all. Until the day I was arrested. As the police were taking me away, he unceremoniously announced, *"I guess you're more like your mother than I thought."*

As I changed my clothes, thoughts transitioned to the Reynolds family. I started working for Reynolds Home Care part-time when I was in high school. It was a great job. I started by running errands, cleaning houses, placing rental ads. Mr. Reynolds was the perfect boss. He was constantly teaching me new tasks. At his encouragement I enrolled in some accounting classes. When I graduated from high school, he trained me to take over Mrs. Reynolds' job as bookkeeper. Eventually, I ran the office—until twenty-five-thousand dollars went missing from one of the business accounts, and Mr. Reynolds and I were the only ones with access or opportunity.

I needed to stop thinking. The worst thing I could do was fall down the rabbit hole again. Walking through the lobby toward the garage-transport station, I turned my attention to the hotel's panoramic views. Their beauty was always calming. That's when I noticed a couple on one of the decks, hand in hand, looking over the railing. It was snowing lightly, as it had been doing periodically throughout the day. The pair didn't seem to notice the snow, even though neither was wearing a jacket or sweater. They just stared at the town lights below. I grabbed two of the afghans we have stashed around the lobby for guests who are unprepared for the weather and went outside. At first, I thought it was the woman Brian introduced me to when I served them lunch today, but when they turned, I saw it wasn't her—though they could be sisters. The couple was in their late thirties, both athletically built, both brunettes. He stood well over six feet, she around five foot seven. They accepted the proffered blankets with such warm smiles, it made me smile. As I reentered the hotel, I felt we'd just had a conversation without words. Oddly comforted by the experience—I was no longer preoccupied with my history of disillusionment. Turning to get one last glimpse of them, I saw only the afghans, sprinkled with snowflakes, draped over the railing.

J, the consultant

There was no wait for the sleigh to the garage; I was its lone passenger. Glancing back at the hotel, I thought I saw Mary and Bob standing on the lobby deck watching me. Stretching around to see if it was them, I almost fell out of the sleigh. Fortunately, I was strapped in tight. Then we entered the trees, and the hotel was out of sight.

The spring snow made it particularly cold on the way back to the garage. Once dropped off next to my Subaru, I got in, cranked the heat up to maximum, and drove to the grocery store. Earlier this morning delivery pizza had sounded fine to both of us for dinner, but as the delicate diamond ring on my left hand confirmed, this was a special day that called for a more proper meal. One of our favorites was roast chicken, and that was what we would have. Besides, cooking would give me a chance to think—and I had a lot to think about.

By the time I'd unpacked the groceries and found two little bottles of Armagnac—*thank you, Brian*—I was dizzy with questions. Was Aileen really an embezzler? Her conviction was strong evidence she was. Were the sexual harassment claims against her legitimate? I poured myself a glass of Brophy Clark chardonnay and started to brine the chicken.

The trick to not becoming overwhelmed at the beginning of a job is to focus on the primary objective. In this case it was to build a strong management team for Couloir. As I peeled and sliced the potatoes, it became evident that reading Aileen's file should happen *after* I had a clearer understanding of Couloir's work culture. Though unquestionably a key component of the current situation, her issues should not drive the process. I turned the oven to five hundred degrees and butterflied the chicken. By eliminating some of the drama from the equation, it appeared this could be a more interesting assignment than I first thought.

Just as I finished rubbing the chicken with a tarragon-butter mixture and placed it on top of the potatoes, my cell buzzed with a text from Ross. He said he was running late; and, asked if he should pick up a pizza. I texted him back it was all taken care of, and there was a cold martini waiting for him in the freezer. I placed the chicken in the oven and went to change out of my work clothes.

I heard Ross come in as I was putting on a pair of jeans and a new moss-green sweater—hoping he would notice it showed off the green in my hazel eyes. I found him in front of the fire with his martini in one hand, and a refilled chardonnay in the other. He looked exhausted.

"Smells like you decided to forgo the pizza. Must be a special occasion."

I dangled my left hand in the air.

He grinned, then fell more than sat on the couch.

"Long day?"

He nodded. "We got a call just as the mountain was closing that we had a lost twelve-year-old, last seen at the Mill restaurant for lunch by his parents. Scott—that's the kid's name—asked if he could ski for a while by himself because they were too slow and didn't want to go on any of the 'good runs.' They agreed as long as he returned to the bottom of Chair 2 by three o'clock. After waiting half an hour for Scott and not getting any response on his cell phone, they started taking turns going to look for him while the other waited at the meeting place. When they still couldn't find him, they called Patrol." Ross took a slow sip of his drink.

"Where did you find him?"

"We didn't." This time he took a bigger sip.

"Somebody must have, or you wouldn't be home. What happened?"

"While we searched, Scott's parents waited in the patrol room. After a while, mom went back to the condo to get her inhaler for her stress-induced asthma. That's where she found him, playing video games."

"His parents must have been embarrassed."

"And angry. Scott's father asked if Scott could come to the patrol room tomorrow and do chores for the day. When we explained the room was a restricted area, he made a five-hundred-dollar donation to our end-of-the-season party and asked for the name of every patroller who looked for his son. When I asked why, he told me Scott would spend tomorrow writing individual apologies."

Over dinner I gave Ross an edited version of my meeting

with Brian, eliminating any reference to the two sexual harassment charges. Ross had lived in Mammoth much longer than I had so I was most interested in his take on Fred and Maureen Reynolds. When I described their demands, and Brian's responses, Ross was visibly surprised.

"That sounds nothing like the Fred Reynolds I know. Fred's always been the guy you could call in the middle of the night for help, and he would come. He's either started or led every civic group in town and is on the boards of most of the nonprofits. Years ago, long before I moved to town, his sister and her husband were killed by a drunk driver coming back from dinner in June Lake. Fred took in their two boys who were elementary school age and raised them as his own. The oldest, Mike, is one of the rental shop managers on the mountain. He thinks his dad is the greatest in the world, and I've never seen any evidence that he's not."

"Are you sure there aren't two Fred Reynolds in town?" I asked, dumbfounded.

"Not who have a home care and rental business and a wife named Maureen."

Ross started clearing our plates as I continued grilling him. "Tell me about the family. What's Maureen like? Is it just the two boys, or do they have children of their own?"

He returned from the kitchen with the two little bottles of Armagnac, saying, "Let's open these and sit in front of the fire."

I poured the brandy into snifters while Ross positioned my favorite wingback chairs facing the fireplace. Once he revived the fire with a few logs, we sat next to one another, as we did most snowy nights, and rested our stockinged feet on the hearth. Before I could reinitiate the interrogation, Ross took my left hand, kissed my ring finger, and said, "I'll answer all your questions in the morning. I promise."

Brian, the hotelier

After Aileen left, I stared at my desk. A couple of hours' work stared back. Normal workdays ended around seven, when I would take a tour of the facility, often stopping in the bar for a drink, and sometimes the restaurant for dinner. Today had not been a normal day. I justified closing the computer by telling myself I needed to check in on Matteo.

I was still confused about Matteo's accusation of sexual harassment against Aileen, and now that the investigation was concluded, I could talk to him about it. Matteo had been with Couloir since it opened. I'd lured him away from another bar in town. He was the perfect lead bartender—tall, good looking, charming—and he could run the full bar when it was packed with no assistance if he had to, without complaint by the customers or by him. He was born in Mammoth to a French mother and a Spanish father—both ski instructors on the mountain. Which meant he could converse fluently with many of our non-English-speaking international guests. His only downsides were his fondness for women of every age, and his disdain for cleaning up at the end of an evening. Which brought me back to the question, why would someone, who never saw a woman he didn't like, accuse his quite attractive supervisor, who guarded her personal space with a vengeance, of coming on to him? It didn't fit.

Entering the bar, I passed a table of six whose attire and excited conversation confirmed they had been skiing all day. There was a smattering of couples at the window tables, watching the snow dance in the fading light, and a few singles at the bar, looking at their phones. Nodding at Matteo, I sat at the end of the bar closest to the kitchen and away from the guests. Within moments he placed a tall vodka and soda and a bowl of warm cashews in front of me—just the way I liked them, sweet and salty with a hint of rosemary.

"Hi, Boss. Sounds like you had a bittersweet day. Rumor is Taylor's sexual harassment complaint was dismissed and then she quit." He rolled his eyes and added with a wry grin, "Don't worry, I'm not going to follow her."

I looked around the room to make sure Matteo wasn't needed by any of the guests, then quietly said, "You know, whenever a complaint is filed against me or any of my managers, I always remove myself from the process and hire an outside investigator. It's important staff know the probe will be fair and the results unbiased."

Matteo's face turned serious. "I know, Boss, you explained it to me when…" His eyes left my face and studied an invisible speck on the bar. "…I um, made my um, my claim." His discomfort vanished as quickly as it had appeared. He smiled as he looked at me and said, "I have no complaints." He chuckled at his play on words.

His easy manner helped to relieve some of the tension I was holding in my neck and back. "Now that your process is over, I would really like to hear what happened with Aileen that made you file…"

I was cut off mid-sentence by a couple approaching the bar, speaking in loud, rapid French. While I couldn't understand a word, they seemed more excited than angry. Matteo turned to his customers. By the pair's delighted expression, they had to be acquainted. As he made his way toward them, Matteo said something to me over his shoulder. All I heard was, "Easy, Boss, … said I should do it… didn't want … down." The few phrases I heard didn't make sense. But I snapped back to my surroundings as most of the bar crowd ran over to one of the windows while the French woman yelled, "*Regarde l'ourse et ses petits*!" I was clueless until other guests started pointing outside with shouts of "bear" and "cubs". Ahh. The magic of the Eastern Sierra in spring. I would postpone my chat with Matteo.

Aileen, the food & beverage director

I had every intention of driving home but found myself in the parking lot of Bleu—my favorite bar, eatery, and market. At some level I knew I would be climbing the walls if I was alone in the house, even though it hadn't been a conscious decision. Today had been long and emotional. Worst of all, I'd criticized Brian to his face, and cried in front of him. Some truffle mac and cheese and a glass of sauvignon blanc seemed like a perfect antidote to a bad mood.

The entry was crowded with people waiting for a table or takeout, but I headed to the bar, hoping to find a vacant seat. As I slipped by a young couple and their daughter, someone behind me roughly grabbed my arm. The tension I held in all day surged through me. I turned, then felt all emotion leave my body. I was face to face with Maureen Reynolds. The one person I had successfully avoided since my return to Mammoth.

"Why did you come back?" she yelled loudly through clenched teeth. "Have you no shame?"

The waiting patrons went still. Everyone was looking at me. I was paralyzed with panic. It felt like all the air had been sucked out of the room. I wanted to run but couldn't.

"It wasn't enough to steal thousands of dollars from Fred and me, now you're sleeping with your boss. You *do* realize Couloir's best manager quit because of your..."

Theresa Brocia, half of the couple who owns Bleu and a new friend, gently pried Maureen's fingers off my arm. Without acknowledging Maureen or the scene she'd created, Theresa said, "Aileen, there you are. I've been saving a seat for you at the bar." I burned with embarrassment as she took my arm and guided me through the crowd.

I tried to thank her as she sat me down, but the lump in my throat and tears spilling down my face made it impossible. She ordered me a glass of white wine, then whispered she'd be back in a bit. She said something to the bartender, which included a glance in the direction of Maureen who was in animated conversation with her companions.

In addition to public humiliation, my encounter with Maureen took me back ten years—a place I tried never to go. Standing in court with a public defender at my side, I believed the jury had seen through all the biased testimony and knew my arrest had been one big mistake. I was so positive, I was almost giddy with excitement to have the trial over. When the guilty verdict was announced, I was so shocked I sat down in my chair and threw up all over my shoes.

A hand on my back startled me back to the present. I cringed then decided I must face Maureen and let her finish her tirade. Because I was sure that's who it was. I just wanted to get it over with.

Hoping I wouldn't get sick, I turned to face her, but it was the young girl who had been waiting with her parents in the reception area when Maureen confronted me. Whatever she saw in my eyes caused her to take an apprehensive step backwards. I held up my hands, "I'm sorry. I thought you were…"

Her face lit up. "I know," she said earnestly. "You thought I was the bully."

Nodding in affirmation, I noticed her hand was still resting on my shoulder. She appeared to be around thirteen. Her long blond hair, green-blue eyes, petite frame, and air of determination made her look like a princess from a Disney movie. I couldn't help but smile.

"I know you're older than I am," she continued, "but I thought you might want to hear how I handle bullies."

I saw her peek over her shoulder toward a bench in the front of the restaurant where two faces watched our interaction. Her mother, an older version of the princess, was nodding encouragingly. Her father, a big guy who clearly spent time working out, was flashing a *that's my kid* grin to anyone who was interested. And with some embarrassment, I realized many of the patrons were listening.

Focusing on the child and not the room, I asked, "I would really appreciate your advice, but first, may I ask your name?"

"I'm Lissa. Lissa Cole. Pointing to her parents, she said, "That's my mom, Alysa, and my dad, Jon."

Extending my hand, I said, "My name is Aileen."

Lissa's handshake was surprisingly strong, as if shaking the hands of adults was a frequent occurrence. Even before she let go, she began speaking.

"Never back down from bullies, that only gives them power over you. Of course, if the bully is going to hurt you, you may want to find an adult to help." As if hearing her words, she giggled, "I guess you are an adult, Aileen."

We both laughed, and then Lissa turned serious again. "Mom says that how you look at a bully is more important than what you say. She told me to look straight into the bully's eyes, so you look confident and brave. It shows you can't be intimidated." She smiled again. "And it works, I tried it, and it really works. Let me tell you about it…"

Lissa's mother gently interrupted her. "Our takeout is ready, and daddy is paying the bill. Besides, I think this lady probably wants to order dinner."

Lissa looked a little deflated but said, "Okay. Mom, this is Aileen, and I told her almost all the things you told me about bullies." Then she gave me a hug, and whispered in my ear, "If the bully still won't go away, call my dad, Jon Cole. He's a cop."

Hand in hand, mother and daughter joined dad and left the restaurant.

Twenty minutes ago, I thought this had been one of the worst days of my life, and now I wasn't so sure.

Day 2
J, the consultant

A sound alarmingly similar to a snowplow startled me awake. I refused to open my eyes to confirm what I knew to be true: it had snowed all night. I reached over for Ross only to discover rumpled sheets cool to the touch. The house was still. No sounds of a shower running or Ross moving around in the kitchen. He had already left for work.

I donned a pair of sweats and went to make a cappuccino on my DeLonghi—a habit and machine I acquired from a neighbor who stayed with me last year after her house blew up. Next to my mug was a note from Ross, unnecessarily explaining his need to go into work early because of the weather and promising to share all he knew about the Reynoldses when he got home tonight.

As I debated about having a second coffee, my cell came to life with the repetitive sound of a golf ball falling into the cup. It was a ringtone to remind me summer would eventually arrive. It was Kate, my twin Mary's former assistant and dear friend, and since the plane crash, one my closest friends.

Before I could say hello, she started, "Have you set a date? Do you like the ring? Were you surpri…?"

I interrupted. "How did you know? It just happened yesterday."

"Ross called. He was pretty excited…" Kate paused. "Why didn't *you* call and tell me?"

As I struggled for an answer, she laughed, "Oh, don't worry. Just tell me all about it. How did he propose?"

I put her on speaker, making a second cappuccino while I gave her the details.

The conversation was winding down when she said, "Your engagement is not the only reason I phoned. I have a favor to ask."

"Anything."

"You better hear what it is before you agree. It's not just for me, it's for *Hope For Our Children*. I don't know if I mentioned it, but Jean McBride moved from Executive Director to running the Board after last year's fundraiser. She asked if I would take Mary's position on the Board, and I accepted."

"That's wonderful, Mary was always passionate about *HFOC*, and I'm impressed with the work they've started here in Mono County. How's Jean?"

"Well, that's a good place to begin the story." Kate said slowly. "The day before my first board meeting last fall, Jean phoned and asked if I could meet her for lunch. She wanted to give me background on unexpected business, which would require board action." Kate sighed.

"First, she said the current executive director was leaving, and the assistant director would be replacing him. This had been anticipated, because the ED's father had been failing, and his mother needed him. Gail Edwards, the assistant director, had assumed many of his duties over the past few months in preparation. Jean explained that she had the full support of the Board. I remember thinking, wow, this organization has it together." Kate made a small sound that sounded like a snort.

After a few seconds of silence, I asked, "I take it there's more?"

"Sorry, J. Next, Jean said two of her strongest board members would be unable to complete their terms. One had been offered an opportunity on the East Coast she couldn't turn down, and the other learned he had adult-onset diabetes and wanted to reduce the stress in his life. Jean fully understood there was nothing she could do but wish both well, though she was concerned about the unfortunate timing."

"Wow. No wonder she wanted to meet with you and explain. That's a lot for a new board member. So, I take it you two and the remaining board have your work cut out for you."

"Not quite." I could hear her sadness. "Jean said she had one more bit of news. Her husband had been diagnosed with lymphoma. She needed to take a temporary leave from the Board while he received treatment. She would be available by phone, but only for emergencies."

Neither of us spoke. Jean was a force of nature. She had taken a small Northern California nonprofit with a commitment to help abused and neglected children and grew it into one of the largest and most effective statewide providers of resources and programs for vulnerable children and their families.

"How many remaining board members are there?"

"There are eight members left, including myself. Two of us are new; three only occasionally attend meetings but don't seem to offer much input when they are there; and, of the three who are active: one is quite outspoken, and the other two support him."

"Doesn't sound ideal, but it should work."

This time the sound that came through the phone was definitely a snort.

"Okay, Kate. Spill. Tell me what's happening."

Kate sucked in her breath. "Jean made her announcement in November. We're on an every-other-month meeting schedule, so our first meeting without her was in January. It went smoothly, as did the March meeting. Probably because Jean had prepared detailed agendas. This month three of the board members decided to ignore Jean's agenda and came to the meeting with their own. They demanded a thorough review of program operations and personnel issues instead of focusing on planning, policy, and fundraising, as the board normally does. The meeting ended with the new executive director leaving in tears. She emailed her resignation the next morning."

"You *do* have a problem. What did Jean say when you spoke with her?"

"She told me to call you."

A long silence was followed by intense discussion. We agreed the actions of the rogue board members could jeopardize the organization's reputation and fundraising ability, as well as disrupt current operations. Kate agreed to meet with Gail Edwards to see what it would take to rescind her resignation, and I would go to San Francisco to meet with the Board.

As we ended the call, I cautioned, "Kate, I'll call in the next few days to let you know when I can be there, but I don't think it will be too soon. Yesterday I committed to a new project that is fraught with personnel issues, and I can't back out now. I suggest you do whatever it takes to keep Gail on board, and if you want me to speak with her, I will. In the meantime, would you send me all the contact information with your take on each of the board members. I'll draft a letter for Jean to email out to the Board when we've set a date for my visit, introducing me, and explaining I will be contacting each of them prior to the board meeting."

Aileen, the food & beverage director

I awoke with a feeling of resolve. The young girl from Bleu—what was her name? Oh yeah, Lissa—made me realize I was acting like I actually *had* stolen from the Reynoldses. Nothing could be further from the truth. It was time to quit acting like a thief, or worse yet, a victim. I was finally home, had a good job, and even possibilities for the future. I must stop sabotaging myself, or let anyone else sabotage me, for that matter.

I left for work early, planning to stop on the way to pick up a chai tea. The line at the Looney Bean gave me time to plan the day's priorities. Number one was to convince Brian to do whatever it took to get Taylor to rescind her resignation. The thought of confronting him again made me sick to my stomach, but if I was going to be more assertive, this was a good place to start. I was trying out strategies in my head when I heard someone gasp. One glance made, and I felt my newfound confidence drain away. *No! Not Maureen again!* In the next instant I saw she was too young to be Maureen, but her open-mouthed stare made me uneasy.

"Aileen?" whispered the woman.

It was *Cindy* Reynolds. When I left for prison, she was in her early twenties and still looked like a teenager. Now she was grown up. She was talking to her companion—almost her clone. Both were petite, around five-four, identically dressed in designer high-waisted jeans, silky white turtlenecks, high-heeled ankle boots, and silver Patagonia jackets. But it was Cindy who had my attention. I flashed back to the awkward young teen I met when I first started working at Reynolds Home Care. Within weeks of starting my part-time job, the thirteen-year-old had declared to anyone who would listen that we were long-lost sisters. When it was my turn to cover the phone, she would do her homework at my desk. When I copied contracts, she would be ready with extra copy paper. Whatever I did, she was there. The memory bubble burst as I also remembered that I never saw or heard from her again after my arrest.

Someone calling my name brought me back to the coffeehouse. It was Cindy. Looking around, I saw her friend waiting by the front door. Cindy looked nervous. "I'm sorry I didn't contact you when you got back to town," she said awkwardly. She stared at her shoes as she added, "The family was against any..."

I shook my head. "It's okay. I under...."

Cindy held up her hand, "No. I'm not a kid anymore. I should have..."

She was interrupted by the man behind me, "Do you want coffee, because the rest of us do!" It was my turn to order. A line of perturbed, under-caffeinated patrons glared at me. When I turned to Cindy, she and her friend had gone.

The encounter threw me off kilter. Should I call her? Or would that just cause more family angst? Her apology sounded genuine, but she was stiff and distant, like she was talking to a stranger. Our meeting made me yearn to see her again. But it didn't seem she wanted to see me.

I left the car in the employee section of Couloir's parking building, shoved Cindy to the back of my mind, and prepared for my encounter with Brian.

His office was dark and vacant. Surprising, since his routine was to come in early, order breakfast in his office, and answer emails as he ate. Well, he had to come in sooner or later. Knowing if I left, I might never have the courage again to speak my piece, I sat down on the bench in front of his desk and waited.

Twenty minutes later I began to wonder whether he was even planning on coming into the office today. Perhaps I should check his schedule. I pulled the laptop out of my bag and was turning it on when the office outside door opened. Brian was munching on a croissant, a bit of berry jam smudged on his upper lip, more noticeable when he grinned at me.

"Aileen, I thought I might find you in my office. Had time to reconsider last night's demands? I thought you might have second…"

"What demands?" asked a voice behind us.

Taylor stood at the inside entrance to the office, with what could only be described as a shit-eating grin on her face. "I knew there was something going on between you."

My insides constricted. I tried not to cringe without

much success. Picking up my bag, I turned to Brian. "Actually, I wanted to reiterate my position. Consider it so." I turned and fled before either of them could see my shaking hands.

Once I was in the kitchen with the staff, my confidence returned. I was in my safe place and, despite the morning's commotion, easily ran our daily staff meeting. It made me feel more like my pre-incarceration self. I was really going to have to do something nice for Lissa Cole. As we were wrapping up with the review of dinner reservations, Taylor walked in, speaking as if I were the only one in the room. "We have to talk. I don't know what your game is, but it's not going to work."

I heard myself respond calmly, "I'll be in my office when we're finished here." Glancing at my watch, I added, "That should be in about fifteen minutes." Proud of myself for not backing down, I returned my attention to a wide-eyed team. After a huffing noise, the door swished closed.

The long, narrow corridor at the back of the kitchen complex was filled with the rhythmic sound of someone pacing in my office. Taylor was waiting for me. Yesterday's me would have returned to the kitchen to perform mindless tasks until she got tired of waiting. Today's me was committed to no longer acquiescing by melting into the background. If an adolescent could stand up to bullies, so could I. One bully at a time.

I entered the small, cluttered room. "Barging into my staff meeting was rude and disruptive. Next time you want to see me, please..."

Taylor sprang toward me, getting into my face. "You told Brian to do whatever it takes to hire me back? What kind of bullshit is that? What if the only way I will return is if he kicks your bony little, convict ass out?"

I grabbed a piece of Kleenex and wiped the spittle off my face. "Did you?" Relieved my voice sounded calm, without a hint of fear or emotion. I guessed some of my prison experiences prepared me for life, after all.

All of a sudden, this amazon of a woman deflated. She fell into the only guest chair in the room, a stainless-steel contraption I had filched from the kitchen. She opened her mouth, but nothing came out. Taylor, a tall, attractive, big-boned, athletic woman around my age looked like a confused child.

She shook her head. Again, she tried to say something and failed. Tears of frustration filled her eyes.

I pushed the Kleenex box across the desk and said nothing.

I stared at my hands while debating whether I was handling this situation right, when I heard a soft, "Why?" Looking up, I saw she had regained a bit of her stature. "Why, Aileen? Why would you tell Brian he should do anything to get me to return?"

When I didn't respond, Taylor said, "Please. I really want to know."

I took a deep breath, slowly exhaling, and spoke to my feet. "I'll tell you what I told Brian. You're really good at your job. You always put the hotel and guests first. While no one is irreplaceable, you come close. And I can understand why you might not have viewed my joining Couloir favorably. I don't blame you."

Taylor just stared at me, shaking her head. As she headed

toward the door, she turned. "I hope this doesn't hurt your feelings, but when did you get the guts to make demands of Brian, or to stand up to me? What happened to you?"

I smiled. "I met a young girl who is a lot more savvy than I am."

When it became evident I wasn't going to elaborate, Taylor said, "You're a piece of work. I'd sure like to know what the future has in store for you."

An involuntary shudder passed through me as the office returned to silence.

J, the consultant

After I drafted a letter for Jean McBride to send to *Hope For Our Children* board members, I perused Aileen's file and related documents, including notes from yesterday's meeting with Brian. It was tedious work that demanded absolute concentration. Stiff, bleary-eyed, and hungry, I took a midafternoon break for some tabbouleh, but barely tasted it. I could see only one strategy to bring Brian's senior management team together, and I was fairly certain Brian wouldn't like it; it wasn't his style.

Lunch finished, I knew I had to quit procrastinating and phoned him. I explained my idea and the rationale behind it; then anxiously sat listening to the deafening silence coming from his end of the connection. As I was about to ask if he was still on the line, I heard his intake of air, and what could only be described as a deep belly laugh that wasn't happy.

"You want me to leave town and turn over the management of Couloir to you?"

"To be precise, I want your management team to run Couloir, I would just serve as the… uh… facilitator."

"And this is a good idea because…?"

"If you want," I read from my notes, "'A management team that finishes each other's sentences, helps one another out, believes in each other, owns and solves problems as a team,' then they need to solve issues together."

"They already do." Brian sounded defensive.

Taking a deep breath, I was about to learn how Brian handled feedback. "Not based on the management team meeting notes you gave me with Aileen's personnel information. You present a problem to the team and ask for each person's input. There is little to no discussion. Sometimes you make a decision while the team is still in session; sometimes you say the decision will be made by the next meeting. This approach fosters competition among the managers, not teamwork."

A grunt of protest came over the phone, then nothing. The good news was he hadn't disconnected, I could hear him breathing. I took the time to get my heart rate down, an inevitable biological response to my being blunt with a new client.

After a long pause, Brian said, "I was told you don't pull any punches." I could feel his shrug in the silence on the phone. "But isn't the purpose of a team meeting to get perspectives from every aspect of an operation so you can make the best decision?"

"That's certainly one viable style of management. And in particularly complex organizations, quite effective. Each manager represents and lobbies for their piece of the operation to ensure they continue to provide peak performance. It encourages a flow of information and keeps decision making at the top. But if you're serious about having a team that can solve Couloir's problems together, you need all your senior managers to represent not just his or her part of the hotel, but to accept a broader role and find the best solution for the entire enterprise. In my experience this approach to management is well suited to smaller organizations and helpful during times of limited or reduced resources."

"Hmmm. I'm not going to lie to you, you're taking me out of my comfort zone. Turning over operational decisions, even for a short period…"

"Who runs the daily operations of your other two hotels?"

"They both have general managers."

"When one of those general managers goes on vacation, who manages the hotel?"

"The team… Okay, I get your point. I just need to spend a little time with the idea. Let me think it over and I'll call you back later today, tomorrow morning at the latest."

"I'll wait for your call."

No sooner had I disconnected when there was a pounding on the front door. Followed by the creaking of the door opening. Before I could become alarmed, my neighbor Charlotte yelled, "Oh good, it's unlocked. Can you believe this fucking snow? Is it ever going to quit? J! J, where are you?" And then all four-feet-eleven inches of her stomped into my office.

Charlotte shook the snow out of her red orphan-Annie curls without stopping her rant. While she nattered on, I couldn't help but smile—unrelenting monologues and pacing were just two of her many charms. When I purchased my home, Charlotte's family had a vacation home at the end of the block they'd used for a few holidays and occasionally in the summer. A little over a year ago at the age of forty, Charlotte retired from a lucrative management position for a web design company, purchased the house from her father, and moved in. Then her father died under suspicious circumstances, and one of her siblings blew up her home. That's when she moved in with me while all could be resolved and rebuilt. Now she and Mrs. Simpson, a longtime family employee cum best friend, were building a duplex in the footprint of the house, so each would have her own space.

Suddenly Charlotte's freckled face was just inches from mine, ocean-blue eyes piercing their way into my consciousness. "Are you even listening to me?"

I laughed. "Hanging on your every word."

Haughtily, she said, "You and Ross are invited to dinner tomorrow night." When she saw the fear in my eyes, she added, "Mrs. Simpson will be cooking. We're celebrating the completion of the duplex's interior."

My grateful sigh was not lost on Charlotte. "We wouldn't miss it for the world."

"Good. Now please drive me home, it's ugly out there."

Raising my eyebrow, I looked at her. "To the end of the block?"

She ran her hands over her stocky frame. "When the workout room is completed in the back of the garage, I'll start exercising." She headed to my garage without the grace of looking back to see if I would follow her.

Brian, the hotelier

I was distracted all afternoon, unable to make up my mind whether I was for or against J's teambuilding strategy. It had a certain kind of logic that appealed to me, but did I really want to give up that much control of our daily operations despite my abhorrence of personnel management? I knew my board would want me to, but I liked being in the mix of things. I needed to talk to J. I put in my earbuds to make a call, and before I could, the phone vibrated. The caller ID said Patrick O'Toole—Les Bosses GM, and the most trustworthy member of our hotel family.

"Patrick, your timing couldn't be more perfect."

"Not sure, Boss, if you're going to feel that way after I tell you why I called…"

Minutes later when J answered my call, I asked, "Can you begin the teambuilding tomorrow?"

Her surprise was evident. "Uh… sure. What was the deciding factor?"

"An avalanche just outside the entrance to our Aspen hotel."

"Oh, no. Have there been any injuries?"

"Yes, but, fortunately, not critical. A couple, first-time visitors on their way to the resort, saw some deer, got out of the car with their rifle, and shot at them. Fortunately, the couple had moved about a hundred yards from the car to get a good angle. The slide took the car; they were hit by some side debris, but it's not life threatening." I couldn't help myself, adding, "How can people be so stupid?"

"You and Ross should talk. Some of his ski patrol stories... well, they defy imagination," snickered J.

We spent the next several minutes talking about the hotel, upcoming events, and ongoing issues. "I'm sending out an alert to the six team members, telling them you are in charge."

J interrupted. "Six team members? There's Aileen, Food & Beverage Director; Charles, Facilities Director; Sierra, Human Resources Director; Tom, Controller; and Beth, IT Director. Have you already hired someone for Guest Services?"

"No. Taylor has taken back her resignation at my request."

J made no response.

I continued. "My plane leaves in two hours. Just call or text if you have a problem. If you can't reach me, I'll text you the GM's info and you can call Patrick. He can speak for me. Oh, and I'm not sure if you remember, but he's also Aileen's twin brother."

My mind raced. There were so many things I had planned to do over the next few days. Like think through J's unusual teambuilding strategy and make a deliberate decision; see Matteo and find out the real reason behind the complaint he filed; and respond to the advance letter to the editor I'd received from a local newspaper an hour ago authored by Maureen Reynolds. I'd considered telling J about it but thought it might be necessary the team deal with it as it unfolded. Then I had second thoughts.

"Oh, J, one last thing. I just received a copy of a letter that will appear in tomorrow's paper. I suspect it may be the team's first order of business. I'm forwarding it to you now."

Constantly amazed by the lack of humanity among some I knew, I reread the brief but damning letter on my computer screen before tapping forward.

Dear Editor:

For those who aren't aware, there has been a hire at our newest hotel that is an insult to the community. The nameless hire was convicted for embezzlement against a local business, served time, and is now accused of sleeping with her boss. This is not a big city with indifferent and immoral citizens. Mammoth Lakes is a small town with community values. How can we continue to support businesses and people who demean those values?

Concerned citizens led by Reynolds Home Care

Taylor, the guest services director

As we entered the crowded bar, Missy suggested I find a table and she would get our beers. I began to relax for the first time in a couple of days. That was the effect my evenings with Missy had. Spotting a table in the back of the room where we could have a little privacy, I hurried before someone else sat down. There was a lot to share with Missy and I didn't want to be overheard. Missy was the only person I could talk to these days. We'd known one another since elementary school, though hadn't been friends. The seven-year-old me thought she was selfish and pushy. When Missy as executive chef and I as guest services director started at Couloir on the same day, she seemed a much nicer person. I suppose we all grow up.

Glancing at the bar, I saw her standing behind other patrons all trying to get the lone bartender's attention. With time to kill, I checked my email. At the top of the list was one from Brian marked urgent. "Oh, dear God, what now?"

I was dumbstruck as I read: *"There has been an incident*

that demands my immediate attention at Les Bosses. J Westmore will provide the details at tomorrow morning's team meeting. Serendipitously, I met with J yesterday to engage her services to strengthen our team's communication and problem-solving skills. In light of unexpected events, I have asked her to lead the team in my absence. Please give her the respect you would give me."

"What the hell?" I flung my hands up in the air in disgust and knocked the beers out of Missy's hands as she was setting them on the table.

Once she and the table were cleaned up, and I'd purchased us new drinks—stronger this time—I showed her the email.

She just sat there, long blond hair slightly damp, hazel eyes wide open staring at me in confusion. Finally, she said, "Before we get to the email, I know why you quit Couloir, but can you tell me what made you decide to come back?"

And just like that, I relaxed, and we started to laugh.

After a piss-poor job of explaining the morning's encounter with Brian and subsequent meeting with Aileen, Missy asked, "Did it change your opinion of Aileen?"

I thought about her question. As executive chef, Missy reported to Aileen. From past remarks, I thought she respected her work but found Aileen to be single-minded and oddly private. "The jury is still out. It blew me away when Brian told me that Aileen had demanded he do whatever it took to get me to rescind my resignation. And again when she told me Couloir needed me. Usually she's so… so mousy, like she has no feelings or emotions. And I'm still not convinced she and Brian don't have something going on. What's odd is that I definitely can see her having an affair with him.

I mean, who wouldn't? But I can't imagine the ice queen embezzling money. Who could have known?"

We sipped our drinks in companionable silence. Then Missy picked up my phone and read Brian's email.

She scrunched her face, "J Westmore? Sounds familiar. Should I know her?"

"I think she's the one who nailed Ray Ratonne over at Snowline for sexual harassment a couple of years ago."

"I remember. What a sleazebag that guy was."

"And I think she helped find the twin toddlers who were kidnapped last year."

"Impressive, but how does any of this make her qualified to run a hotel?"

"Beats me. But for the moment it's an SEP!"

We smiled at each other, lifted our drinks, saying in unison, "Somebody else's problem."

Aileen, the food & beverage director

As usual, the three brothers from across the street were sledding down my driveway when I arrived. A tap on my horn brought irritated looks but cleared my path to the garage. Grocery-laden and emotionally exhausted, I entered my home and immediately felt like a new person. I would never get tired of walking through the front door. It was a small A-frame, two bed, two-and-a-half bath house in the part of town locals refer to as the snowbelt. The walls and furniture were pine, the décor 1980s mountain rustic. And it was all mine!

After prison, I went to work in Aspen and lived with my twin, but my heart was in Mammoth. I had some great jobs, but I drove Patrick nuts constantly talking about my plans to return. I'd start and he'd walk out of the room. Then last summer instead of leaving, he said, "Good. Because if you pass the phone interview with Brian Jeffries, who is going to call you shortly, you should be working as the food & beverage director at the new hotel in Mammoth within a few weeks, if not days." I couldn't believe it. I peppered him with so many questions he finally went out for a drink with friends and did not invite me to join. As predicted, Brian phoned, and arranged for us to meet the next day. In the morning as I was packing, Patrick told me to take everything I needed with me, and he'd send the rest when asked. He handed me a manila envelope and made me promise not to open it until Brian offered me the job. I scoffed but Patrick made me swear. Hours later, after Brian offered me the position he said, "Now, don't you have an envelope you need to open?" I asked Brian how he knew, and he laughed. I opened it up right in front of him, and there were two identical keys, the deed to a house in my name, and a note. "Congratulations, Aileen. It's time for you to be happy again. I bought the house sight-unseen, but Brian saw it and thinks you'll like it. He also sent out a cleaning crew and stocked it with linens and other basic items from the hotel. Love you, Sis. Patrick."

My newfound plan to start trying to take charge of my life needed to be celebrated, so I'd splurged at the grocery store. I placed red tulips in a jar on the kitchen table and began to prepare some albondigas soup. The ingredients soon covered the small kitchen counter: minced beef, eggs, a small red onion, tortilla chips, carrots, celery, canned plum tomatoes, fresh cilantro, and a plethora of spices and herbs. I poured myself a glass of white wine, asked Alexa to play James Taylor—my mother's favorite musician—and began to prepare the soup.

When the meatballs were simmering in the broth, I sat at the counter that served as my desk and checked my email.

There were two from Brian: one marked urgent, the other your eyes only. I started with urgent.

So that was why Brian was meeting with Ms. Westmore. It made sense. The team, if you could call it that, was in disarray. Everyone doing their own thing. I texted Patrick to find out what was happening at his hotel without expecting an immediate response and moved on to the second email.

I read the 'your eyes only' email twice, then made it to the bathroom in time to throw up. Just as I was hoping to get some footing in my life and put all the injustices behind me, it was happening all over again. I was back in the newspaper. I'm not sure how long I stared at the screen on my laptop. It was long enough for my wine to warm and the soup to boil over. I picked up my phone and searched for the number. In a small town it was easy to find. I punched in the number and said, "I'm sorry to disturb you. May I speak with Lissa, please? Would you tell her this is Aileen, the woman she met at Bleu last night, and I need a pep talk?"

Day 3
J, the consultant

In my experience, people who attend regularly scheduled meetings together generally tend to sit in the same seats every time. I took a position at the head of the rectangular table that seated twelve, assuming it was Brian's position, interested to see who sat where and next to whom.

The small room's atmospheric pressure changed as all six managers filed in at exactly eight o'clock. For a moment, I experienced an unusual stillness. It felt like the five seconds before a major earthquake—when order was about to be replaced by chaos, but your brain hasn't yet registered the shift. Four clutched coffee drinks—even though a full coffee service with croissants and fruit was waiting patiently on a sideboard—three also held onto the local newspaper.

Part of last night's meeting preparation was to augment Brian's descriptions of each of his senior managers by visiting the hotel's website to read their bios, and more importantly, familiarize myself with their pictures. As they took their seats, I mentally reviewed the little I knew about each.

The oldest member, Facilities Director Charlie Benjamin,

led the procession. In his mid-fifties, he'd worked over twenty years for the town, and retired as soon as he was offered the position at Couloir. Married with four children aged twelve to eighteen—all girls living at home—he was grateful for the increase in his monthly income. Brian said Charlie was an outstanding facilities manager but had little interest in being on the hotel's management team. He frequently tried to talk Brian out of requiring his attendance at team meetings. Charlie's complaints mainly revolved around the time wasted, and the drama involved, which he likened to a weekend night at home with his daughters. He took the chair closest to the door and gave his full attention to his cell phone.

Next came Beth Simpson, the IT Director, in deep conversation with Sierra Thomas, head of human resources. Both women were in their mid-thirties, but that's where similarities stopped. The contrasts were striking. Beth was dark-skinned, long, and all angles. Her close-cropped black hair, deep brown eyes, high cheekbones, and expertly applied makeup made me think more of a runway model than a technology expert. Sierra was petite with soft rounded features, and a cellophane-blue streak through her long dark-blond hair that closely matched her blue eyes. Her only cosmetic was bright red lipstick. They took seats next to one another on my right.

Brian had engaged Beth as a consultant to develop the IT plan for Couloir before it was built. After working together for a few months, he was so impressed, he offered her the department head position. As a single parent, Beth refused until Brian agreed to let her son stay in her office when he wasn't at school or participating in an activity. And if he became ill, he gave her permission to work from home. Brian learned what a bargain he'd made when he went into Beth's office to get assistance with his smart phone, finding only her ten-year-old son, Michael, present. He left minutes later, phone fixed, and an offer from Michael to come back if he had any more issues.

Neither Brian nor the website bio gave me any feel for Sierra Thomas. It was worrisome, since my presence in an organization usually was most awkward for the human resources professional. What I did know about her was that she'd been the HR manager for two other hotels in town before coming to work at Couloir. Brian found her competent and timely but thought her a better technician than manager. Since she had a two-person department, this caused him little concern. The only personal background he shared was that her parents had come to Mammoth over thirty years ago on a college ski trip and—like so many full-time residents—never left. Brian had met them at the grand opening and thought they were a hoot.

The controller, Tom Ruiz, was the only one who appeared angry. A recent transfer from Les Bosses, one of Couloir's sister hotels, where he'd been the assistant controller. Brian confessed he regretted promoting Tom. *"You know, J, when Patrick, Les Bosses' GM, refused to promote Tom to controller, I should've paid attention. I just wrote it off to a personality conflict. So, when I heard Tom was looking outside for a job, I called and offered him the controller position at Couloir. What I've learned since is that he's strung pretty tight. His work is solid, but his interpersonal skills are lacking."* I watched as the short, wiry man twisted his newspaper into a ball as he fell into the chair directly opposite me and glared at Aileen who entered just in front of Taylor.

Both Aileen and Taylor seemed subdued. Neither made eye contact with any of the room's occupants. They took the two seats to my left, leaving an empty seat between them.

After a long sip of coffee, I began. "I'm sure you all have a lot of questions. I'll introduce myself; explain my assignment and basic strategy, then…" holding up my copy of the newspaper, "we can get down to business. My name is J…"

"We all know who you are. You're the chick who was involved in the bombing last year. What I want to know is what are we going to do about *this*?" Tom threw the balled-up newspaper down the table at Aileen. It landed limply, well short of its goal.

"Let me begin again," I said evenly. "My name is J Westmore, and I've been asked by Brian…"

"I don't give a flying fuck who you are," Tom said loudly. "You're just some consultant that's going to run a few meetings while Brian is away. But we have an emergency that needs to be dealt with immediately." Turning toward Aileen, he yelled, "You and Brian are sleeping together?"

Tom had everyone's full attention; even Charlie set aside his phone.

I stood up. "Please leave, Mr. Ruiz." For emphasis, I added, "Now."

I finally had sparked his interest. "Who the hell do you think you are? You can't fire me."

Giving him a slight smile, I said, "So we've come full circle—back to introductions. My name is J Westmore. No, I'm not firing you, you're still Couloir's controller. However,

I am removing you from the senior management team while I'm leading it."

"You can't do that. I'll…I'll call Brian." He was quickly devolving back to adolescence. "What if I refuse to leave?"

"I sincerely hope that's not your intention. But, if you insist, I'll call Security and have you removed."

Tom abruptly stood and picked up his coffee and phone. "You know what? I don't need this shit." When he reached the door, he looked back. "Enjoy your power trip while it lasts." And he left.

As I returned my focus to the rest of the group, Charlie said, "I've always wanted to see someone stand up to that little…" All it took was a raised eyebrow for him to stop. He shrugged and leaned back into his chair, eyes glowing with a look of satisfaction.

After a brief bio, I outlined our charge. "Brian's vision is for this group to become a functional management team rather than a group of managers who only pay attention to his or her own department. He told me it's a concept he's been discussing with you both as a group and individually. Does this sound familiar?"

To my surprise, Charlie was the first to respond. "Yeah, he's talked about it, but I'm not sure what it means?" Scrunching up his face, he added, "Practically speaking, that is."

Taylor and Beth appeared to be interested in hearing my response. Sierra doodled on a pad of paper, looking bored. Aileen was in the same position she'd been in since the beginning of Tom's attack, looking at her lap.

"Let's see if I can give you a hypothetical example. It's

Couloir's annual budgeting process, but it's been a lean year and rather than covering each department's basic expenses, there are limited resources for upgrades, replacements, and new technologies. IT wants to update the routers and servers; Food & Beverage has a refrigerator and an oven ready for replacement; Administration is in line to update the point-of-sale system; and Facilities needs to expand garage facilities and buy two new vehicles to move guests up and down the mountain. Human Resources has run out of office space. The current practice is that each manager lobbies for his or her priorities and waits for Brian's decision. With a functional management team, each manager would present their arguments to the team. Then based on the strategic plan, projected performance for the upcoming year, and combined experience, Couloir's management team would rank needs, make recommendations for both the current year's budget, and propose a plan for how other needs could be met in the future."

Taylor queried, "So *we* would be making annual operating budget resource allocation decisions?"

"You would begin by preparing the annual operating budget for his approval. But, yes, ultimately that's one of Brian's goals. First, however, you have to prove yourself as a team in which each member is able to represent his or her functional needs, and simultaneously advocate for what's best for the entire operation."

Beth gasped, "Brian wants *us* to run Couloir?"

"From an operational vantage point, yes. Then he can give his attention to either enriching the experience at all the hotels or adding to the hotel family. But he can only do that if you can reliably operate as a team. I need to stress, though, he does not want to *leave* the team; he just doesn't want to *be* the team. He wants to lead you, not be you."

Aileen spoke so softly, I had to ask her to repeat herself. "I think we're all committed to Couloir, but I'm not sure we all…"

As Aileen hesitated, Taylor turned toward her with an odd, haunted expression. She finished Aileen's sentence, "… trust one another."

"Trust takes time and experience. That's why I'm here. By the time we're finished, you should think of each other as one-sixth…" Looking at Tom's empty chair, I amended, "… one-fifth of the single brain that manages Couloir."

Sierra spoke for the first time. Her voice was neutral; her question was not. "Are you really kicking Tom off the team? Brian won't like it. He brought him here from one of his other hotels." While I wasn't surprised by Sierra's question or her attitude, I found the question a little out of left field.

"Until Tom demonstrates the willingness and ability to constructively participate on a team, yes." I could tell by the expressions around the room my answer only addressed part of the question. I needed to address the proverbial elephant. "Being part of a team requires objectivity, as well as compassion. If tomorrow morning I reviewed all of Couloir's personnel files, I would probably find arrests for DUIs, drug possession, battery. All sorts of crimes have been committed by employees that resulted in jail time, probation, or community service judgments. But, because you don't know the details, you don't treat these individuals any differently than anyone else you work with. And you shouldn't." Both Beth and Charlie shifted uncomfortably in their chairs. I'd hit the mark. "But Aileen's experience was made public, in what I will politely describe as an offensive manner. Is that fair? No. She should be judged by her performance at Couloir and the successes that brought her here, which I understand to be considerable—not judged on speculation and gossip."

"I get what you're saying," Sierra said, again with a neutral, almost monotone affect. "But what about sleeping with Brian?"

I was waiting for this topic, though I was surprised it was from HR. As I formulated my response, Taylor said softly, "The accusation was mine, based on speculation, and if I'm honest, jealousy." Turning to look at Sierra, she continued. "As head of HR, you *know* a reputable, independent investigator found no evidence of impropriety." She stared at Sierra. "So, I'm not sure I understand your point?"

Sierra opened her mouth to respond, glanced at the other managers, and said nothing.

Beth intervened. "I like this new program. To return to the letter to the editor, I think no response is the best response. The paper only comes out once a week; surely the editor isn't going to reprint the same letter." She tentatively looked around. "Besides, the Reynoldses tried to start a boycott of the hotel when Aileen arrived, and we all saw how effective that was. Our numbers couldn't be higher."

Noticing the surprise on Charlie's and Aileen's faces, Beth grimaced, and said to the inside of her coffee cup. "Sorry, I thought everyone knew."

"I agree to no public statement," Charlie chimed in, "but we do have to agree on how we will respond to employee questions. You know there will be a lot of them."

Wow, I thought Charlie was the one who had little interest in being on the management team. "That's a great question, Charlie." Looking around the table, I asked, "Ideas?"

After a moment, Beth said with surprising candor, "Regarding the… er… uh… criminal reference, I think you said it best, J. I don't know about the rest of you, but I had a few… um… experiences in my youth I would not like to have made public." She reddened. "As far as the improper relationship goes, Taylor, your point about an outside, independent investigation with no finding of impropriety is on point."

It was Taylor's turn to blush. "I'm hoping we can keep the part about my role as the accuser in this room?"

The group spent the next half hour crafting answers to questions, then briefly going over the operational plan for the coming week.

I concluded the meeting with a ground rule. "If something comes up outside your department's purview while Brian is away, I want us to meet in his office to discuss and come up with a plan of action. Team management only works when all are present to discuss and help shape the strategy. At our next meeting we can work out communication strategies for team members who are absent. I realize this will impose a time burden, but I think you will find it worth it. And the big winner will be Couloir."

Everyone was gathering belongings when Sierra asked, "What do we tell our staff about Tom not being part of the team?"

"Nothing. Since personnel matters are confidential, the

only way I can see the question coming up is if Tom tells a staff member. If this happens and someone asks you, send the employee back to Tom. Don't share or volunteer your impressions. The facts are Tom is the controller of Couloir and a senior manager."

As everyone left, the mood was distinctly different. Taylor was speaking softly to Aileen, Charlie was whistling, and Beth was animated as she prattled on to Sierra—the only one who did not look happy.

Finally alone, I closed my eyes and stretched out my legs, mentally reviewing the meeting. Tom's anger and Sierra's odd behavior were uncomfortable, but not inconsistent with my expectations. Brian had said Tom was strung a little tightly. His former manager, Aileen's brother, had refused to promote him at Les Bosses, which made Aileen an easy target to vent his vitriol on. Sierra's affect was off-putting, but she did ask some good questions. I was going to have to make an effort to involve her so she didn't view me as competition. Beth seemed engaged. What surprised me the most was Taylor's candor, and Charlie's focused participation. I took out my phone and began to dictate observations and questions while they were fresh in my mind.

It vibrated. "That was fast," I answered. "Tom said he would call you."

Brian chuckled. "Not just Tom. Sounds like you made quite an impression. After I heard from Tom, who I understand had a head start, I got a call from Charlie, texts from Beth and Taylor, and an email from Sierra."

"Anything I should know about?"

"Let's see…" I could hear the smile in his voice. "Tom

wants you gone; Charlie's decided this 'management team-thing' is more interesting than he first thought; Beth can hardly wait until the team is running the hotel; and, Taylor wanted to apologize for filing her complaint."

"I hope you told Taylor she had every right to file."

"I did. She was also concerned about how the Reynoldses knew about her charge."

"A valid concern. And Sierra?"

"Her communication was more complicated and quite confusing. Lots of words, but few sentences, if you know what I mean. Phrases like 'doesn't understand our culture,' 'what about confidentiality,' and 'limits of authority.' I think she feels threatened, but there may be more to it. I want to ponder this one a while. When I have a handle on it, I'll call and we can discuss it."

"So where do we stand with Tom?"

"If you're asking what do I think of your actions? My answer is well done. I told him you were in charge, and if he wants back on the team, he needs to ask you what he needs to do to be reinstated, and then do it."

Finished with both the call and recording my notes, my stomach grumbled. In search of some lunch, I saw Aileen at one of the lobby's large windows, staring out onto a snowy deck. Good time to check up on her. "Hi Aileen," I said softly.

She startled slightly and turned. The look on her face was so peculiar, I asked if she was all right.

"I'm better than when I arrived this morning, thanks to how you handled the meeting," she said timidly. But it was the window that held her interest. "It's the oddest thing. Yesterday I brought some afghans out to a jacketless couple who were standing right there on the deck while it snowed. At first, when I only saw their profiles, I thought the woman was you." She flashed another slight smile. "But she was taller with darker hair."

"Did you speak with them?" I asked, feeling the familiar ache in my chest.

"No. Though something was so compelling about the couple, when I returned to the lobby I decided to go back out and…" Aileen's voice fell off. "They'd disappeared. All I found were two blankets on the railing. A few minutes ago, I saw them again in the same place…"

"And…?"

"They faded away, as if they were an illusion or mirage." Shaking her head, she added, "You must think I'm crazy."

I turned so Aileen couldn't see my face. "No, I don't think you're crazy," adding in my head, "I think you must be special."

Taylor, the guest services director

I could smell the espresso as I walked down the hall toward my office. Missy stood, holding two steaming mugs, an expectant look on her face. "Sounds like you had quite the meeting."

"Tom?" I queried.

"He told me the consultant tried to fire him, but Brian intervened." Her eyes were wide with excitement. "Guess she didn't last long."

Unfortunately, I was taking a sip as Missy made her pronouncement, and I snorted the coffee up my nose. After the tense morning, it felt good to laugh, even if I did sound slightly hysterical. Missy stared open-mouthed. She tried to ask what was so funny, but I held up my hand until I could regain control.

She was getting irritated, so between gulps of air I stuttered, "No one fired Tom. He acted like such a jerk, J kicked him off the team and basically told him he could come back when he was ready to act like an adult."

"But he said…"

"When did you start believing anything Tom said?"

That was when I saw Tom standing in the doorway. We locked eyes.

Missy's back was to him, so she was unaware we were not alone. I held up my hand to stop Missy from continuing.

Looking more than a little confused, she asked, "What's wrong?"

Before I could answer, Tom was gone.

Somehow Missy understood even before I could find the words to explain what just happened.

We finished our espressos in awkward silence. I didn't know what Missy was thinking about, but I chastised myself for breaking confidentiality, especially since I knew it would come back and bite me.

Missy picked up the coffee cups and started to leave. "I almost forgot."

"Hmm?" I responded as I scrolled through emails.

"Could I come and stay with you for a few days while I get some issues settled with my landlord?"

"Sure," I automatically responded, my thoughts a million miles away.

"Great. Let me know when you're leaving, and I'll ride home with you?"

I was suddenly aware I just made a commitment. "Huh?"

"No sense in taking both cars since we'll be back here tomorrow morning."

"What about your things?" Now wondering what she meant by a few days."

Missy grinned. "They're in my office." She turned to go.

"What if I said it wasn't a good time for…?" She was

gone before I completed my sentence.

Late in the afternoon I returned to my office to find Charlie doing spins in my desk chair. He looked up and said, "This chair is making an odd squeak."

I listened as he continued doing circles. "I don't hear anything."

"Probably because you're used to it. I'll come by tomorrow and see if it needs to be fixed or replaced."

"So, you came by to check my office furniture?" I asked, irritated he was still sitting at my desk.

"No." He laughed. "Came by to tell you my crew will be working on the maintenance issues in the two back units starting tomorrow."

I began to protest. Holding up a hand he said, "Both units are vacant for the next few days, and we'll be careful not to disturb any nearby guests."

"Okay." I made a mental note to stop by mid-morning to make sure his crew was onboard with the 'careful not to disturb' promise.

"Anything else?" I asked a little impatiently since once Charlie started talking, he could go on forever. There were a million things that needed to be done before I could go home, and it had been a long day.

"Yeah. What in the hell did you do to Tom? I don't know who he's angrier with, you, Aileen, or the consultant."

I slumped into one of my guest chairs, considering fight or flight, when Missy walked in with two large suitcases, saying, "This is going to be fun. Every night will be a slumber party."

I held in a groan.

J, the consultant

I was relieved to hear the sounds of the garage door closing and Ross's heavy footfall on the stairs. It was almost time to leave for Charlotte and Mrs. Simpson's. But instead of taking a left at the top of the stairs, Ross headed toward the kitchen. I peeked out from the bedroom half-dressed, curious why he hadn't come in to get ready for dinner, and heard him mutter, "All I want is a cold martini and a quiet evening with some mindless television…" Damn, I'd forgotten to tell him about the dinner invitation. My mind was working fast to find the right words when he caught sight of me.

"Not tonight! Please tell me you're changing into sweats, not into going-out clothes."

"I'm sorry. Charlotte invited us for dinner so we can see the finished duplex."

He dropped onto the couch, staring at the ceiling. "We're going to eat at Charlotte's? Do you remember the last time Charlotte cooked for us? Please, tell her I send my apologies, but I'm stuck at work."

"You just drove by her house, and she can see your car in the driveway. Besides, Charlotte assured me Mrs. Simpson is preparing the meal."

After a long, uncomfortable silence, his face twitched. He was going into negotiation mode. "I have tomorrow off. Why don't you take the day off and we'll go down to Bishop and golf?"

I frowned. "Not possible. I have to be at Couloir by eight o'clock."

He did a full body stretch, making himself comfortable on the sofa. As he kicked his shoes off, he said, "We can leave at eleven."

We scowled at one another.

Thirty minutes later, we were walking hand in hand to Charlotte's.

The house was a three-story, clean-lined split level with two front doors. Faced with the question of which doorbell to ring, we chose the one with a country wreath and welcome mat— rather than the one with a pair of dirty boots. Before it was answered, a silver sports car pulled into the driveway. I smiled to see a tall, elegant blond woman and a scruffy, stocky man with unruly black curls emerge from the vehicle: The recently wed principal of the local elementary school and the chief of police.

"Linda. Ian. What a lovely surprise. Charlotte didn't tell me you would be here."

From behind me, Charlotte said, "You mean you would have shown a little more enthusiasm for coming to the house if you'd known? Why are you standing out here? It's freezing." She turned and stomped up the stairs. The four of us followed her through the door with the dirty boots.

It was a different world—of white birchwood floors,

white walls, cleverly recessed lights, lots of windows and splashes of primary colors. In whichever direction you looked the home was happy. We found Mrs. Simpson, who was perfectly coordinated with her new digs in white leggings, white tunic, and necklace of chunky red, yellow, and blue ceramic beads, making martinis in the large great room.

After hugs, she handed each of us a drink while Charlotte started talking with all the enthusiasm of a tour guide who had recently received a cut in pay. "As you can see, our common area is on the second floor." Pointing to doors on either side of the room, "Each of us has our own den and smaller kitchen, if…" She looked at Mrs. Simpson with a raised eyebrow, "one of us thinks she needs a little space."

Mrs. Simpson's laugh was warm and playful. "Don't sulk Charlotte, it's impolite. Besides, you must admit sometimes your enthusiasm can suck all the air out of a room."

Ian held up his martini. "I'll second that." He took a sip then made a beeline for a large platter of appetizers on the coffee table.

Charlotte continued as if no one had spoken. "The top floor houses our individual living suites, which include a large bedroom, ensuite, and sitting room. Downstairs we each have a guest bedroom, bathroom, and office. Unfortunately, this room is the only room that is furnished enough for guests. Any questions?"

"Just one," said Linda. Addressing Mrs. Simpson, "Is your name really Mrs. Simpson?"

Of course, Charlotte started answering for Mrs. Simpson. "Your bright husband over there accused her of using an alias."

Ian called from across the room. "Hey, all I did was ask her for her full name. If you recall, the question was precipitated by the second attempt on your life."

While Charlotte and Ian bickered, Mrs. Simpson motioned for Linda to sit on the couch, and picked up a small photo album from the coffee table. As she flipped through the pages, she said, "As the saying goes, a picture is worth a thousand words. Then she turned the book around so Linda could see it. "This is me the first day I went to work as a personal assistant to Charlotte's mother."

Linda's eyes widened as she studied the tall, gangly, early twenty-something young woman with a blue beehive hairdo. "My real name is Marge Bouvier, but once the kids started calling me Mrs. Simpson, it stuck."

The first course was butter lettuce salad dressed with tarragon vinaigrette, and Prosecco. Our banter was as light as the course, mostly focused on the new home, and the journey Charlotte and Mrs. Simpson had taken to find the perfect design and style.

As we moved to the lamb shoulder with chickpeas, plum tomatoes and North African spices, the wine—a Spanish Ribera del Duero—our conversation became heavier. It started when Charlotte said, "I hear you've been making some waves at Couloir, J. What's up?"

"How do you know I'm working at Couloir?"

Ian chuckled. "Everyone knows."

I looked around the table, and *everyone* nodded. "I just started the day before yesterday." I knew it was a small town, but this was crazy.

"Let's start with you, Charlotte. How did you find out?"

"Beth Simpson told me. We're doing a project together." She made a face. "What's the big deal?"

I held up my hands. "Mrs. Simpson? You're fairly new in town, did Charlotte tell you?"

With an apologetic look she said, "No. I overheard a discussion while buying produce for this evening's dinner."

"The grocery store! Linda, you?"

"Charlie Benjamin helps out with maintenance problems at the school when we don't have the budget to hire someone," she said, shrugging her shoulders.

I closed my eyes. "Ian?"

"I'm the chief of police. I know everything." While I glared at him, Linda kicked him under the table. "Okay, I overheard Beth and Charlotte talking."

"You were spying on us?" Charlotte demanded.

"I need to know everything that goes on in my department," he said defensively.

"In your department?" I was totally confused.

"Charlotte and Beth are doing a little project for me," Ian said, unusually subdued.

"Yeah," smirked Charlotte. "He has a little internet security problem."

"Your assignment is confidential," Ian growled.

I put my head in my hands, muttering, "Like everything else in this town."

Mrs. Simpson stood up. "I think it's time for dessert." The tension was broken.

Linda and Ross cleared the table, while Mrs. Simpson began assembling the dessert. I took cappuccino orders, and Charlotte placed a bottle of Courvoisier on the table next to a small bowl of sugar cubes.

Mrs. Simpson outdid herself. Dessert was individual meringues with vanilla ice cream, fresh blueberries and raspberries, sprinkled with shaved dark chocolate. "I special ordered the berries from Bleu. Aren't they beautiful?"

As we started our dessert, I asked Ian, "Were you Chief when Aileen O'Toole was arrested?"

"I'd just been promoted." He stopped eating. "It was an odd case."

"How do you mean? Everything I've heard made it sound pretty cut and dried."

"Oh, don't get me wrong. She did it. No one but family members were permitted in the back offices. There was video surveillance that showed no intruders. And Aileen and Fred Reynolds were the only ones who knew the computer access code, which changed weekly. Besides, the Reynoldses weren't going to steal from themselves. No, what made the case so strange was none of us could believe Aileen was capable of such a crime." He stared longingly at his half-eaten dessert then continued.

"I had a few encounters with Aileen's father, Rory O'Toole, mostly alcohol-related charges or disputes with neighbors. He was a sullen, mean-spirited man whose wife had left him. Rory moved to Mammoth with Aileen and Patrick when they were seven or eight. From what I understand, the twins raised themselves. They were good students. By the time they reached high school, Patrick worked with a local construction company on weekends and in the summer. And, of course, Aileen worked for the Reynoldses. Patrick and Aileen were respectful, hard-working, polite kids who deserved loving parents." Ian took a large bite of his dessert and sighed contentedly.

"When we received the complaint about the missing money, I was sure there was some mistake. The Aileen I knew would never steal." His voice became almost a whisper. "But I was wrong. She did it. The evidence locked it down."

"What did she do with the money?" Charlotte blurted.

"Don't know. We never found it."

There was a sad silence.

Charlotte broke it. "Well, that was cheery. Glad I invited you to dinner so we could celebrate the new house. Have any more uplifting stories?"

Ian and I looked a little contrite until Mrs. Simpson said, "They are our *guests*, Charlotte. Now, would anyone like seconds on dessert? I have plenty."

Ian lit up. "Thought you'd never ask."

Day 4
Taylor, the guest services director

Looking down at my to-do list made me want to cry. I was overwhelmingly behind. I knew I'd be stuck on the computer for hours. A sudden rap on my door was the last straw. I could feel tears of frustration filling my eyes. If it was Missy, things could get ugly. She'd only stayed at my condo one night, and already it felt like a month. My precious privacy gone. From the time we carpooled home yesterday until we returned this morning, she never quit talking. There may have been a couple of hours when she let me get some sleep, but I felt so foggy I couldn't remember. I thought work would provide respite, but in the last five hours she visited my office three times to propose ideas about what we could do tonight.

When the second, louder, knock came, I heard myself yell, "WHAT?" I sounded like a madwoman, even to my own ears.

Sierra walked in, leading with raised palms. "Wow.

Someone had a bad night."

"Sorry. My nerves are a little frayed." Blowing out a long breath, I asked, "What can I do for you?"

My gut tightened as I watched her settle onto a chair and slip out of her heels. "So, the rumors are true."

"What rumors?"

"Missy moving in with you."

"She did not move in with me." My shrill response made me pause. In a more subdued tone, I continued. "It's just for a few days while she settles an issue with her landlord."

Sierra smirked. "Uh huh."

"What the hell does that mean?"

Head shaking, she said, "Missy frequently has issues with her landlord."

"Missy and I are friends, and I've never heard of landlord issues before."

"Maybe she wanted to keep it from you, but now no one else will take her in. Her issues tend to last a long time."

Just what I needed. I wanted to cry. After a few calming breaths, I asked, "Is this the reason you came to see me, Sierra?"

Hearing the change in my tone, she straightened. "No. There are two reasons for my visit. First, thought you'd like to know Tom has made a formal complaint about you."

"A complaint? Tom? What's his problem now?"

"You violated his confidentiality when you told Missy that he was kicked off the management team."

I remembered him standing in the doorway when I was talking to Missy and groaned. "Tom told her J fired him, and that Brian intervened, implying Brian fired J."

Sierra held up her hands in surrender. "You know the process, Taylor. You'll have a chance to share your side of the story. Just giving you notice."

I rolled my eyes. "And the other reason you're here?"

"Since Brian is in Colorado, he wants you to fill in for him at Mammoth High School's career day. And it's tomorrow."

"You're just letting me know now?"

"I just found out. It will be you, Tom, and Aileen."

"Oh, that's just great. Tom who just filed a complaint against me, and Aileen against whom I filed a complaint."

Sierra's smile was almost gleeful. "You know the drill. Give the kids an overview of your responsibilities with practical examples, tell a few interesting stories involving your job, and answer questions."

"I have so much on my plate right now. Couldn't you do it? Recruitment is part of your job description, isn't it?" I pleaded.

"Recruitment *is* my responsibility, but Brian asked for you. Besides..." Sierra added petulantly, "I'm sure they want directors speaking to the students, not a manager."

A moan battled to escape my lips. Please, dear God, not the *I'm only a manager* whine.

Beth walked into my office, and I let out a small sigh of relief. She looked at her watch when she saw Sierra. "You did say you wanted to meet at two, didn't you, Taylor?"

Sierra started to put on her shoes then stopped. Leaning back in her chair, she said, "I have a question for the two of you. She looked back and forth at Beth and me. "What do you think of J?"

Beth shrugged. "I thought she was very professional at

our management meeting. She certainly handled Tom well. She has a solid reputation in town. And a woman I'm doing a project with is a neighbor of J's. She can't say enough about her."

I could feel Sierra's eyes on me, but I focused all my attention on my computer screen.

With the hint of a smile Beth took up the slack. "Why do you ask?"

Sierra straightened in her chair. Using her important voice, she said, "J came in just to see me this morning. She apologized for not meeting with me to get my input before yesterday's management meeting, but said it was impossible because of Brian's sudden departure. She asked if I would send her my thoughts about how I see the role of HR, and ideas for the management team." Sierra paused for our acknowledgement or reaction, but neither Beth nor I said a word.

Finally, Sierra slipped on her shoes, stood, and looked pointedly at Beth. "I didn't know you were doing outside projects. I'm familiar with your personnel file and I've never seen an authorization."

Beth shrugged. "I told Brian. He gave me the go-ahead and never asked me to sign anything."

The sound that came from Sierra as she left the office was a cross between a growl and a sigh.

We waited until her footsteps faded down the hall. Beth shook her head, "I better warn Missy."

"What do you have to warn Missy about?"

"She occasionally helps out with my outside projects."

I was confused. "But she's a … a chef?"

Beth laughed. "She is. But she knows a lot about computers and can always use the extra money."

"That's for sure. She's always short of cash."

Beth turned serious. "Is Sierra getting stranger or is it my imagination?"

"Something's been off with her ever since we opened. Do you remember how great she was to work with during Couloir's planning stage? I mean we're all aware how upset she is about being a manager rather than a director, but..."

Beth rolled her eyes. "She didn't bring that up again, did she?"

"Yeah, but this feels like something more."

"Well, hopefully our consultant can fix it." Beth opened her laptop, signaling she was ready to get to work.

I sighed. "At least Brian's decision to hire J to work with the team probably means he's not going to promote Aileen to general manager any time soon."

Beth abruptly closed her computer. "What? Who told you Brian wanted to make Aileen GM?"

"Sierra told me several weeks ago."

Beth covered her face with her hands. "And you believed her?"

"She's head of HR. Of course I believed her."

Beth was still for a moment. In almost a whisper she asked, "Is that why you filed the sexual harassment complaint against Brian and Aileen?"

I felt my face grow hot. Then said softly with little conviction, "He *must* be sleeping with her."

J, the consultant

Up before dawn, I stared at the cappuccino machine, telepathically commanding it to complete its warm-up cycle quickly.

"We should play hooky more often, J. Golf yesterday was perfect." Ross finished packing his lunch, kissed me on the back of the neck, and left for work.

"That's because you won all the money," I yelled as he disappeared downstairs.

I was still waiting for coffee when my cell buzzed. Refusing to take my eyes off the machine, I answered blindly, forgoing caller ID. "Uh huh?"

"J? Is this you?" Kate asked.

Before I could answer, a second voice chimed in. "Kate, are you sure we have the right number?"

"I think so." She said in a muffled voice. Much louder Kate said. "May I speak with J Westmore?" After a moment, adding, "Please."

The expresso machine roared to life, and Kate hung up.

My coffee was finally ready when the phone buzzed again. I answered as if this was Kate's first call. "Hello, Kate.

What a nice surprise."

There was a long silence, then Kate said. "Hi, J, I'm with Jean McBride and we're hoping you've freed up your schedule so you can be in San Francisco tomorrow. Things are getting a little dicey."

"Sorry, I can't leave my assignment here right now."

Kate and Jean were murmuring to each other. While I couldn't make out the words, I could hear defeat in their voices.

"Jean, your Board has always been top notch. Mary loved being on it. Tell me as explicitly as you can, what or whom you believe to be the problem."

"I was hoping you could take an objective look. I could be wrong." This strong, confident woman sounded like a beaten child. Then I remembered her husband had just been diagnosed with lymphoma.

"Me too. But let's try this approach. When was the last time your Board was functioning up to your standards?" I asked more gently.

"Last fall," she said quietly.

This was going to take a while. I quickly texted Sierra to say I'd be delayed. "What happened last fall, Jean?"

"It all happened in the span of two months. First, Emily Grant, one of our most active members, had a fatal heart attack in the middle of a board meeting. Next, Marshall was diagnosed with Parkinson's and announced his resignation; and Kelly was offered a promotion if she moved to the east coast. Both were productive Board Officers. It ended when my husband learned he had cancer and needed a bone marrow transplant, which necessitated my current leave of absence."

"I'm sorry," I said softly. "So, how were the remaining members?"

"Concerned, but they all pitched in. Even a few of our less active members started participating." Jean's tone started to gain some strength. "We'd already invited Kate to join. Kelly recommended a colleague to replace her, who was interviewed and accepted. The members seemed excited about some fresh perspectives." Jean paused, and I heard Kate murmur something. "Oh yes, and Emily's husband called to ask if he could fill her chair. It seems George had retired from his company shortly before Emily's death, and he had a lot of time on his hands."

"Tell me about the Board dynamics with the new crew."

Kate chimed in. "It pretty much happened as I described it to you when we spoke. For the first few meetings all went smoothly. Jean prepared agendas, and we adhered to them pretty closely. But at the last meeting George and two of the old Board members, close friends of Emily's, ignored the agenda and wanted to get involved in day-to-day operations. It was so bad the executive director left in tears and quit the next day."

"Were you two able to convince the new exec to rescind her resignation?"

Kate answered. "We did, J. But I just saw their proposed agenda for the next board meeting, and my money is that Gail won't even show up when she sees it."

"You said two of the old members were friends of Emily's? Did they go off script when Emily was still alive?"

"Oh no," Jean said. "Never. Not until Colonel Grant arrived."

"Colonel Grant? George Grant? Why does that name sound familiar?"

I was racking my brain when Kate said, "I know there was some press in local papers when he sued his son, but I never really paid much attention."

"I don't remember anything about George suing his son." Jean said. "But I didn't do any real research on him. I thought if he was anything like Emily, he would be a welcome addition to the group."

It came to me. "I remember." I ran down to my office and rummaged through some professional journals. "Here it is." I shared the highlights. "Colonel George Grant started a manufacturing business that produced generators for homes and small businesses about thirty-five years ago... His son, Craig, who is now forty-eight, had worked for his father ever since graduate school... At retirement, the Colonel signed over the business to his son, in keeping with an agreement they had struck years before.... He and his wife were going to travel the world... Craig immediately undertook a workplace culture shift—something he'd been planning for several years... He involved managers in the process of pushing decision-making down the ladder, bringing back former high performers who had left for advancement and a better work environment, introducing performance indicators so employees knew how they were doing, supporting work-related educational programs, establishing childcare centers in the plants, offering long-term employees an opportunity to buy into the company... When the Colonel's wife suddenly died, he wanted the business back, but Craig knew that his father's authoritarian practices would end in workplace chaos. So, he refused to give or sell back the company."

As I blew out a long breath, Kate asked, "How do you know all of this?"

"When the article came out, I was one of many in my profession who was impressed with Craig. In the world of organization development, Craig Grant is a rock star. He took a slowly failing company and made it vibrant, relevant, and profitable in a matter of months, not years."

"Do you think Jan and Kay are just going along with George?" asked Jean.

"You said they'd never gone off script until George came. I suspect they cared for Emily and are trying to support her husband."

Jean sighed. "Of course. I've just been so distracted." After a moment she asked, "What do you suggest we do? We can't kick him off the Board. Not after he's lost his wife and his business. We're an organization about hope not abandonment."

"I have the beginning of an idea, but first tell me who's assumed the leadership of the Board while you're on leave, Jean."

"It's all my fault." Emotion evident in Jean's voice. Kate and I started to protest, but Jean stopped us with a "No." We remained quiet and listened.

"When Emily died, I was devastated, both as a friend and as Board chair. Emily had a unique ability to engage the disinterested and calm down the raucous. Her death took a big toll on Board functioning, and I needed to step up my game. My confidence started to fail when Marshall and Kelly announced their departures. But when Johnny and I..." Jean emitted a small, agonizing groan. "Sorry… when we learned about his lymphoma, I could no longer pay attention." She took a deep breath. "Which is a long way of saying we currently have no leadership. I was hoping if I drafted agendas that focused on routine business and processes, the Board could coast until the new members were comfortable and I was back from leave." She chuffed. "Guess that didn't work."

The silence that followed was so long, I thought we'd been disconnected.

Kate broke it. "So, J, have any ideas?

I did. Roberta Hart, a.k.a. Berta to her friends, whom I met last summer when she underwrote a golf gala in Mammoth for *Hope For Our Children.* The goal was to raise a million dollars for building facilities and providing programs for Mono County's at-risk and vulnerable children. A goal that was exceeded by an additional eight-hundred-eighty-five thousand dollars. Berta was born to money and married more. Her life's work was to protect and nurture every vulnerable child in California. In her mid-sixties, Berta was formidable in stature, nature, and determination. I was sure that if we told her what was happening, she would take charge. Jean could concentrate all her attention on her husband and know she would return to a focused, productive, schooled board.

I couldn't keep the smile out of my voice. "Berta." Jean and Kate gasped in agreement.

Day 5
Aileen, the food & beverage director

My resolve to stand up for myself was taking a beating. This morning in line at the Looney Bean I spotted Cindy Reynolds and her lookalike sidekick ahead of me. This time they were dressed in long-sleeved, mid-calf, fleece dresses that hugged every curve to stunning effect, and cowboy boots. Cindy in gray and silver; her companion in black and white. Confident and charismatic, Cindy appeared to be the dominant one in whatever relationship the two had. Until she spotted me, that is. I watched recognition transform her into a smaller, less dense version of herself—a transformation I had undergone many times when I was in prison. It was eerie. I decided to get my coffee at work.

I spent the morning in the kitchen working with some new staff. Around noon I finally made it to my office, finding a reminder from Sierra about my participation at high school career day. Something I had managed to forget because the task required that I return to a high school I hadn't entered since I graduated, and the need to be in a very public situation. Exacerbated, of course, by the recent letter in the newspaper recapping the details of my incarceration, and implying I was sleeping with my boss. But it was the second part of Sierra's note that made me want to go home and pull the covers over my head. I knew Tom, who hated both my twin brother and me, would be participating but didn't worry about it, because Brian would be our third. Now I learned Taylor, who had accused me of sleeping with Brian, would be replacing Brian.

A knock at my door forced me to pick up jacket, gloves, and scarf. Taylor stuck her head in. "It's time to go. Thought we could leave together. But first I wanted a word." Without waiting for a response, she closed the door and said, "For what it's worth, Aileen, I'm really sorry."

Maybe I shouldn't always expect the worst.

As we walked through the lobby, I registered Taylor's attire. "You look like you're dressed for a storm. When I arrived this morning, it looked like it was going to be a nice day. Besides, the sleigh is always warm and comfy."

Taylor laughed. "I never ride if I don't have to. I'll be upfront, driving the snowmobile. In my opinion it's one of the perks of the job. Besides, the last person I want driving is Tom. He's an adolescent when it comes to snowmobiles. He doesn't pay attention to the terrain or the passengers."

This meant I would be in the sleigh with Tom. Before I could object, we were almost mowed down by an angry Missy. She said nothing, but her expression was so venomous, the sound was startling.

"I thought you two were friends. You've known each

other for years, haven't you?" I whispered to Taylor.

Taylor nodded, looking hurt but resigned. "I told her last night I considered her a dear friend, but I couldn't live with her. We're too different. My neatness verges on OCD; Missy thinks counters are where you put the trash. I like yoga and reading before I go to sleep; Missy wants to party. I gave her until the weekend to find another place to crash."

"I take it she didn't understand."

"That's an understatement. She went ballistic. Said she'd never stay where she wasn't wanted. Ranted for a couple of hours while she threw her stuff in boxes. She left around midnight."

"Ouch. Where did she spend…" Taylor was no longer paying attention to me. She ran down the outside stairs to the snowmobile and sleigh where Tom was sitting on the snowmobile.

"No, Tom. I'm driving. I always drive and you know it." They started to argue.

Regardless of who won the argument, I knew I wasn't driving. I slipped into the sleigh, happy the weather had warmed. Patiently, I awaited the outcome, as did a growing number of guests and staff.

Just as I thought the two might come to blows, Sierra strode out of the lobby. "Stop. You two are making a scene. And if you don't leave now, you'll be late. Taylor, Tom is already on the snowmobile, so go sit next to Aileen."

Taylor was fuming as she climbed in next to me. Tom was laughing as he started the engine.

Predictably, once out of sight of the hotel, Tom increased his speed. Each curve slammed Taylor and me into the sides of the sleigh like dolls. The snowmobile's revving engines made it impossible for us to communicate with each other, much less with Tom. Hope returned as I saw we were almost at the last turn, when suddenly Taylor yelled "JUMP" and pushed me out of the sleigh. My last thought was wondering how I could hear Taylor so clearly when there was so much noise.

J, the consultant

It was almost noon by the time I reached Couloir's garage. Sierra had sent me a text saying Tom, Taylor, and Aileen would be out of the office for the afternoon, but she was looking forward to meeting. She'd been working on some "observations and ideas" and was eager to share them.

Since I'd called ahead to let the garage know I was coming, Frank, my favorite snowmobile driver, was waiting for me, ready to go. I liked him. Not only was he affable, but he was also a good source for what was going on at the hotel.

A few yards before I reached our sleigh, I spied a large root sticking up through the snow too late and did a face plant. Frank collected my purse and computer. As he helped me up, I said, "This is dangerous," pointing to the non-existent tree root I'd stumbled over.

Frank smiled indulgently.

I felt my face grow hot. "Seriously. A big tree root was sticking out of the packed snow. I saw it."

Frank nodded, trying to contain his grin. "I believe you. I'll have a look around as soon as I get back."

Damn. I KNEW the root was there. I SAW it. But

arguing wouldn't make it reappear. I was just embarrassing myself.

Sensing my frustration, Frank asked if I'd hurt myself. I stopped just short of telling him about the large bruise I knew I was going to have on my hip. "Fine. Just scraped my hands and my pride...Thanks for picking me up."

We'd just started toward the trail when there was a tremendous banging sound from the trees and something large shot by the front of our snowmobile and slammed sideways into the side of the garage.

As heart rates slowed down, comprehension dawned. Guests and staff ran to the burning heap: a barely recognizable passenger sleigh. Relief came only after confirming no passengers were inside.

The sound of an approaching snowmobile slowly making its way down the trail drew our attention from the wreck. Frank and I moved toward the trail to see who the driver was. As we walked, he took my arm. I thought he was afraid I'd fall again, but when I looked at him, his face was white. "You do realize if you hadn't stumbled, we'd be toast. Don't you?"

His words were just beginning to register when we heard Tom, the driver of the snowmobile, yell, "Call 911. Call 911." Then he started to cry.

Between sobs, Tom said Aileen and Taylor were unconscious on the trail. He'd covered them with blankets, and then came down for help. Eschewing our vehicle, Frank and I ran up the trail. It wasn't long before we found them. Aileen looked like she was regaining consciousness. Taylor was still out, which was probably good because her right arm lay at an unnatural angle. Tom was wise not to try to move them. Frank went to Aileen. I could hear him murmuring soft assurances as small groans escaped her lips. I sat with Taylor until the paramedics arrived. She was still unconscious. Somehow while we were with the women, all seemed quiet. But walking back down the trail, we heard the growing roar of chaos.

As we stepped out from the trees, I heard a loud familiar voice bellow, "We need order and quiet. No one will be leaving for the time being. So, get comfortable. This is a crime scene."

What the hell was our chief of police doing? What did he mean this was a crime scene?

Frank and I approached Ian. As soon as he spotted me, he said, "Why am I not surprised to see you, J? At least this time you weren't in the middle of the action and didn't have to use any of that strange luck you have."

Before I could stop him, Frank said, "Wow. It's happened before?"

"What do you mean?" Ian demanded.

Frank sputtered, pointing to the twisted hunk that was a passenger sleigh. "If J hadn't fallen on the ice, we would have been taken out by that."

Before Ian could come up with a snappy comeback, I asked, "Who called you? What do you mean a *crime scene*?"

Charlie walked over. "I called him when I..."

Ian held up his hand, stopping Charlie midsentence. "Son," he said to Frank, "Why don't you give your name and contact information to one of the officers over there, then wait with the others. We'll need to interview you."

Frank gave me a quick questioning look. I nodded, and he left.

Ian crooked his head toward the destroyed sleigh. "Charlie, J, Let's talk over there." With a stern look at me, he added, "Don't touch anything."

Charlie said quietly, "As soon as the paramedics were called, I went over to see how we could move the vehicle." He gave a sardonic grin. "Guests don't find smashed passenger sleighs comforting."

Ian waved his hand in a *get on with it* gesture.

"I couldn't believe one of our sleighs would disengage from the snowmobile. We inspect them every day. Hell, I inspect them every day." Charlie's voice was rising. Ian gestured for him to quiet down. More softly, he said. "When I..."

We were interrupted by the paramedics taking stretchers down the hill to the ambulance. Aileen looked dazed but conscious. The small part of her face that wasn't covered was bruised and torn. Taylor wasn't moving at all.

Sierra approached us, announcing, "As soon as the paramedics clear the area, we will resume normal operations. We're in the middle of a shift change."

"No," said Ian. "I want all the employees who were working at the time of the crash in the banquet room. We need to question them before they leave."

"There were only a few employees who saw what happened. I'll tell them to meet you there and send the rest home."

"I don't think you understand, Miss..." He looked at her name tag. "Sierra. I want to meet with all the employees who were working at the time of the crash, including managers. I understand there are guests to be attended to. I need a list of the essential staff who cannot leave their posts."

Sierra looked like she'd had a very long day. "I don't understand," she said forcefully. "Why would we pay overtime to off-duty employees while you investigate an accident?"

"Because," he glared at Sierra, "we need to make sure it *was* an accident."

Rolling her eyes, Sierra stomped off. I turned to Charlie. "You were saying?"

"When I inspected the sleigh, the safety pin wasn't damaged."

"Not quite sure I understand what you're saying."

Ian rolled his eyes. Charlie said, "The safety pin connects the sleigh to the snowmobile. But I found it undamaged, and not fastened."

"Someone forgot to engage the safety pin?"

"A logical question, but I personally inspect the sleighs every morning. And this morning it was attached. Since it wasn't damaged, it didn't break. The only scenario I can think of is that someone disconnected the safety latch, but left the pin in. When the sleigh went around a corner or hit a bump, it separated from the snowmobile. That's my take. What we have here, J, is not an accident. It's attempted murder."

Aileen, the food & beverage director

I was dizzy and disoriented as emergency room staff assessed my injuries. As soon as they quit prodding and manipulating my body parts, the pain medications took over and I fell in and out of consciousness. A nurse entered the emergency room cubicle as the drug-induced fog started to lift. Suzy, I think the nurse said her name was Suzy, was so nice. "I don't think you have to wait much longer. Your room is almost ready. Can I get you another blanket?" I tried to read her nametag, so I could make sure I had her name right, but my vision was still off kilter and blurry. I'd been x-rayed, scanned, examined, cleaned, wrapped, and coddled since I arrived. I couldn't quite grasp what had happened. I was having problems putting all the pieces together in my head, so I quit trying.

Instead, I closed my eyes and remembered the last time I felt like this. It was in prison. Someone hit me hard on the back of my head on our way to breakfast. The next thing I knew I was sitting in a steel chair in the doctor's office being asked questions I couldn't understand, the ringing in my ears blocking out the guard's words. That time no one asked me if I wanted a blanket.

Maybe I fell asleep, or perhaps I just spaced out, but when I opened my eyes, a policeman was sitting in a chair beside my bed. I panicked. Was I back in prison? Loud beeping started, and Suzy came in and told the policeman to leave. She held my hand, making soothing noises. I closed my eyes.

Day 6
Aileen, the food & beverage director

The next time I woke I was in a different room and there was a breakfast tray on the bedstand. I hurt all over. My left arm was cast from elbow to fingertips and in a sling. I tried to sit up, but my body wouldn't let me. "Aileen. You're awake." It was Patrick. I started to cry. Patrick would take care of me. He always had.

Patrick and a doctor told me I was very lucky. I had a broken wrist, a few cracked ribs, a lot of bruises and abrasions, but nothing that wouldn't heal.

Before the doctor left, he asked, "Aileen, you're one very smart woman. Jumping out of the sleigh when you did couldn't have been easy, but it did save the two of you. How did you know when to jump?"

I looked at the doctor and Patrick. "I don't know what you're talking about..."

Patrick looked concerned. "Still fuzzy?" he asked.

"No." I tried to sit up, but again thought better of it when my ribs protested. "Taylor yelled 'jump' and then pushed me out of the sleigh."

Patrick and the doctor were giving each other a strange look, when I finally remembered to ask, "How's Taylor?"

The doctor gave a half-smile. "You two are almost mirror images of one another. Though she broke her right shoulder instead of her wrist."

"Where is she?"

"In the next room. If you want to see her, I'll ask a nurse to come in and help."

"I'd like that. Please. If it isn't too much of a bother?"

Patrick and a nurse who wasn't Suzy took me in a wheelchair to see Taylor.

Before I could stop myself, an involuntary "Oh no," escaped my lips. Sitting up in her bed, Taylor's face was so black and blue and swollen, I almost didn't recognize her.

To my surprise, she snuffled, "You look like shit."

"Not as bad as you do." Immediately I felt bad about the criticism.

Taylor offered me a hand mirror from her side table.

My shock was instantaneous. There was no unmarred skin on my face. I was black, blue, and purple. Where I wasn't bruised, I was scraped. I tried to take it in.

A horrifying moment later, I said, "You're right. I do look like shit." We both laughed. Or at least, tried to—damaged ribs and swollen faces complained about the movement.

We looked at one another anew. "You saved my life," I said softly. "Thank you."

Taylor looked puzzled. "You must have hit your head harder than I was told. *You* yelled 'jump' and pushed me out of the sleigh. You saved *my* life."

I looked at Patrick. "I don't understand. She saved mine."

The nurse hovering in the background, seeing the distress in both Taylor's and my demeanor, said, "That's enough for now. You two can talk about who saved whom tomorrow."

She rolled me back into my room, Patrick following.

Day 7
Aileen, the food & beverage director

The next morning the policeman was back. I wasn't afraid because my mind had cleared, and Patrick was with me. The man looked vaguely familiar, but I couldn't place him. He told me his name, but I referred to him as Chief. I was not comfortable with law enforcement yet. That would probably take a long time, if ever.

Patrick asked if they knew what caused the accident. The chief said the investigation would take a few days. After I briefly described the events leading up to the accident, the chief began the questions:

"Did you hear Taylor and Tom argue over who would drive the snowmobile?"

"Yes."

The chief frowned. "Was it a heated argument?"

I looked at Patrick. He gave me a *ride with the tide* look.

He was right. I wasn't in prison anymore. "No, it was more of a contest. Two strong-willed people who would not be happy if the other was driving."

The chief's face started to relax. "What did you do while they were arguing?"

"I knew I wasn't going to be driving, so I got into the sleigh and rooted for Tom."

"You rooted for Tom?" The chief sounded incredulous.

I think my lips formed the hint of a smile but couldn't be sure. "I didn't want to sit next to him in the sleigh."

The chief snickered. "My understanding is the HR manager came out and decided Tom should drive. Is that what you remember?"

"Actually, Sierra seemed more concerned that we would be late to the high school career day. She said something like, "Tom is sitting on the snowmobile, so let him drive."

"Then what happened?"

"Taylor got in the sleigh with me, and Tom took off."

"And…"

"As soon as we got into the trees, Tom started driving really fast, knocking us around in the sleigh. Then Taylor yelled 'jump' and shoved me out of the sleigh. That's the last thing I remember until I woke up in the snow."

The chief seemed to contemplate my answer.

"Do you have any enemies, Aileen?"

My laughter was arrested by my injuries. "You must know my history."

I was surprised when the chief laughed too. "Do you have any enemies besides the Reynoldses?"

The list was assembling in my mind when Patrick spoke. Staring at the floor, his voice held a slight tremor of emotion. "Besides being Aileen's twin, I'm the general manager for one of Brian's other hotels. Tom used to work for me as assistant controller. I wouldn't promote him because… well it doesn't matter why. Let's just say I wouldn't promote him. Brian wanted to give him a chance and made him controller at Couloir. It would be a gross understatement to say Tom does not like me, and by association, Aileen."

"Would you agree, Aileen?"

I took a deep breath. "Chief, in my experience, there's a difference between people who don't like you and enemies. But in the case of Tom, I would agree with Patrick."

The chief's eyes widened. "Well said. Let's start with enemies, then move to people who don't like you."

Taylor, the guest services director

I was hurting, bored, and groggy from pain killers. Aileen and I were going to be released this morning, and I was looking forward to getting out of the hospital. I never wanted to be in a hospital again. Missy sent me a text asking if I wanted her to stay to take care of me, and I immediately and tactfully, I hope, declined. I never wanted to spend a night with her in the same house again. But I *was* concerned about how I'd manage for the first few days with a broken shoulder.

Suzy, the day nurse, came in. "Taylor, Police Chief Williams is just finishing up with Aileen and was hoping you would feel up to talking with him."

My first impulse was to claim drowsiness, but an interview would happen eventually, and best to get it out of the way before I went home. "Sure."

Nervous, I started to comb my hair—anything to improve my appearance. But one look in a mirror told me that was useless. Besides, I didn't comb so well left-handed. So, I went back to my newest favorite pastime, trying to find a sitting position in bed that didn't hurt.

There was a knock and the door opened. I was surprised to see a red-haired man instead of the police chief. "Uh, sorry to disturb you. I'm Patrick, Aileen's twin brother."

I stared at him, thinking he looked nothing like Aileen. As I gawked, his name rang a bell. He was one of Brian's general managers, but my foggy brain couldn't remember which hotel.

Patrick interrupted my reverie. Looking concerned, "Perhaps I should drop by later?"

"No, I'm sorry. Still a little spacey, I guess."

"Aileen and I wanted to ask you a question."

"I'd rather answer your questions than the police chief's."

Patrick smiled. "I understand. Aileen is still with him. She wanted to know if you'd like to stay with her for the next few days. I'm going to be waiting on her, and I can just as easily take care of both of you. If you're right-handed, maneuvering with that shoulder is going to take some getting used to."

I was stunned. After all that had happened over the past several weeks, Aileen was concerned about my well-being. I didn't know what to say.

Taking my silence as discomfort, Patrick said, "No pressure. Just think about it." He headed toward the door.

"Patrick, I don't have to think about it. The invitation was just unexpected. Yes, please. The doc said the morphine is masking the pain. Once I leave, I'll be on traditional painkillers, and the first few days won't be pleasant."

"Good. Aileen will be happy you accepted."

The relief I felt surprised me. The doctor had been quite adamant that I shouldn't be alone for the first few days, until I got through the worst of the pain and understood my physical limitations. But there was no one I felt comfortable asking to help me. I closed my eyes, trying to imagine what Aileen's house would look like, and dozed off.

I was awakened by Suzy. "Sorry to disturb you, dear, but Police Chief Williams would like to ask you some questions. Do you feel up to it, or should I ask him to come back later?"

The chief popped his head through the open door. "It'll just take a few minutes."

Suzy said, "I thought I asked you to wait…"

I broke in. "It's okay. I'll talk with him."

Suzy made an irritated sound. "I'll be back in a few minutes to see how you're doing, Taylor."

"Thanks for talking to me now, Taylor. Please call me Ian. Why don't we start with a description of what happened? Start with the discussion over who would drive the snowmobile."

The chief roamed the room as I started to describe the events leading up to the crash. It seemed he was more interested in looking out the window than at me. Becoming a little irritated, I changed the topic, "I guess I haven't told you anything you haven't already heard?"

"Sorry, Taylor, I really am listening. Hospitals have always made me edgy." He sat down in the chair next to my bed. "You were saying: Aileen yelled 'jump' and pushed you out of the sleigh..."

"Yes. But what's odd is that she thinks I pushed her out. Guess the drugs they're giving us are messing with our heads."

"Do you have any enemies?"

"What does that have to do with our accident?" A shot of adrenaline cleared my head. "You don't think this was an accident, do you? You think someone tried to hurt us?"

He grimaced. "Let's just say until we can confirm it was an accident, we'll be looking at all possibilities. So, any enemies?"

"Not really."

"How about Tom? Didn't he recently file a complaint against you?"

"How could you know that?" I demanded. Answering my own question, "Ah, you've been talking to Sierra. Yes, I was told he filed a complaint, but I haven't seen it. Tom is always unhappy with everyone. It doesn't mean anything. He's just an unhappy, annoying guy."

"It sounds like he gave you and Aileen a pretty rough ride?"

"That's because he has the maturity of a fifteen-year-old. But he would never try to intentionally hurt us."

"How about Missy?"

I was indignant. "Missy is a good friend."

"But you kicked her out of your house in the middle of the night."

"Oh, for God's sake, just because we can't room together, albeit for a short time, doesn't mean we're not still friends. And for the record, I asked her to be out by the weekend. She's the one who decided to leave immediately. Next, you'll be..."

Suzy stuck her head in the door. "Are you about through in here?"

Before Ian could say anything, I said, "Yes. Thanks, Suzy. The chief just finished."

Brian, the hotelier

I barely made it onto the plane from LAX to Mammoth Lakes before the doors slammed shut. A harried-looking young woman escorted me to the only empty seat on the flight, while irritated passengers glared at me. Pointing to my chair, she took my bag and instructed me to secure my seatbelt so the plane could take off. Her request for haste was reinforced by those buckled in around me. I did as instructed, taking a deep breath to calm my already frayed nerves. The letter in the newspaper, the avalanche, my controller's unprofessional behavior, now an accident that almost killed two senior staffers. *What more could happen?*

Eyes closed while I searched for a thought that would bring respite, it took me a moment to register that my seatmate was talking to me. My stomach clenched when I turned to see a smiling Fred Reynolds.

"Brian, it's good to see you. I was planning on calling you when I got back to Mammoth, and here you are."

I managed a half smile.

Fred held up his hands. "I totally understand. That's why I wanted to talk to you. About that little email exchange, we had last fall, I'm sorry. For some reason Maureen just can't forgive Aileen. She's become downright irrational. You know she threatened to leave me if I didn't contact you when you announced Aileen's hire." Letting out a long sigh, Fred leaned back in his seat and placed his hands on his knees. "Glad to finally get that off my chest." He gave me a wide grin. "I hear around town that Aileen is doing well. Good for her."

I couldn't stop myself. "Who are you kidding, Fred? You couldn't possibly care about Aileen after the letter you published in the newspaper this week." I was so angry I was shaking. Other passengers began to stare.

"What... what are you talking about? What letter? I wasn't even in town this week..."

I held up my hand to stop him. Flipping through files on my phone, I found a copy of the letter. "Then tell me how you explain this."

Dear Editor:

For those who aren't aware, there has been a hire at our newest hotel that is an insult to the community. The nameless hire was convicted for embezzlement against a local business, served time, and is now accused of sleeping with her boss. This is not a big city with indifferent and immoral citizens. Mammoth Lakes is a small town with community values. How can we continue to support businesses and people who demean those values?

Concerned citizens led by Reynolds Home Care

The color drained from Fred's face as he read. "This was in the newspaper?" he asked in a hoarse whisper.

I nodded, trying to determine if this was an act or he really didn't know about it. The way he was squeezing my phone, I suspected the latter. Gently removing the phone from his grasp, I asked in a more conciliatory voice, "You really didn't know?"

Now his color was rising. "I had no idea. Who's seen this? Never mind, that's a stupid question." He lowered his head to his hands. "Oh, Maureen. What have you done now?"

There were tears in his eyes when he looked up. "I don't know what to say. Maureen's had it out for Aileen ever since she started working for us full time. I couldn't understand why. Aileen was smart, professional, a hard worker. For so long she was one of the family. If I hadn't been there, I would have staked my reputation on Aileen's innocence during the embezzlement debacle."

We both sat back, mulling over the ramifications of our exchange. The pilot announced our imminent landing, but neither of us stirred. As we taxied down the runway, Fred said, "Brian, I'm sorry. I'll try to find some way to make it right. For what it's worth, would you please pass on my apologies to Aileen?" He wiped his eyes. "Please."

There was a small crowd waiting behind the airport's chain link fence. Two figures, unaware of each other, stood on either side of a screaming teenager who was waving flowers over her head like a flag—Maureen and Patrick.

Walking to the truck, I delayed telling Patrick about my exchange with Fred, and asked for a detailed update on his sister and Taylor's conditions.

"Considering what happened, they're in remarkably good condition. I brought them home this morning."

"Home?" I asked.

"Ah. That explains it."

"Explains what?"

"I guess you didn't see my text. I thought you would when the plane landed."

I checked my pockets for my phone.

Patrick held up one hand to stop me. "I'll give you the live version. In answer to your first question, Aileen knew Taylor lives alone, so she asked Taylor if she'd like to come home with us so I could take care of both of them until they're comfortable on their own. The doc said they'll both need support, especially for the first few days."

"That's nice of the two of you, but I don't get it." I shook my head, feeling stymied. "Taylor files a complaint against your sister. Aileen is vindicated. Taylor resigns in protest. Aileen insists I convince Taylor to rescind her resignation. The two get in an accident…"

Patrick interrupted me. "About that. Chief Williams is pretty sure it wasn't an accident."

"What do you mean *not an accident*? What else could it be?"

"Right now, he's calling it a suspicious accident, but he believes attempted murder, and so do I."

I was speechless.

"I'm taking you to see Aileen and Taylor while they still have hospital-grade meds in them. They're expecting us. Then we can go to the police department and see the chief."

All I could do was nod.

We pulled up in front of Aileen's A-frame, and despite all that had happened I couldn't help but smile. The last time I'd been to the house was almost a year ago when Patrick asked me to check it out before he purchased it for his sister. At the time I suggested he wait until I actually interviewed Aileen and offered her the job, but he was certain that was just a formality. In the end, he was right.

The stiffness of two plane rides and hours spent in airports made getting out of the car a challenge. I was stretching when Patrick yelled from the back of the truck, "Could you give me a hand with this?"

"This looks a lot like the recliner from the lobby library." I said as I helped heft the leather chair to the front porch.

Patrick chuckled. "That's because it is. With a broken shoulder Taylor needs to sleep sitting up for a while. Nice to have an entire hotel full of furniture, don't you think?"

I almost lost my grip on the chair when I saw them. Aileen and Taylor sat at opposite ends of the couch, their injured appendages covered in icepacks. They rested on throw pillows, eyes peering out from swollen, bruised, and cut faces, looking eerily like bookends. I froze, while Patrick awkwardly tried to maneuver the recliner to a small bedroom just off the living room.

"Close your mouth, Boss, and help Patrick before he breaks something," chided Taylor. Aileen added, "When you're finished, Bro, I think you better offer Brian something to drink." Their voices listless but clear.

As Patrick handed me a beer, he whispered, "Let's not bring up the attempted murder hypothesis until we know more. These two have enough to worry about right now."

"Got it."

Patrick and I grabbed dining chairs and sat across from the injured women. "You'll never guess who I saw on the plane…"

Aileen interrupted. "Sorry, but we have a question that can't wait. Does the police chief really think the crash was intentional?"

I gave Patrick a shrug. So much for not worrying them. "I don't know. Patrick just told me about the possibility. When we leave here, we're going to the police station to find out what's going on."

While their faces were too obscured for me to see their reactions, both women visibly sagged in their seats.

Taylor spoke. "Ian asked both of us about enemies. No one ever asks about enemies when you're in an accident. We think he found something, and we want to..." Her voice lost strength mid-sentence. She finished with an involuntary yawn.

A quick check of Aileen indicated she too was beginning to fade.

"Patrick and I will head over to the station and let you two get some rest. He can tell you what we found out when he returns." I stood. "Anything we can get…" They were both asleep.

Patrick filled their water glasses and made sure all their medications were accessible. He scribbled a quick note, and we left.

J, the consultant

The morning was consumed by reading California's workplace-violence regulations. After a while the words blurred together. I needed a break. My stomach growled. I needed lunch. Leftover tamales screamed from the refrigerator, "Eat me." I needed tamales. I took the stairs two at a time. Perhaps I could eat one cold, while I heated the other two. They were small. My mouth was watering. The cell buzzed. It was MLPD. Reluctantly, I said, "Hello."

"How quickly can you be in my office?" Ian asked.

"What's this about?"

"Couloir, of course." An indignant note hung in his voice.

I looked at the refrigerator. "Let's say an hour."

"Let's say twenty minutes."

Now I looked at the old sweats I was wearing. "I have to change. I'll make it as close to twenty minutes as possible." The note in *my* voice was resignation.

"Do that."

I was hanging up when he said, "Oh, and, J, I ordered sandwiches from Bleu. Pick them up on your way over."

"You want me to what?" But he had already disconnected.

Twenty-five minutes later I was sitting in Ian's office. When he reached for the sack of food, I narrowed my eyes, saying, "One of those better be for me."

He looked alarmed. "Why didn't you order your own sandwich?"

"Because…" I said, stretching out the word. "You said I needed to be in your office in twenty minutes." I thought about his urgency. "Why did I?"

Ian rolled his eyes at me. "I was hungry."

Furious, I snatched the bag out of his hand, opened it to find three sandwiches. It was my turn to roll my eyes. I grabbed a sandwich and gave him back the bag. He started to protest until I took out my cell.

"Who are you calling?" he asked dubiously.

"Your new bride."

He handed me a napkin and explained the real reason for our meeting. "I'm ninety-nine percent certain the sleigh mishap was attempted murder. I have an interview in…" He glanced at his watch. "…thirty minutes with my lead suspect. I know this is unorthodox, but I'd like you to be here for the questioning."

"You want me to be in your interview?"

He slapped his forehead. "Is everyone around here stupid?"

I glared at him.

"Not in the interview. I want you in the observation room."

"Why?" I protested. He held up his hands, settled back in his chair and quickly consumed his first sandwich. I started on mine when he bit into the second.

The door flew open, framing a red-faced Charlotte. "Where's my sandwich?"

Ian smirked. "J's eating it."

"There were three sandwiches," I protested.

Through clenched teeth Charlotte yelled, "I know. One-and-a-half for each of us."

How could she yell with clenched teeth? I'd have to try that when I got home.

They were staring at me. Charlotte, hands on hips, ready to explode. Ian, leaning back, enjoying the show.

Without another word she walked over, took my half-eaten sandwich out of my hand, and left.

I should have stayed home and had tamales.

I sighed. "Who is this suspect you're…"

The door opened again. This time a bit more civilly. A female officer I'd never met before said, "He arrived early. I have him in the interview room. Officer Cole will be with you."

Ian stuffed the last of his lunch into his mouth. Between chews he said, "I'll be right in. Will you take Ms. Westmore to the observation booth? And make sure she doesn't touch anything."

Officer—her name tag said Garcia—picked up my coat and asked me to follow her. I caught up with her when she was halfway down the hall. "Please, Officer Garcia…"

She held her finger to her lips and picked up her pace. I followed her into what appeared to be a closet. When the door was firmly closed, she said, "I'm sorry." She faltered. "Your presence is a little … unusual. We can talk now. The room is soundproof."

I'd been right. It was the size of a large closet. Most of the space was taken up by a high counter with three high chairs on one side, facing a large wall screen. "The interview should begin in a few minutes. Good thing you arrived early so the chief could brief you."

I shook my head. "Officer Garcia, I don't know why he wants me to listen to this interview. And I don't know who is being interviewed. Ian was too busy eating lunch."

Officer Garcia's laugh was low and throaty. "First, please call me Elli."

"Please call *me* J. Do you know why I'm here, Elli?"

"The chief said you're working with the management staff at Couloir, and you know the suspect. He's hoping you can watch how the suspect responds and share your observations with him. He said he's worked with you before under some peculiar circumstances..." Elli cocked her head, looking at me curiously, "...and trusts your opinions. He also knows you will keep everything you see and hear confidential."

Suddenly the room darkened, and a live shot of the interview room appeared on the screen—the picture was crisp but had a slightly turquoise hue. I whispered, "I thought we would be watching through a one-way mirror."

She smiled. "I'll explain after."

Officer Cole escorted Tom Ruiz into the interrogation room, followed by the chief. Both police officers took chairs, leaving only the one facing the screen for Tom. Tom glanced at the wall mirror behind his chair and sat down.

Tom was Ian's lead suspect? The guy may be a jerk with a temper, but kill someone? I didn't think so.

He looked around the room. "This is much nicer than

I expected." Nodding toward Elli and me, he added, "Nice artwork. Very soothing."

Artwork? I turned to Elli, but her eyes were glued to the screen.

I leaned forward in my chair and studied Tom. He was trying to act nonchalant, but a slight tremor in his voice betrayed him. I wondered if only I heard it.

Ian thanked Tom for coming to the station, explaining everyone who was involved or witnessed the accident was being interviewed. He looked at his notes and began. "Please describe what happened from the time you got to the snowmobile, Mr. Ruiz."

"Tom. Call me Tom. It's really pretty simple. Taylor, Aileen, and I were scheduled to participate in the Mammoth High School career day. A snowmobile with sleigh was waiting for us at the bottom of the lobby steps. I got there first so I could drive." He raised his eyebrows and quipped, "Girls don't know the first thing about driving snowmobiles." When no one responded, he continued. "Taylor and Aileen showed up a few minutes later. Aileen got into the sleigh. Taylor wanted to drive, but I said no. Eventually she got into the sleigh too. We took off. The next thing I knew, the girls were flying out of the sleigh as it broke away from the snowmobile. I stopped, but both were unconscious. So, I went to the bottom to get help. It all happened quite fast."

Ian nodded. "How do you like working at Couloir?"

The abrupt change of topic rattled Tom, but he quickly recovered. "I like working for Brian."

"How about the rest of the management team?"

Tom leaned forward, narrowing his eyes. "I thought you

wanted to talk about the accident. How is my opinion of the team relevant?"

Ian held up his hands. "I only ask because you're in an important position and I value your opinion. I'm trying to get a feel for how everyone gets along."

"You don't think it's an accident?"

"I'm not saying that. Even when I know for certain it's an accident, I would be remiss if I still didn't explore all alternatives. I thought you would be a good person to get a feel for the organization. But if you're not comfortable..." Ian let his words hang in the air.

Damn. Ian was good at this.

Tom leaned back in his chair. "No, that's cool. I get it. What do you want to know?"

"I don't know." Ian shrugged his shoulders. "I have a list of the management team members somewhere..." He looked at Jon who started flipping through the files he'd brought with him.

"No problem. Brian is a great boss. He stole me from one of his other hotels to be Couloir's controller. He seems fair and gives me a lot of leeway."

"How'd they feel about it at the other hotel?"

Tom laughed. He was comfortable. He was in charge. "My old boss Patrick was pissed with Brian. He had a lot of problems replacing me."

Ian chuckled conspiratorially.

"Beth is our IT Director. She's pretty good at her job. Keeps our systems current and running. When an update screws up the financial data, she sorts it out quickly. Beth sticks with the program and doesn't get involved in other people's business. Charlie is a lot like Beth. He's always on top of the physical plant and lets me know in advance whenever possible if we're going to have any unexpected maintenance or capital expenditures. Sierra is a competent human resources manager, not much more to say."

"And Aileen and Taylor?"

He straightened slightly. "They're okay."

"Okay?"

"They do their jobs."

"But…?"

"Hey. They both just got hurt. I wouldn't want to badmouth them."

Ian threw up his hands again. "Never mind. I just thought you seemed like a pretty astute guy, and I could get some insights from you." Ian started paging through his notes.

Tom let out a deep breath. "If you put it that way. What can I say about Aileen? I'm the controller, she's a convicted felon who got the position because of her brother and is keeping it because she's sleeping with Brian. Hell, he even gave her a big, unbudgeted raise after she'd only worked at Couloir for a few months. As for Taylor, she's a drama queen, a gossip, and given her need to dominate, probably a lesbian. Not a pretty combination." There was a long silence in the room, while Tom contemplated what he'd just said.

Ian broke it. "And you were the only one of the three of you who wasn't injured in the accident."

Tom stood up, angrily. "Am I under arrest?"

"No."

Tom walked out of the room.

In the observation room, Elli raised her eyebrows. "Hmmm." She stood, "Let's go back to the chief's office."

"Would you show me the artwork in the interview room on our way?"

Elli smiled. "Sure. I think you'll like this."

To my surprise, the small room felt inviting. The square table was a polished dark wood; the three chairs matched. On one wall was a large rectangular mirror. On the opposite was a stunning, intricate weaving of turquoise, green, blue, and some pewter thread or yarn, with different sized beads woven into the piece. The entire hanging was encased in acrylic.

"Wow. This doesn't belong in a police station; it belongs in someone's home."

"Interesting you would say that. The furniture was in Ian's home. He donated it to the department when he married Linda and moved into her house. It's reclaimed hardwood, so it's sturdier than almost everything in the department that isn't metal. The textile art was made by one of the locals. Among the beads, she weaved in miniature cameras that are Bluetoothed to the computer. For most, the room seems so out of place in a police department, it throws them off balance. When the interviewers sit on the side of the table facing the ubiquitous mirror, the witness or suspect feels less threatened. So far, this new set up has proved quite helpful in gathering information." Elli laughed. "Here at the station, we call it our version of enhanced interrogation."

Ian walked in and barked, "What are you two doing? I've been waiting for you."

Elli started. "J wanted to…"

"I don't care what J wanted. We need to debrief while everything is fresh."

"Great interview. You blew me away." I waved my arms. "Then I learned staging this room was your idea. Wow."

Ian's face colored. "I heard about something similar at last year's California Police Chiefs annual conference, and thought I'd put my own spin on it. Glad you can appreciate it."

I winked at Elli as we followed a smiling Ian to his office.

There was standing room only. I'd expected to see Jon Cole, but not Brian and Patrick. Ian's under-his-breath expletive screamed neither did he. "What brings you two gentlemen to my office… unannounced?" he asked without humor.

Brian stood. "Sorry, Chief, but I just got back to town and Patrick tells me you don't think the sleigh incident was an accident. What's the story?" Brian looked at me. "Is that why *you're* here, J?"

Ian's sigh was loud and long. Then he recounted in detail Charlie's discovery that the safety pin linking the sleigh to the snowmobile was neither damaged nor engaged, and Charlie's assurances that he had made sure it was secured the morning of the accident.

Brian was still processing the implications of Ian's information when an officer walked in and said, "Sorry for the interruption, Chief, but we just received word that Aileen O'Toole and Taylor Hunt have been rushed to the hospital."

Patrick gasped. "What happened?"

The officer said, "It appears they've been poisoned."

Chaos ensued then I was alone. What little I had been

able to decipher from the shouts and barks, Patrick and Brian were on their way to the hospital, and Ian, Jon, and Elli to Aileen's house. I decided to go to Couloir. It wasn't clear if Aileen, Taylor, or both were the targets, but chances were whoever was behind these attacks worked at the hotel.

Brian, the hotelier

Patrick left the hospital waiting room to speak with Aileen's doctor, leaving me alone and numb. What the hell was going on? Why would someone want to hurt—I couldn't use the word murder—Aileen and Taylor? Or was it only one of them, and the other just happened to be in the wrong place? Who could possibly hate either one so much? Could it be Maureen? She certainly had it out for Aileen. Would she know how to sabotage a sleigh? This was absurd. Maureen's actions had been cruel and ugly, but she wouldn't resort to violence. Would she? Or was it someone at the hotel? That's even more far-fetched. I would know if I had a sociopath working for me, wouldn't I? Nothing makes…

Someone placed a hand on my arm. It was a young girl with long blond hair and blue-green eyes. "I thought you might need this," handing me a box of Kleenex. I must've looked confused. "You're crying." I touched my face. She was right, I was crying. "My mother told me to sit quietly and not talk to anyone, especially strangers. But she's always told me to help people in need, so I thought I'd take a chance."

I started to respond, but she wasn't through. She held out

her hand. "My name is Lissa Cole." I shook her hand as she continued. "My mother is getting an x-ray because she fell off a stepladder. Why are you crying? Are you hurt? Should I get a nurse?"

"Hello, Lissa Cole. I'm Brian Jeffries. I'm all right but thank you. I didn't know I was crying. Two of my empl… er…friends are hurt, and I'm waiting to hear how they are…"

Ian stormed into the waiting room, decked out in all his police gear, and headed toward me.

Lissa's eyes widened. "Are you a bad guy?"

"No," I said. "The chief is here to help find the person who hurt my friends." Clearly, Ian was scaring the girl.

He startled me when he said, "Hi, Lissa. Why don't you give me a minute with Mr. Jeffries? Your father should be in shortly."

She gave him a hug and retreated to the other side of the room to watch for her father.

"Did you find anything at the house to explain what happened?"

Ian looked down at the box of Kleenex in my lap. "Did you bring anything for Aileen and Taylor when you saw them earlier?"

"No. I didn't know we would be going to Aileen's. Why?"

Ian held up his hand in a *be patient* gesture. "Did you send a gift to the house?"

"No. What's this all about?"

"Are you sure? You didn't bring them some food or whatever?"

"I did not," I snapped. Lissa turned to watch us. Ian told me to lower my voice.

"Ian?"

Ian scrolled through his phone. When he found what he was looking for, he handed it to me. "This is what we think made the ladies sick." It was a picture of a gift basket filled with fruit, boxes of tea, and fresh cookies. "Now scroll to the next picture."

I did. It was a Couloir gift card. The typed message read "This should help with your recovery—BJ."

Ian started talking, but I wasn't listening. I was studying the note. Something didn't work. He tried to take the phone back, but I wouldn't let him. I just stared at his phone. When it clicked, I looked up to discover Patrick and Jon had joined us. "I did not send the basket, and I did not write this note. The proof is right here."

Patrick looked over my shoulder at the phone. He made a snorting sound, "Of course, you didn't."

An irritated Ian said, "How can you take one look and be so positive?"

Patrick chuffed, "Because Brian once fired a manager because he kept calling him BJ." He looked at me. "Wasn't his name Skip? Skip…"

A nurse pushing a wheelchair-bound patient gave us a stern look, and the reality of why and where we were almost knocked me off my feet.

"Patrick. Aileen? Taylor?" Was all I could say.

"They're stable and sedated. We can't see them until tomorrow."

"I need to know what happened," I said to Ian. "Let's go back to Aileen's."

Ian and Patrick gave each other a quick glance. "There

are still officers at the house collecting evidence. They'll be out later tonight." Clearing his throat, he added, "You may want to consider getting a cleaning crew in tomorrow morning. The sooner, the better."

The chief suggested the police station and delivery pizza. After all that had happened, I thought a drink might be in order. I suggested Couloir and a private dining room. We headed for the hotel.

The sun was setting and temperatures dropping by the time we arrived. We almost bumped into J who was on her way out. I told her we would catch up in the morning. Ian surprised me for the second time today when he said, "J, turn around and join us for dinner. We have a lot to discuss." J opened her mouth to respond. Ian cut her off. "No excuses. We've had a second murder attempt." As we filed into the private dining room, I heard J say into her cell, "Sorry, honey. Looks like we have to reschedule our date."

Despite the day's horrors, I felt myself relax as I walked into the dining room. Decorated like a library in a private club, it was my favorite room in the hotel. The walls were lined with floor-to-ceiling bookshelves that housed an unusually good library. Leather wingback chairs framed a roaring fireplace; two couches and a long coffee table offered comfortable seating conducive to informal conversations. The other side of the room had an oak dining table that seated ten. All tastefully illuminated by floor and table lamps.

The group chose seats close to the fire, while I ordered appetizers from the kitchen. Patrick went to one of the bookcases as if he were choosing a book and pushed a hidden button. The bookshelf glided open to reveal a bar. I took drink orders. The only one who chose a non-alcoholic beverage was Jon, who looked at Ian as he claimed he was still on the clock. Ian paid no notice.

Appetizers on the table, drinks in hand, Ian called for quiet. As he collected his thoughts, I asked, "Before you begin, Chief, not that I mind, but why did you invite J to join us? She's an HR professional, not a cop." I gave her a *hope-I-didn't hurt-your-feelings* shrug. She smiled back.

"Interesting question. No, she's not a cop, as I have reminded her on several occasions. But Ms. Westmore has a knack for... how should I put it? In the last few years, she has somehow sorted out a variety of crimes, including kidnapping, extortion, and attempted murder, surviving with only scrapes and bruises. For the most part this has been accomplished on her own. By including her, we may benefit from her insights." He looked sternly at J. "More importantly, since she just happens to be working at Couloir, we might keep her from doing something stupid. Again."

This was my consultant? I looked from J—who sat quietly sipping on her martini—to Ian. I just nodded, unsure of what to think.

"Any thought the sleigh crash was an accident vanished with today's attack. For J's sake, I'll sum up what we know." He looked around for agreement, stuffed an eggroll in his mouth, and began. "According to Patrick, he picked Aileen and Taylor up at the hospital late this morning and brought them both to Aileen's home. Patrick is staying at his sister's and taking care of both women until they no longer need him. After they were settled, he picked Brian up at the airport around noon and drove to Aileen's to check on the women.

Patrick said he saw no gift basket in the house at any time."

Ian looked at me. Miffed at his earlier insinuations, I barked. "Neither did I!"

Ian's look said, "Get over it." He continued. "When the ladies began to doze off, Patrick and Brian came to the department to see me—without calling ahead, I might add." This guy was a real character. "According to Aileen's neighbor, she found a gift basket on her front porch addressed to Aileen. Clearly delivered to the wrong house. She took it to Aileen's. After several knocks and no answer, she tried the door and found it unlocked. Aileen and another woman were asleep on the couch, so she set it on the coffee table so Aileen would see it when she woke. Approximately an hour later, as the neighbor was leaving to meet friends, she noticed Aileen's door was slightly ajar. Thinking she forgot to close the door all the way, she hurried to do so. When she reached the porch, she heard moans coming from inside. Finding both women in a state of major distress, the neighbor called 911. When we arrived on scene, the women had already been rushed to the hospital. From what we could determine, only a few cookies were missing from the basket. We'll have all the items in the basket tested, but pretty good chance it was the cookies. The emergency room physician told me Aileen and Taylor owe their lives to the concerned neighbor."

I turned to Patrick, disconcerted. "How could we have forgotten to lock the door?" Immediately regretting the question when I saw how upset he was.

J asked. "Was there a gift card in the basket?"

The mood shifted. Everyone laughed, except me.

J looked confused. Patrick told her about the note, Ian's

suspicions, and my irritation. J did a poor job of hiding her smile.

We were interrupted when dinner arrived. Missy outdid herself on short notice. She offered a choice of grilled New York steak, roasted asparagus with parmesan and garlic, and fingerling potatoes; or Dover sole piccata, cold asparagus in a champagne vinaigrette, and wild rice. I asked her to just bring a simple white and red wine pairing. This was a working dinner, and I was paying for it.

Over dinner we discussed the crucial question: Who was the target? Aileen or Taylor or both? Initially, everyone but J—who wanted to keep an open mind—thought it had to be Aileen, because of the public attacks the Reynoldses had made. That is, until I told them about my encounter with Fred Reynolds on the plane today. Then some doubts started creeping in.

Ian said, "If you believe Fred, then the only alternative is Maureen. She's certainly nasty enough. And poison is often a woman's weapon. But how could she have engineered the sleigh sabotage?"

A skeptical Patrick said. "It's only a question if you buy Fred's story."

J asked, "Who knew Taylor was staying with Aileen?"

Patrick thought a moment. "I phoned Sierra this morning to give her an update on Aileen and Taylor, and that I would be taking them home." He paused. "I can't remember if I said anything about Taylor coming to the house or not. I do remember asking her to update the senior managers."

"Well, that's not very helpful." Ian said as he helped himself to a bite of J's fish.

She slapped his arm away. "Remember, this is Mammoth. The whole town probably knows."

We went back and forth through espressos and dessert, never coming to any agreement. As the conversation wound down, Ian said he would be interviewing the Reynoldses, and conducting second interviews with some of the employees who had been nearby during the sleigh incident. He asked me to get a list of all the employees who had worked today, their arrival times, and if they had gone offsite.

Everyone was getting ready to leave when I asked, "J, why did you come to Couloir this afternoon?"

The question halted the group. Ian said, "That's a good question, what were you doing here?"

J shrugged her shoulders. "My guess is whether the target is Aileen or Taylor or both, probably someone at Couloir is responsible. I wanted to hang around and see what I could pick up."

"Did you learn anything?"

J hesitated for just a second. "Not really. When I do, Ian, you'll be the first to know. I promise."

J agreed to meet with me in the morning. The group bundled up in their coats for the ride down the hill, while I headed to my lodgings, trying to comprehend the implications of the day.

J, the consultant

Stripping off my coat and hat, I heard Ross talking on his cell. "Don't worry. I'm sure we'll be there." There was a pause. Ross laughed. "Because she stood me up for our date this evening." Another pause. "See you tomorrow night. Looking forward to it. Let me know if we need to bring anything."

I was formulating an objection, until I remembered how Ross acquiesced to dining at Charlotte's a couple of nights ago. "So, what's on the docket for tomorrow?" I asked as I slowly climbed the stairs to the living area.

"An impromptu, informal *wish-the-season-was-over* party given for and by mountain employees. Everyone's so beat up, Jeff thought it might be good for morale. I agreed with him."

Despite the chaos in my head, I smiled. "Jeff always thinks a party is a good idea... and he's most often right." I tossed my purse onto an ottoman.

Ross studied me. "I can't tell whether you're exhausted or wired?"

"Both."

He moved the wingback chairs closer to the fireplace. "Want to talk about it over a glass of wine?"

"Hoping you might ask; I had Pellegrino instead of wine at dinner." I gave a happy sigh when I saw the bottle of 2013 Freemark Abbey Josephine red from our special occasion stash open and breathing on the dining room table.

Once seated, chairs touching, feet on hearth, fire roaring, wine in hand, Ross asked, "Were a couple of Couloir employees poisoned today?"

I almost spilled my wine. "How did you know?"

"You know how closely ski patrol and paramedics work. When I helped put an injured skier into the ambulance this afternoon, one of the medics mentioned something to that effect. I assumed that's the reason you worked late."

"Yes. Aileen and Taylor. I was meeting this afternoon with Ian, a couple of his officers, Brian, and Patrick when we got the news."

"To say they're having a tough week is an understatement. Are they going to be all right?"

"The Doc told Patrick both were stable and sedated. Aileen's next-door neighbor found them when she went to check on why their front door was open." I was surprised to feel tears on my cheeks. "I guess I haven't had a chance to process everything that's happened."

Ross sat back. "Why don't you tell me about your day as it unfolded?"

A little of the tension left my neck and shoulders. "That would be good. Thanks." I stared into the fire. "Ian phoned around lunchtime, asking me to come to the police station immediately." Ross looked surprised but didn't say anything.

"He wanted me to observe his interview with Tom Ruiz regarding the sleigh incident."

"I thought Ian didn't want you involved in any police business?"

"So, did I. He told Brian since I was working at Couloir, he felt the need to keep an eye on me." I rolled my eyes. "Anyway, turns out the chief is a very good interviewer. I was impressed. After asking Tom to describe the events leading to the crash, Ian asked if he would tell him a little about each Couloir senior manager. Tom was positive about his interactions with Brian, Beth, Sierra, and Charlie. He started to balk at saying anything about Taylor and Aileen because they were injured, but Ian subtly encouraged him. Basically, he said Aileen is an embezzler who's sleeping with the boss, and Taylor is a gossip and probably a lesbian."

"Wow. He really said that? Didn't he think it would make him look guilty?"

"Like I said, Ian is a good interviewer. When Ian pointed out the obvious, Tom left."

"What was Ian's reaction to his meeting with Tom?"

"Never got to discuss it. When we returned to his office, Brian and Patrick were waiting for an update on the sleigh incident. Apparently, Brian didn't know it was being investigated as attempted murder until he arrived back in town today. While Ian was trying to brief Brian, we were notified of the poisoning. Brian and Patrick took off for the hospital; Ian and his officers headed for Aileen's house, where the poisoning took place; and I decided to go to Couloir."

"Why Couloir?"

"I'm not sure how to explain it. I think the answers are

there. The poisoning had just happened, so I was hoping no one knew yet. Guess I wanted to see if anyone in management was acting strangely."

"And?"

"Charlie was a basket case, but his focus was on the sleigh accident. Beth was locked up in a meeting with vendors about a new point-of-service system. But I did find Sierra. Actually, to be precise, she found me. Sierra wanted to share some of her ideas for strengthening the role of human resources in the organization. Sometime after five I asked her to put her thoughts in writing, and as I was leaving, I ran into Ian and the group."

Ross laughed. "Did Sierra have any good ideas?"

"Only if you think hiring three additional HR staff and promoting her to senior vice president will improve Couloir's guest experience."

"You're saying the trip up to the hotel was a bust?"

"Up until I ran into Brian, Ian, Jon, and Patrick coming into the hotel for the dinner meeting."

"Did the Reynoldses come up in the dinner conversation? They've made their feelings about Aileen very public."

I told Ross about Brian and Fred's encounter, finishing with, "Brian believed Fred was being truthful. Fred's account does seem consistent with your impression of him. Besides, if Fred planned on murdering Aileen, I doubt he would've gone after her in the press."

"Do you think they're both targets, or just one of them?"

"That's what we spent most of this evening talking about. We couldn't come to any conclusion."

"Yeah. But what do *you* think?"

"Well, the obvious target is Aileen. The Reynoldses have attacked her in the press, and she's had two sexual harassment complaints against her, for which she's been exonerated. The sleigh crash facts seem to support this since Aileen was the only one of the three involved who was certain to be in the sleigh. Remember, Tom and Taylor argued about who would drive the snowmobile. From what Aileen said, if Sierra hadn't made the decision, they might still be arguing. Today's attempt is different. Patrick said he called Sierra to update her before he picked up Taylor and Aileen and asked her to pass along the information to the rest of the management team. But he can't remember whether he told her he was taking both women to Aileen's. And the gift basket note wasn't addressed to anyone, it just said: *This should help with your recovery.*"

"I understand. But you're not answering my question. What do *you* think?"

I gazed into my glass of wine. The dark, ruby color in the firelight made it as beautiful to look at as to drink. "As I said, after we got the news at the police station, my first instinct was to go to Couloir. What I think is that someone at Couloir is behind the attacks."

"And..."

"It's complicated. On one hand..."

"Gut feel."

I closed my eyes, feeling only the warmth of the fire, and whispered, "I know Aileen has seen Mary and Bob, but I only found out by accident. I can answer you when I find out whether Taylor has or not."

"How are you going to find out?"

"Good question."

Day 8
Taylor, the guest services director

I kept trying to open my eyes, but my lids were stuck. No matter how hard I tried, they wouldn't budge. I was starting to panic. Something bad was going to happen, I could feel it. How could I stop whatever it was if I couldn't see it? After what seemed like an eternity, my lids cracked ever so slightly. Everything was blurry. Nothing felt familiar. I strained to open my eyes all the way. Help me. I couldn't open them.

Someone stroked my cheek, making soothing sounds. "Breathe. Just breathe," she whispered.

I took a long breath, and my eyes slowly opened. A woman with long brown hair, warm brown eyes, and a Mona Lisa smile stood in front of me. Her voice was calming and familiar. I can't explain it, but I instantly felt safe. She held up a glass of water with a straw, and I took a long, slow sip. Our eyes locked. It felt like she was streaming calmness directly into me. I was flooded with a sense of inner peace. Then I noticed she wasn't alone. There was a tall man standing behind her with the same deep brown eyes, smiling at me. As they watched, my eyelids grew heavy. I started to drift off. They touched foreheads, and I fell back to sleep.

The next time I woke, the room was bustling. A nurse was talking to Aileen and another was asking me how I was feeling. Physically, I felt like I'd been hit by a truck, but I was infused with a strange sense of serenity. After a whirlwind of activity that included a check of our vitals, some poking and prodding, and a lot of questions, Aileen and I were finally alone.

She sat on the edge of her bed and looked at me for the longest time. Finally, she said, "You saw them too, didn't you?"

It took me a moment to grasp what she meant. I thought they were a dream, but if Aileen had seen them… "How did you know?"

Her laugh was light and real. "Because under all those bruises, you look peaceful in a way I've never seen you."

To my chagrin, tears trickled down my face. That's exactly how I felt, but something was niggling at me. "The woman who spoke to me?" I took a deep breath, trying to muster the strength for my next words "Do you remember how we disagreed about who said 'jump' in the sleigh accident?" I knew I sounded crazy but felt compelled to share my thoughts. "I think it was her voice."

Aileen nodded tentatively then more vigorously with what I hoped was dawning understanding. We smiled at one another and shrugged. It could have been her voice, or side effects of the hospital meds we were taking. We'd probably never know.

Aileen said, "You know, I've seen them at Couloir. Once I brought them afghans when they were standing on the deck in the snow…"

Aileen was still talking, but I couldn't hear her. Suddenly my head was flooded with thoughts of my recent behavior. I'd always been an ordered, methodical person who believed public displays of emotion were crass. Now I thought about all the horrible things I'd said and done to her over the last several months. My shame and embarrassment seemed overwhelming. And Aileen's response was concern about my well-being. Crap, she'd invited me to recuperate in her home. I tried to stifle a sob, but when she stopped mid-sentence and looked up in alarm, I knew I hadn't been successful. She walked a bit unsteadily to my bed and took my hand. Before she could say anything, I blurted, "I'm so sorry, Aileen. I feel so ashamed for all the times I've undermined or ignored you…" I was hiccupping between sobs.

Aileen said softly, "Breathe. Just breathe." And I stilled then, giving her a curious look. She nodded. All my anguish evaporated in a breath.

Brian, the hotelier

Sleep never came. Every time I shut my eyes, I saw Aileen and Taylor, bruised, broken, and poisoned. Could someone at my hotel really be at the root of this? Had I hired a psychopath?

Just after dawn I heard a knock on my door. I opened it to an equally exhausted Patrick, still dressed in yesterday's clothes. Bless him, he carried a tray with four large espressos, warm croissants, butter, and blueberry jam. We drank the first espressos in silence. As I reached for the second, Patrick said, "I spoke with my staff at Les Bosses this morning. They understand my twin is my first priority and are prepared for me to be only electronically available for the foreseeable future. I just left housekeeping, and they agreed to give Aileen's house a thorough cleaning today. We need to remember to give them a bonus; the house is pretty nasty. I was going to have a security system installed today, but I know Aileen. She will never turn it on. So, instead I decided to have Joe Cocker come out and stay with Aileen. He loves her, and will take good…"

Patrick was talking so fast his words blended together. I

held up my hand, and he stopped, looking anxious and a little irritated at my interruption. "Joe Cocker? Is he still alive?"

He rolled his eyes. "You know Joe. My boxador."

"Boxador? I thought Joe was just a mutt."

Patrick clenched his teeth at my interruption. "Joe's not a mutt! He is a highly intelligent boxer-Labrador retriever mix. Do you have any more trivial questions?"

I gestured for him to continue.

"Joe won't let anyone with bad intentions get near Aileen. And, I'm having Apple watches delivered tomorrow morning for both Aileen and Taylor. Then if they can't reach their phones, they still can call for help from their watches. I've already arranged for Beth to go over to the house tomorrow and teach them about the emergency and health monitoring apps. I still have to work on security arrangements for the times the girls are alone." Patrick finally ran out of steam and reached for his second coffee.

I was about to chide Patrick about being so hyper, when I realized my best friend had gone very still. He sat slumped, staring at the floor. I'd never seen Patrick like this. "Are you okay?"

Patrick's response was a sharp intake of breath. "This just isn't fair. Aileen's been through so much. She's never done anything to hurt anybody, yet people are always trying to hurt her."

Unsure what to say or do, I just watched and waited. Finally, Patrick looked at me, "I can't lose her, Boss. I just can't!" And he began to quietly cry.

We were wrecks, but once showered, shaved, and in clean clothes, Patrick and I entered the conference room for our meeting with the acting management team. I was pleased to see J had received my text inviting her to the meeting. She was sitting quietly in the back of the room against the wall. All looked up expectantly as we took our seats except for Tom who was tapping frantically on his laptop. I looked around the table before starting. Charlie was sitting on the edge of his chair, clearly distraught. I had to remember to assure him we in no way believed he had anything to do with the sleigh accident. Next, Beth, who looked like she always did, all business. Then Missy, who I'd asked to step up while Aileen was out of commission. Missy looked simultaneously excited and nervous. Of course, it was her first management meeting. Sierra looked at me expectantly. And Tom kept his head down, focusing on his computer.

"The purpose of this morning's meeting is to provide a brief update on our injured managers, and to clarify everyone's role during this, uh…" I couldn't think of the right word.

"Crisis?" Beth offered.

"Yes, unfortunately it's quite appropriate. Thank you. I believe Sierra has been keeping you informed." Everyone nodded. "But I wanted you to hear it from me. The sleigh incident was no accident. It was attempted murder. In addition, yesterday someone or someones succeeded in poisoning Aileen and Taylor at Aileen's house. Had it not been for an observant neighbor, both women would have died."

To my relief there were no questions other than Missy's; she asked when they would be well enough to return home. Patrick told the group they were expected tomorrow, but given the circumstances, they would not be seeing well-wishers.

The team seemed to understand.

My next agenda item was to clarify roles. "Charlie, Beth, Sierra, and Tom, you will continue in your regular roles, though there'll be a few extra assignments. Sierra, I appreciate you continuing to keep all members of management fully informed, and if there are any questions from staff, guests, or the community, please direct them to me. Charlie, first I want to acknowledge your astute observation the day of the sleigh event and your immediate call to the police. You are to be commended. I want you to continue liaising with the police in that matter, and of course, keep Patrick or me informed. Beth, I understand you already have an assignment from Patrick. I want to assure all of you, if Patrick asks you to do something, he speaks for me."

"That leads me to Patrick and Missy. Patrick and I will be assuming Taylor's duties for the duration. And Missy…" I tried to smile because she was clearly excited about her temporary new role, "…will step up to cover Aileen's responsibilities. If you have any problems or questions, Missy, please see me immediately. Other than monitoring the investigation, my sole focus will be on working with you all to keep our guests happy, and our hotel running."

I looked around the table. "Any questions?" No one spoke up. "Comments?"

Without taking her arm off the table, Missy raised her hand. "Missy?"

"I just want to thank you for this opportunity. I'll do my best." As if sensing the inappropriateness of her excitement, she added, "I'm just so sorry it's under these circumstances."

I smiled at her. It wasn't her fault Aileen and Taylor had

been injured. "If that's it..."

Tom spoke for the first time. "I have a point of business to bring up." Without waiting for a response, he continued. "Over a week ago *before* all the trouble started, I began working with Missy to conduct an inventory of our premium spirits. As you know, this includes all the wines and spirits worth over one-hundred-fifty dollars per bottle. They are kept in a locked cage in the wine cellar." Tom pulled out some sheets of paper from under his computer. "This first document is the inventory list from the latest stocking. The second is a summary of what has been consumed, and what should be the remaining units. Lastly, the inventory list Missy prepared last week. I was there when she conducted the inventory, so I can vouch for its accuracy." Tom passed the sheets to me. "You will note that five cases of wine, and ten bottles of high-end whiskeys and cognacs are missing. This represents approximately eighteen thousand dollars of missing inventory." He paused. With a strange look of satisfaction and a glance at Patrick, he said. "I checked with all members of the bar staff. The only person who has the key to the storage cage is Aileen."

All the air was sucked out of the room. Patrick started to get out of his chair, but I held his arm and would not let go.

Charlie jumped up, yelling, "You little shit, who the hell do you think you are?"

"Sit down, Charlie. Everyone, be quiet." I took some deep, slow breaths in an effort to keep calm. I looked at Patrick, saying softly, "I've got this." He was still straining against my hold. "Did you hear me, Patrick, I *will* handle this." After a moment, he relented, but his look said: *you better.*

"Tom, were you aware that as owner of this hotel, I also have a key?"

Tom looked like I was speaking a foreign language.

"And if you had spoken with either Aileen or me before you undertook this unauthorized investigation, you would know I have set the spirits you mentioned aside for this year's charity auctions." I paused to let my words sink in. "Why don't you join me in my office…" I glanced at my watch, then at J. "At noon." Turning to the rest of the group, I said, "Sierra, J, why don't you head to my office. I will be there momentarily. For the rest of you, let's get back to work."

Tom sprinted out the door. The rest of the team quickly followed. I held onto Patrick's arm until we were alone.

As soon as I let go, he started to pace. "You should have let me take him apart. I told you he was a jerk. I'll never understand why you brought him out here and promoted him, when I was in the process of building a case to fire him." Patrick's rants were getting loud.

The door opened, and both of us looked up annoyed at the interruption.

"Wow. I could hear you down the hall. You two may want to keep your voices down, you're scaring your employees," Ian said as he strode in. Without waiting for an invitation, or response, he took a chair. "J and I…" He looked around, "Where is she? She was here a minute ago."

J entered the room, closing the door behind her. She gave Patrick and me a *sorry-about-this* look then said to Ian, "Sierra was a little upset when you told her she would not be needed. You could have been a bit more tactful. I was trying to calm her down."

"It seems everyone is upset around here. I thought you'd want to hear about my interviews with Fred and Maureen Reynolds." He smiled at the two men glaring at him.

"This is a bad time, Ian. Couldn't you have called?" I asked.

"Not really. I needed to come up to serve one of your employees with a search warrant." Looking around, he screwed up his face. "Don't you provide refreshments at your meetings?"

Patrick ignored Ian's question. "Which employee?"

"Tom Ruiz. Before I met with the Reynoldses today, I stopped by Darcy Cheney's office to ask her some follow up questions...."

I was confused. "Who is Darcy Cheney?"

Patrick responded quickly. "Aileen's neighbor. The one who called the ambulance." His eyes still focused on Ian. "What does Darcy have to do with Tom?"

"I asked her if she'd seen any unusual cars hanging around the neighborhood. Social workers tend to be very observant. Did you know Darcy is a social worker?"

Patrick was moving from agitation to anger. "*And* did she?"

Ian raised his hands. "Hey calm down, I'm getting there. Yes, and she wrote down the license plate number the third time she saw the car cruising down the street. That's why I was able to get a search warrant for Tom's office, car, and home."

The door flew open again. Tom was in a rage. He scowled at Ian. "I was told you would be in here talking about me to my employer. You have no right." When Tom spotted J standing against the wall, he yelled, "And what is *she* doing here?"

Ian was unfazed. He pulled some papers out of his inside jacket pocket. "This is a search warrant for your office, car, and house."

Tom ignored Ian and ran out of the room. "I'm calling an attorney."

Ian shrugged and started to follow Tom. I stopped him. "Ian, could you add something to your search warrant?" I could feel Patrick and J eyeing me curiously.

Ian said, "Depends. What is it?"

"This morning in our management meeting Tom accused Aileen of stealing over fifteen-thousand dollars-worth of premium wine and spirits."

Ian's eyes got big. I pulled out the documents Tom had given me. "Actually, he considerably underestimated their value, but that's beside the point. I have all the items listed in his inventory in my quarters. All except one, which I have reason to suspect he may have filched for himself, thinking no one would notice. I mean, what's one more bottle?"

"Well, it's tied to a pattern of behavior against Aileen. I'll have to see if I can add it, though it seems a lot of bother for a bottle of booze."

"This is a Pierre Ferrand Ancestrale seventy-year-old cognac I purchased for fifteen-hundred dollars."

J, the consultant

Ian said he would brief us on the Reynoldses as soon as he gave his officers some final instructions, and he left.

When we reached Brian's office, Patrick said, "Can you fill me in later, Boss. I have a lot to do before I pick Joe up at the airport." He didn't wait for an answer.

It was just the two of us. I wondered who Joe was, but it didn't seem like the right time to ask.

Brian glanced at his watch. "I don't believe Tom will be making our noon appointment," he said, his voice thick with disgust. "I wanted to speak with you alone anyway. How about if we have lunch? I'm hungry."

"I think Ian will be returning soon. Shouldn't we wait for him?"

Brian chuckled. "If we're eating, he'll find us. Let's chat while we go to the dining room; Ian can report over our meal. When we're finished, I want to get over to Aileen's and help Patrick."

He spoke as we walked. "When this is all over, we need to reassess what kind of work the management team requires, which most likely will include at least one new member. But for now, there's not much we can do." I was about to tell him I had anticipated his placing the assignment on hold when he continued. "The thing is, J, if you're willing, I'd like you to stick around. Patrick's priority is Aileen, as it should be. And since Taylor is staying at Aileen's, Patrick can watch over her too. Mine must be Couloir. In the chaos that was once my management team, I need a confidante and sounding board I can trust." He stopped walking and turned to me. "Are you game?"

"I would like that," I said, feeling unexpectedly humbled by his confidence.

"There you are," boomed Ian, as he ran to catch up. "You weren't going to go to lunch without me, were you?"

Brian and I ordered seafood cobb salads; Ian ordered a steak sandwich with double fries. We made small talk until our food was served. I could tell Brian was anxious to get over to Aileen's, so I interrupted one of Ian's battle stories. "Did you interview Maureen and Fred together or separately?"

Brian nodded his thanks as Ian finished chewing some French fries.

"I wanted our initial meeting to be friendly. I called first thing and asked if I could stop by. Fred agreed immediately, said Maureen had hot cinnamon rolls in the oven, and to come on over. Maureen and Fred met me at the door and seemed happy to see me. As I followed them into the kitchen, Fred asked me if this was a social or business call. I said business but got no reaction. It was when I asked about the last time either of them had seen Aileen that Maureen went bonkers. After calling Aileen a number of names including whore and crook, she told me to get out of her house." Ian paused and stared at his half-eaten lunch. "I'm talking about the Maureen Reynolds who I thought was a nice, stable, civic-minded lady. She was screaming so loudly neighbors came out of their houses to see what all the commotion was." Ian looked bewildered. "Clearly, I'd chosen the wrong strategy." He took a sip of his milkshake and continued. "When I got back to the department, there was a message from Fred apologizing, and asking me to stop by his office." Directing his gaze at Brian, he said, "Fred told me pretty much what he told you on the plane. He went along with Maureen when they saw the announcement of Aileen's appointment at Couloir, solely because he thought if he didn't, Maureen would kick him out of the house. He had been unaware of the recent letter to the editor until you showed it to him. Most importantly, he was genuinely shocked to hear about the attempted poisoning." Ian took a large bite of his steak sandwich, and mumbled, "Fred also said Maureen was contacting their attorney, so this would probably be the last time he could speak freely."

We speculated on why Maureen hated Aileen with no new insights as we finished lunch. Looking antsy, Brian thanked Ian for taking the time to brief us, and with a quick apology, said he needed to leave. Ian looked at me questioningly. I grabbed my purse and stood up. He gave the dessert menu one longing look and followed. As we walked out, he said, "I didn't want to bring this up during lunch, but it appears there was arsenic in the cookies." A couple entering the restaurant must have heard the tail-end of Ian's announcement, because they looked at one another and left. Fortunately, Brian didn't notice.

My mobile vibrated in my purse all the way home. I really needed to get a new car with wireless technology. My earbuds would work, but they were always somewhere at the bottom of my purse. I answered without glancing at the caller ID as I pulled into the garage.

"Hello."

"You finally answered!" Kate's voice grew faint, as if she turned away from the phone. "She finally answered."

"Sorry, Kate, I was driving. Give me a second, I'm just walking into the house." Quickly shrugging off my winter gear, I fell into my office chair. "What's up? Who's there with you?"

"Jean is. I have you on speaker. We called to tell you it worked."

"What worked?"

"Your idea of getting Roberta Hart to help with the Colonel."

"What are you talking about? We just talked about this a few days ago. How could it possibly have worked already?"

Jean replied. "Kate and I thought it was such a good idea we called Berta as soon as we got off the phone with you. Apparently, she was a longtime friend of Emily's and knows the Colonel quite well. When we explained the situation, she was not surprised. First, she asked us to send her the minutes from the last board meeting and the Colonel's proposed agenda. Then told us to call an emergency board meeting for this morning to appoint her my proxy until I can return."

"Were both of you able to attend this morning?"

Kate answered. "I did. Jean was skyped in. As soon as

it was over, I drove over here to the hospital so we could celebrate."

"Start from the beginning. What happened?"

"Berta and the Colonel arrived together and sat next to one another. Later we found out she insisted her driver pick him up so they could discuss the agenda. Berta opened by telling everyone how committed she was to *Hope For Our Children's* mission then said, and I quote: "This is a difficult time for Jean, and I believe the Board owes it to her to do something worthwhile while she's taking care of her husband. Since we have a very qualified executive director in Gail Edwards, I want us to spend this time in fundraising mode and start contacting potential major donors." Then she patted the Colonel's hand, saying: "And George is as excited as I am about it." While everyone stared at Berta, a little stunned, she handed out a one-page document with assignments for each of us. It was masterful."

"Did anyone object?"

"No one. She paired us, new member with experienced member, outlined a process for contact, provided us with a list of possible donors, and, sent us on our way. She, of course, paired herself with the Colonel." I could hear Kate's grin.

Jean added, "It was brilliant. I can't thank you enough for thinking of Berta. I'm just embarrassed I didn't."

We continued chatting about Berta and the Colonel until I heard Ross pull into the driveway. "Sorry. Got to go. We're going to a mountain party, and I need to change out of my work clothes."

I was entering our upstairs bedroom when Ross opened

the front door. "J, I'm home. Are you ready? We need to arrive early because I have the kegs."

"Give me five," I yelled.

I threw on a pair of jeans and a forest green turtleneck; tied my hair back into a ponytail and ran downstairs. "Did you get anything besides beer?" I asked hopefully as I hugged him. He opened up a cooler to reveal a bottle of Tito's vodka, a small jar of olives, a shaker, bag of ice, and two steel martini glasses. I hugged him again.

On the way up to Canyon Lodge, I told Ross about the Couloir management team meeting, Tom's indictment of Aileen stealing pricey spirits, and Patrick's visceral response to Tom's accusations. I had just enough time to tell Ross what Brian said really happened to the alcohol before we arrived at our destination, which put the rest of my update on hold.

Mountain parties, especially spur-of-the-moment mountain parties, are great. You run into people you haven't seen all winter, and some you saw yesterday. What was particularly nice about this party was that it wasn't just ski patrol; it was everyone who recently or still worked on the mountain—mostly the outside staff. The staffing essence of what comprised many visitors' mountain experience. Tonight, the group was ready to let loose despite the fatigue visible in their every move. And they knew how to party. I started the evening with my steel martini glass of Tito's and within minutes saw it being passed around until I lost sight of it. Every time the door opened with its rush of alpine air, people entered and left. All happy to be part of a mountain family. The comradery was understated and ever-present. Ross and I started our journey through the room together, separated, and rejoined without noticing. It was how a real party was meant to be.

Sometime around ten o'clock, Ross found me and asked if I was ready to leave. I started to demur, but something about his manner made me find my coat and follow him outside. Instead of walking to the car, he led me over to an icy bench. He placed a small blanket that looked suspiciously like it had been filched from the ski patrol room on the icy seat, and we sat. The air was freezing, but the night crystal clear. The sky was littered by a billion points of light. We took in the gift of a Sierra winter night, cold but for once without wind.

My party-buzz faded, and I was beginning to feel the chill when he said, "What if we get married next week? No crowd, just you and me? We could ask Kate and Nathan to be our witnesses. Then we could have a big party this summer." Ross stared down at his hands while he waited for my answer.

I closed my eyes, a million questions flooding my brain, that is, until someone poked me in the back. I turned to see Mary and Bob looking at me like I was hopeless. Ross looked up when I leaned against him. "It's perfect." We were really going to do it. We were really going to get married.

We passed two tall blond, curly-headed men and a petite woman walking toward the party as we headed for the car. I couldn't make out their faces in the dark, but Ross stopped and offered his hand, "Hey, Phil, Mike, it's been a while."

They shook hands, as the woman addressed me. It was Sierra. "Have you read my recommendations for HR?" Before I could answer, she said, "Of course you haven't." Was that anger in her voice? "Don't worry. Now that there's no management team, we don't need you anymore. Couloir can save some money, and I can help Brian rebuild the team." She grabbed onto both men's arms and headed into the party without another word.

Ross looked surprised. "I didn't know you knew Phil and Mike."

Still reeling from Sierra's rebuke, I asked, "I don't. Who are they?"

"Phil and Mike Berne. The two guys I was speaking to. They're Maureen and Fred Reynolds' adopted sons."

I stopped in my tracks, looking back at the threesome. "But you said their last name was Berne?"

"I thought I told you. When Fred's sister and her husband died, he and Maureen adopted them. But Fred was adamant that the boys keep their father's name."

"They work on the mountain?"

"Just Mike. He works in the rental shop. I think his brother works for the geothermal plant." Ross studied me. "You know Phil's girlfriend?"

"You could say that. She's the human resources manager at Couloir."

"You look upset. What did she say to you?"

I paused, pondering her words in light of her relationship with the Reynoldses. Deciding it was all too complicated this late in the evening, I said with a half-smile, "It doesn't matter. She was just being pissy."

Ross gently pulled my chin up to get my full attention. "Well, we can ponder all the implications tomorrow. Let's go home and call Kate and Nathan."

And we did.

Day 9
Aileen, the food & beverage director

It was almost noon when Patrick drove Taylor and me home from the hospital—for the second time in less than a week. Patrick and I argued while Taylor stared out the front passenger seat window with a hint of a smile.

"Patrick, I appreciate everything you are doing for us, but Taylor and I are not—I repeat *not*—going to have some musclebound security guard stay with us when you're at work. We're perfectly capable of taking care of ourselves while you're gone."

"Who said he's musclebound? Besides, I'm supposed to believe eating poisoned cookies from a gift basket was just the two of you reenacting Little Red Riding Hood?"

Taylor turned a little green but giggled anyway.

"Taylor, you're not helping. Do you realize we will have zero privacy?"

Patrick established eye contact in the rearview mirror. "I'll make you a deal, Sis. If you don't like him, you can ask him to leave."

"Don't think I won't. Remember, you can't back out. I have a witness."

We rode the rest of the way in silence. Every time I caught Patrick's eye in the mirror, he winked. Something was up. As we pulled into the driveway, I recognized Brian's car in front of the house, and groaned. "You're not going to tell me you talked Brian into staying with us?"

Taylor flinched her understanding. Now we were both glaring at Patrick, who annoyingly said nothing. We both understood. He knew there was no way we could tell our boss to get out of the house.

I was approaching the front porch when the front door opened. A smiling Brian stood on the porch watching us. Something flashed by him toward me. Seventy pounds of butterscotch fur sat down in front of me, drooling on my boots. "Joe. You brought me Joe Cocker." I hugged Joe with my good right arm, then asked him to follow me back to the car.

Patrick was still helping Taylor out of the car—my broken left wrist was much less awkward and painful than her broken right shoulder. Joe sat down waiting for introductions—he was a very intelligent and well-trained companion. Patrick took over. "Joe, this is Taylor, and you need to be very gentle with her." He stroked Taylor's back as if he were petting a dog. Cocking his head, Joe gave one soft bark, then stood still to accept Taylor's clumsy but happy pats.

A strong scent of cleaning solvent filled my nostrils when I walked up the porch steps, reminding me what the place must have looked like after Taylor and I were whisked away to the hospital. Entering, a feeling of apprehension gripped me, but the place was spotless. Actually, better than spotless. The couch and living room rug had been replaced with items that looked remarkably similar to items we had recently purchased for Couloir's honeymoon suite. The filched recliner now positioned next to the fireplace had a small table and lamp, which completed the room. Taylor and I looked at Patrick and Brian, who beamed with pride.

"You two are phenomenal. Thank you. Somehow, I'd not considered the mess we must have made of this place." Feeling badly, I added, "You know, we'll have to move the recliner back to the guest bedroom tonight so Taylor has some privacy."

Brian laughed. Patrick said, "No. The original chair is still in the bedroom. When the Boss and I went shopping at Couloir yesterday, we decided we might as well take the companion chair so Taylor can sit more comfortably out here."

The process of checking out of the hospital and driving home had been exhausting. Once Taylor heard the chair was for her, she headed for it. I dropped onto the couch. Joe paused, looked back and forth between Taylor and me, and managed to find a comfortable spot on a rug halfway between us. Patrick picked up our coats and belongings as Brian emerged from the kitchen with two mugs of chicken broth and handed them to us. Taylor thanked him but stared morosely into the cup.

Patrick caught the look. "Don't worry, the doc said you can start the brat diet tonight."

I should never have left Patrick in charge of getting our

home-care instructions. "Brat?" I said a little indignantly.

Grinning, Patrick responded, "Bananas, rice, apple sauce, and toast."

I took a few sips of the soup. The warm liquid felt good on my raw throat. So much had happened, my head was spinning. I'd become a different person in the last few weeks, going from invisible to target; meek to making a stand. Hell, the drowsy friend across from me had filed a complaint against me, then quit when I was exonerated. Now we were becoming friends. Emotionally and physically, I was confused and tired. My eyelids grew heavy. Glancing at Taylor, I saw she too was fading. My last conscious thought: who wanted to kill us?

It was getting dark when I opened my eyes. Taylor was still asleep, occasionally emitting a soft snore. Brian and Patrick were talking quietly at the dining room table. Only Joe, who was licking my uninjured hand, knew I was awake. I realized I really hadn't had a moment alone in days. I stared at Patrick. Despite everything that had happened, it was worth it to have him here. Leaving him had been my only reservation when I moved back to Mammoth. I loved my house, but it was only really home when he was here. Joe quietly chuffed, as if he could read my thoughts. "You're right," I conceded telepathically. "It's only home when *you* and Patrick are here." He smiled in a way only his human would recognize and lay down next to the couch.

Thoughts of my twin were interrupted when a phone vibrated in the kitchen. Brian picked it up. His irritation was apparent as he walked out of the room to take the call. Shaking his head with a half-smile, Patrick peered into the darkened living room. I waved, then put my finger to my lips. Brian returned and whispered to Patrick that Ian was outside. Startling us all, Taylor said, "Well. Invite him in." She sat up in her recliner, reflexively starting to stretch, until her shoulder reminded her what a bad idea that was.

Patrick turned on the lights as Brian escorted the chattering police chief in. Ian was ranting about almost running over the brothers from across the street who were sledding down the driveway. Ian stopped midsentence when he looked at Taylor and me. "Wow. I forgot how bad you two looked."

A flash of anger contorted Patrick's face. When I saw him moving toward Ian, I said, "What? You don't think black, blue, purple, and swollen is a good look? It's scary, but I think the four of us have gotten used to it."

He must have noted Patrick's glare, because he added, "Sorry. It just looks like you two really hurt."

Brian broke the tension. "Ian came to give us an update. Before he begins, would anyone like something to drink?"

In moments we were settled in the living room, drinks in hand—beers for the men, ginger ale for Taylor and me. While Ian focused his attention on the kitchen, waiting for munchies to magically appear, Patrick took the lead. "What did the search turn up?"

Ian tore his eyes away from the kitchen to respond. Taylor and I asked in unison, "What search?"

Brian stepped in and provided a quick summary of Tom being spotted surveilling the house, and Ian's decision to search his office, car, and house.

Patrick started to repeat his question, when Taylor interrupted, "Tom's a first-class bully, but he has neither the imagination nor the balls to attempt murder. He's just not smart or bold enough." Turning to me, "Don't you agree, Aileen?"

Not waiting for my answer, Patrick angrily demanded, "What did you find, Chief?"

Ian cleared his throat. "We did find some interesting items, which I am not at liberty to share with…"

Patrick snapped. "Then why did you come over?"

Looking at his empty bottle of beer, he said, "There is one item I can disclose, actually it's the reason I went out of my way to stop by."

We all looked at Ian. Ian still looked at his bottle of beer. Brian got up and brought him a fresh one. Ian smiled. "We found your fifteen-hundred-dollar bottle of cognac, minus a few ounces, on his kitchen sideboard."

Once again Taylor and I looked at one another confused. Brian briefly detailed the accusations Tom had made in the morning staff meeting. As he did, Patrick got up and started to pace, Taylor slumped back into her recliner, clearly agitated. Everyone started to talk at once.

Except me. I felt like I'd been slapped. The voices faded from my consciousness as I faced the truth. No matter how good I was at my job, someone would always see me as a convicted felon and expect the worst. Every time something was misplaced or missing, I would be suspected. I could never prove my innocence now. No one would believe me. I'd thought I was doing so well at Couloir. I had a good staff and believed we made a formidable team. But a closer examination of the last ten months included a campaign by the Reynoldses to have me fired, two formal employee complaints, and two attempts on my life. Even while I was recovering, I was being accused of theft. What was most devastating was that Missy, my executive chef, must have believed Tom's suspicions, or she would have gone to Brian before conducting the inventory.

Joe's whimpering drew me back to the living room. His head was in my lap. As I stroked him and asked what was wrong, I noticed the room had gone silent. Ian was gone. Patrick and Brian were now flanking me on the couch. Taylor looked at me from her recliner with tears in her eyes. Without a word, Patrick opened his arms. I leaned into him and sobbed.

Brian, the hotelier

The night was cold and dark just like my mood by the time I returned to Couloir. The world had turned upside down. Aileen told Ian we were all used to seeing Taylor and her bruised and swollen. Nothing could be further from the truth. Every time I looked at them my insides clenched. Who could hurt them? Ian and Patrick were convinced it was Tom, but I agreed with Taylor. Tom didn't seem to have the imagination or temerity to pull off two murder attempts. His attacks were petty and juvenile. But if not Tom, who?

After dropping my computer and jacket in the office, I headed to the bar for a well-deserved drink. The kitchen was bustling with the activity of dinner prep. It was heartening to see Missy directing staff as if she'd been born to the job. Finally, something was going right.

In contrast to the restaurant, the lounge was relatively quiet. I took my place at the end of the bar and surveyed the room. From the other end of the bar, Matteo caught my eye and held up a tall glass questioningly. I shook my head and mouthed, "Leave out the soda." He nodded, and a moment later a set down a double Belvedere vodka on the rocks.

"You look like crap, Boss. Aileen and Taylor are going to be okay, aren't they?" He was smiling, but I could hear the concern in his voice.

"Physically they have a way to go, but I think emotionally the two of them are doing far better than Patrick or me."The shame of not being able to protect them was visceral.

"Don't be so hard on yourself, Boss. No one could have anticipated either of the accidents."

The flash of anger I felt when Matteo referred to the attacks as accidents must have radiated across my face, because Matteo held up his hands as he took a step backwards. "Hey, I didn't mean they were accidents. It's clear they were intentional. I just meant, who could have known. They're both great managers and good people."

I exhaled slowly. "Sorry. I hope you know I'm usually not this touchy." Sipping my vodka, I asked. "We never finished our conversation. Why *did* you file a harassment complaint against Aileen?"

And, as if on cue, a large group of local women in their mid-thirties walked into the bar. I knew these women well. The ringleader, a lovely, petite blond dressed in leopard skin leggings topped with a cream-colored turtleneck, brown cashmere cape and matching fur hat with a smile that took up half her face, yelled, "Matteo, we need some drinks, and we need them now." With her unmistakable laugh, Dottie Hartman added, "And get one for yourself, you're joining us." The group shrieked in affirmation.

Moments later, everyone had their beverage of choice. Bowls of warm cashews dotted their table. And Matteo had brought over a barstool to sit on, explaining that he needed the vantage point to keep an eye on his other guests. This is why I hired Matteo; he knew how to balance charm and attention to his responsibilities. Couple that with his ability to speak to most international guests in their own language and his strong local following.

One of the women—her name escaped me— saw me staring at the group and started to wave. *My* charm had vanished a few days ago, so pretending I hadn't seen her, I picked up my phone and listened to voicemail.

The first one was from Ian, informing me his team had confirmed the snowmobile crash was definitely sabotage. I hadn't really thought it was an accident, but hearing the official conclusion killed any late-night hope this was all just one big chunk of bad luck.

The next voicemail was from the Sacramento consultant who had conducted the two sexual harassment complaints. I listened, then replayed it. It had my attention. "Hello, this is Jenn Lee. I recently conducted two internal investigations for Couloir…" A slight chuckle escaped my lips, as I thought believe me, I know who you are. I just paid your invoice; a lot of money to prove nothing happened. "Before I archive a case file, I review the contents, and listen to all the recordings. This includes face to face and phone exchanges." I knew she recorded interviews. I didn't know she recorded phone conversations. "I was listening to the initial call from your HR manager, asking if I was available to assist. After introductions, she gave me a brief overview of the two complaints, and her impressions of those involved." There was a brief pause in the voicemail. When she continued, her professional tone seemed to waver, as if she was unsure how to proceed. "Well, I … ah… understand you've had some recent… ah… problems at Couloir, involving the young woman I was investigating. Otherwise, I probably wouldn't be making this call." I heard her sigh and whisper, "I should have waited until I could talk to him directly." I wasn't sure if she was talking to someone else in the room, or to herself. Her voice returned to its original professional demeanor. "When I asked your HR manager to describe Aileen, she said, and I quote, 'She's been a problem since the day she arrived.' When I asked her what steps had been taken so far, she answered, 'I've conducted my own investigation, and I believe she's…' Sierra paused for almost thirty seconds, I timed it. Then instead of finishing her sentence she said, '…but my boss thinks we should bring someone in from the outside.' The entire exchange didn't feel right. It may be nothing, but I felt you should know. If you have any questions, just call."

The final message was from J. After a long sigh, she said, "I was hoping you'd answer. I wasn't sure I could get you alone tomorrow. Wanted to ask you if you know Sierra's boyfriend is Phil Berne. She lives with him and his brother, Mike. If the names don't ring a bell, they didn't for me either. Apparently, they're Fred Reynolds's adopted sons."

As I tried to process what I had just heard, a steaming bowl of broth and fish was gently pushed in front of me. Without looking up, I said, "No thanks, Matteo. I'm really not hungry."

It was Missy not Matteo. "I'm thinking of putting this on the menu. If you're not hungry, at least try a bite or two and tell me what you think." She was beaming.

I forced a smile onto my face. "Sure." I took a small bite. It was good, really good. I took a second taste. "This paella is great. Is this the only addition you and Aileen are making to the menu?"

"Well…" Missy answered, hesitantly. "I thought I'd experiment with some dishes, and then surprise Aileen when she returns."

How to respond? Aileen never liked surprises, and that was before someone tried to kill her. But Missy looked so ecstatic, and the paella was exceptional. "Probably best to let her know what you're doing, instead of springing it on her all at once. She should be able to go back to her regular diet in the next day or two. Why don't you prepare a container I can take with me tomorrow, then email her to let her know it's coming, and include any other ideas you have."

There seemed to be a slight hesitation before Missy smiled broadly. "I know she's quite particular about what's on the menu, but Aileen also likes initiative. You'll find a package for her in the smaller refrigerator tomorrow morning. Please be sure to tell her your opinion of the dish." And she headed back to the kitchen.

My thoughts returned to J's voicemail. Why did I not know Sierra was dating one of Fred's sons? Was it significant? My thoughts spiraled. How out of touch with the management team was I? This time I was interrupted by a fresh drink, delivered by a more serious Matteo.

"You know, Boss, I've been thinking about your question. All I can say is that filing the complaint was a stupid decision on my part, and I deeply regret it."

I studied Matteo. He rocked back and forth on his heels

uncomfortably. "Did anyone suggest or encourage you to file the charge?"

He looked down. "I take full responsibility."

"That's not what I asked."

Slowly he looked me directly in the eyes. "I take full responsibility. If you need to fire me, I understand. But I can't blame my actions on anyone else. The fact is, I filed the complaint."

Matteo's eyes were wet, but he held my gaze.

I had to know. "Was it Sierra?"

Matteo looked like I'd hit him. I had my confirmation. The tension was broken when Dottie yelled over, "Where's our Matteo?"

He gave me a quick nod and hustled toward his excited guests.

I still wanted to know *why* he did it.

Day 10
J, the consultant

After leaving several messages, Ross and I finally reached Kate and Nathan early in the morning. They'd been on an impromptu golf excursion and left their cell phones at home on purpose. Part of me asked, who does that? The other part answered, newlyweds. Anyway, for two people so difficult to reach, it was incredibly hard to get them off the phone once they agreed to be our witnesses. They wanted to know what we would be wearing, what kind of flowers I would have, even the day and time of the ceremony. It was a little embarrassing to reply we didn't have a clue. So today I would begin making the arrangements.

Given the volatility of the weather recently, Ross and I thought Couloir provided the most elegant options. It gave us the flexibility to have the ceremony outside if it was sunny, or inside if it insisted on snowing. I also could reserve two suites, so Kate, Nathan, Ross, and I could celebrate without getting into a car afterward. Now I was on my way to Brian's office to book the wedding. Preoccupied with making a list of questions in my head, I literally ran into Beth and her son,

Michael, who were headed in the opposite direction. She dropped a bag as we collided, and what looked to be iWatches and charging stations went skittering down the hallway. Beth looked a little annoyed, but ten-year-old Michael was laughing as he skipped down the hall, picking up the spilled contents.

"Sorry. I was so set on seeing Brian before he got too busy, I didn't pay attention."

Beth smiled. What I had assumed was annoyance was just surprise. "We're fine, but I'm afraid if you want to speak with Brian it's going to be a long wait. He's working from Aileen's house again today." Michael handed his mother the scattered items one at a time, so she could put them back into her cloth bag. "We're on our way over there right now. Anything you want me to tell him?"

I was disappointed. This conversation was too important not to be face to face. "How long will you be meeting with him?" This woman who looked like a fashion model let out a loud guffaw. "I take it this is not business, but something personal?" Even Michael was looking at me with interest.

"How did you know?"

"You just turned bright red."

Michael chimed in, "You really did!"

Beth grinned at Michael. "Actually, Michael and I are meeting with Aileen and Taylor to give them these and teach them how to use them." She held up the cloth bag. "Patrick thought the watches would make it easier for them to answer calls or phone for help, since they seem to frequently misplace their phones." I must have looked pathetic because she added, "Why don't you come with us? We'll be there about an hour before we come back. Would that give you enough time with Brian?"

I was trying to find a polite way to decline, thinking I could do a little work, then drive over myself. Michael interrupted my thoughts, saying excitedly, "Mom and I are going to Burgers for lunch after. You could come too and tell us all about the time you almost got blown up!"

It was Beth's turn to blush. "Michael, that's none of our business."

Now Michael looked disappointed, and I caved. Winking at him, I asked, "Which time?" His eyes grew wide.

There was a commotion on the front porch as we pulled into the driveway. Patrick was yelling at someone with his back to us. Concerned about Michael, I suggested, "Let me see what's going on. Why don't you wait here?" I heard Beth's guffaw—a sound that was growing on me—and three car doors opened. Before we got halfway up the walk, Fred Reynolds rushed past us, his face red with fury. Patrick was still on the porch glaring at Fred as we mutely entered the house.

We halted just inside the door. Taylor was trying to comfort Aileen on the couch, Brian was pacing—really pacing, and Joe Cocker stood in the middle of the room watching everyone. No one acknowledged our presence until Michael asked the room, "Why is everyone so upset?"

It was like he broke a spell. Brian stilled and seemed to be searching for the right words. Aileen carefully stood up, using her sleeve to wipe her eyes, and greeted us. Taylor followed awkwardly, looking a little relieved at our interruption. "I'm sorry. Things were going well until our visitor arrived."

"What did Fred do?" I asked, alarmed.

Aileen glared at the open front door. "It wasn't Fred who caused the fuss…"

Patrick stormed back in. Ignoring the rest of us, he yelled, "There is no way I'm going to let Fred or his family near you. You heard what Brian said. Sierra is dating one of his adopted sons. Do you think all these incidents are just bad luck? Someone's out to get you, and like it or not, I'm going to protect you."

"But he just came by to apologize. You can't believe Fred had anything to do with this?" she asked, pointing to Taylor's and her own injuries.

In a more subdued voice, Patrick said, "Aileen, he hurt you before. Wasn't that reason enough to ban him from this house?" He hugged his twin, saying softly, "I won't ever let anything bad happen to you again."

There was an awkward silence while we watched the family drama, until Brian addressed Aileen and Taylor. "I believe Beth and Michael are here to orient you to your new iWatches. Why don't you meet in the living room? Patrick, clearly you've taken possession of the dining room." We all glanced at two computers, a printer, and files littering the table. "So, that leaves the front porch for us to meet, J. Hope that coat is warm."

Aileen offered, "There's a sitting area in my bedroom. Why don't you meet in there?"

As we all moved toward our designated workspaces, Beth whispered in my ear, "Sierra's dating a Reynolds?"

Not knowing how to respond, I just shrugged. I'd been hoping to keep this little tidbit between Brian and me until we could plan a strategy to address it, but that ship had sailed.

Aileen's bedroom was nothing like the rest of the house, which was functionally charming. This was like walking into sunshine. The walls were pale yellow with white crown molding and trim. To the left of the entrance was her bed with a white down quilt and throw pillows in different shades of blue. Next to it was a white dresser with a small bronze sculpture of a ballerina on top. To the right was a large sitting area with two butter yellow upholstered armchairs anchoring a small white table. Two large windows provided enough light that even on the dreariest of days would be sufficient. The room was tied together by a large weaving with multiple textures and shades of yellow and blue yarns accented by beads and glass coins of silver and gold. It was crude but elegant. All encased in an acrylic box. I realized it could be an early work of the same artist who created the hanging in the police interrogation room.

Before I could comment on the décor, Brian sank into one of the chairs, looking frustrated. "Glad you came today, J. I guess you knew we'd have a lot to discuss."

My first instinct was to tell Brian I was here on personal business, but one look said that would be a mistake.

"When I engaged your services, I thought we had a few fixable issues on the team. How stupid was that? Last night I listened to a voicemail from the consultant who investigated the harassment charges against Aileen and learned Sierra may have already made her mind up Aileen was guilty *before* the investigation was conducted. Then I heard your message that Sierra is dating a Reynolds, something I should have been aware of. The final bomb was when I learned Matteo filed his harassment complaint at Sierra's urging."

Shocked at this last tidbit, I was about to ask a question, but Brian held his hand up. "You do realize the only member of the team I've kept fully informed throughout all that's happened is Sierra. How blind and stupid could I be?"

I sat quietly while he took a series of deep breaths. I'd learned a few things about Brian over the past few days. His hotels were his life, his passion. He needed to be in control at all times. His instincts about people were hit or miss. Take two of his hires: Aileen and Tom.

He interrupted my assessment. "Now that I got that out of my system, I'd like your thoughts on my plan for going forward."

I straightened in my chair organizing my thoughts, but he continued.

"It's imperative Aileen and Taylor remain here until an arrest has been made. As far as managing Couloir, Patrick has already taken over Tom's controller responsibilities. Taylor told me this morning she was confident her supervisors could keep Guest Services running smoothly, and that she would stay in regular communication with them. Likewise, Aileen will manage her team remotely. Missy seems to be doing a good job overseeing the kitchen, which makes Aileen's physical absence possible." Brian sighed. "With this new information, we need to decide what to do about Sierra. Do I let her know I'm aware of her relationship with a Reynolds? Do I temporarily place her on a paid administrative leave? Do I pretend we don't know about her boyfriend, and monitor her?"

He looked up at me expectantly.

"Before we decide upon what action to take," I said cautiously, "let's talk about what, as an employer, you can and cannot ask about an employee's private life."

Brian's shoulders started to slump when Joe started barking. The sound was loud and angry. The doorbell rang.

We rushed out to see what the commotion was. Patrick grabbed hold of Joe's collar. "I don't know what's wrong with him. But you better get it while I restrain Joe."

I peeked out the front window to see two unfamiliar cars and a Propane Company truck, while Brian opened the door to Sierra, Missy, and a gas company employee—all their attention focused on the barking dog. Missy held a large food container; Sierra looked determined; the man from the gas company appeared alarmed. He spoke first.

"I can't believe you're all still here. Everyone needs to vacate the premises immediately, then one of you can tell me where the gas leak is." The workman had our attention.

"What gas leak?" demanded Brian.

"The station just received a call from someone saying they lived here and could hear and smell gas. They were instructed to evacuate immediately." As if on cue, a second gas company vehicle pulled up to the front of the house—two men jumped out and ran toward the house. Everyone started talking at once.

Brian held up his hands for quiet. All complied except for the dog who was still barking. "Patrick, can you take Joe into the other room, and try to stop his barking?" Patrick nodded, looked at the newcomers suspiciously then muscled an unwilling Joe into Aileen's bedroom.

"Gentlemen, no one from this house reported a gas leak."

Apparently reading the first workman's name off his shirt, he said. "Rich, why don't you inspect the appliances in the kitchen and utility room, while your coworkers inspect the propane tank at the side of the house?"

As the men went to check for leaks, Missy and Sierra started to speak. Brian again held up his hands. "One thing at a time."

Minutes later the second truck pulled away and Rich returned. "Wow. I'm sorry. Must have been a malicious prank. Pretty crass, if you ask me, especially given their condition," pointing at Aileen and Taylor sitting together on the couch. "I don't mean to be rude, but what happened to you two? Were you in a car accident?"

Taylor responded, "Something like that."

As the door closed behind Rich, Brian turned to Missy. "I'm sorry. I forgot to pick up the paella this morning. Thanks for bringing it by." His tone was friendly but distracted.

Missy said cheerfully, "No problem, Boss. Instructions for heating are on the top." Looking at Aileen. "In case you haven't seen your emails this morning, I sent some new menu ideas for you to consider." She turned to go then paused and asked, "May I use the bathroom before I go?"

Brian responded perfunctorily, "Sure. There's a guest bath just on the other side of the dining room."

Watching Missy's cautious movements, I realized Patrick hadn't managed to quiet Joe.

Brian addressed Sierra stiffly. "And what brings you here?"

"I wanted to talk to you about..." She turned and glared at me. "Some ideas I have for the HR department and strengthening the management team."

Brian closed his eyes momentarily, as if trying to control himself. "This really isn't the time or place."

"Oh… I just thought… well, you might have more time here than at the hotel."

Brian didn't say anything.

Sierra turned red then simply nodded. She turned to go, followed by Missy. Just before the door closed, Brian said, "Ladies, please let the rest of the team know I can be reached electronically, but this house is off limits."

Missy giggled. "I'll tell Charlie when I see him."

I smiled to myself. Missy was right, Charlie was the only member of the team who wasn't here.

As the two women drove away, Aileen's bedroom door burst open and Joe ran to Aileen, looking smug. He'd protected his family. He chuffed, waiting for her praise. What he got was a room full of questions.

Patrick followed, saying to no one in particular, "I've never seen Joe act like that, not even when he was a puppy. Who was he barking at? Why was he so upset?"

Taylor admonished Brian. "What's up? You were really rude, especially to Sierra."

Beth asked, "Did anyone else notice Sierra only looked at Brian and J? And the way she eyed J was scary."

Aileen pondered. "Why would someone call the gas company and say there was a leak in our house?"

I chimed in, "That's a really good question. One I think we need to talk about."

Michael suggested, "Maybe we could do it over lunch?"

Brian sat down hard on a dining room chair and smiled

for the first time in a while. "I think that's a great idea, Michael. J and I can finish our discussion, and Patrick can whip up some lunch while you and your mother finish working with Aileen and Taylor."

Michael tried to hide his disappointment. I intervened. "I think Michael has his heart set on going to Burgers."

Beth started to object, but Brian stopped her. "Michael must have tasted Patrick's food." He winked at Michael. "Besides, I need a little time to wrap my head around everything that's happening. How much longer do you need with Aileen and Taylor, Beth?"

"About fifteen minutes."

"Great, J and I won't need much more than that. He smiled at Michael. "Let's get to work so this young man doesn't starve."

Less than an hour later, Michael was hustling Beth and me out the front door. He tried not to look impatient when I hesitated. "Aileen, the art piece in your bedroom is beautiful. Where did you get it?"

Aileen smiled. "That was a gift from a special friend for my twenty-fourth birthday. She made it. It was the only thing I kept from my earlier life."

"Well, I can see why you kept it. I've been looking for the perfect piece of art for over my fireplace."

"One of my kitchen staff told me she has a small studio in the industrial park, if you're interested."

"Thanks. I just might visit to see what else she's done."

As we drove to the restaurant, Michael asked his mother to explain why Aileen and Taylor asked so many questions about the various apps when it was all so simple.

My thoughts were divided between the genuine excitement Brian expressed when I told him Ross's and my wedding plans, and his angst over the correct steps to take with Sierra. He said he would arrange the former and asked me to come up with a strategy to handle the latter. We agreed he would not meet with Sierra until we met the next morning at Couloir after he had a *soul-cleansing* workout in the hotel sports center.

Putting my concerns on hold as I climbed into the back seat of Beth's car, I said, "Okay, Michael. Let me tell you about what it's like to see a garage explode."

He turned in his seat to look at me. "Awesome."

Taylor, the guest services director

After a lunch of applesauce and rice, I excused myself and went into the guest room to take a nap. The morning's excitement had taken its toll. I popped a pain pill and tried to find a comfortable position on the recliner. Waiting for sleep to come, I pondered how drastically life had changed in the span of a week. I've always been organized—some might call me anal—and outspoken, believing emotion and drama were inappropriate in the workplace. Perhaps I was this way because I was the only child of older parents. When my parents were alive, they worked multiple jobs as many service workers in a resort town did—Mom in restaurants, Dad in hotels. As soon as I was old enough, I took over many of the household chores, pretending our cabin was a grand hotel where everything had to be perfect for the guests. I carried the same obsession with me when I moved into my condo. At home and at work I planned for every contingency so there would be no surprises. But lately all my control had evaporated. First, quitting because I was upset about the outcome of the harassment investigation—what was I thinking? Then telling Missy she could stay with me when, if I'd taken a minute to think, I'd have known it was a disaster waiting to happen. Followed by a sleigh crash and a poisoning. Now I was living in Aileen's house afraid for my life while all manner of people walked in and out at all hours. My sense of control was gone and my nerves frayed. My eyelids grew heavy. My last thought: how did Aileen stay so calm?

It was dark outside when I woke. The house was quiet. After washing my face, a challenge when the only arm you can use is the non-dominant one, I went into the living room. To my great relief, I found only Aileen with Joe sleeping at her feet. "Perfect timing," she said, smiling. "I was going to make some tea. Would you like some?"

I didn't see Patrick or Brian, so I said, "Love some, and perhaps some real food?"

Aileen laughed. "I have some shortbread cookies. How does that sound?"

"Great, as long as they didn't come in a gift basket." Aileen rolled her eyes. "Do you have anything salty to accompany the cookies?"

"Popcorn?"

I studied Aileen as she prepared our snacks. Before I could stop myself, I blurted, "You've changed. Except with your staff, you've always been so... so meek, so invisible, so..."

"Obsequious." She looked upward, considering her words. "When I was young, I believed in myself. On those rare occasions I questioned something I did, or when someone hurt my feelings, Patrick would tell me to get over it. He said if someone treats you badly, it's about them not you.

I believed him. But eventually I forgot his words, especially when people started accusing me of things I didn't do. You know, I think the reason culinary work became so appealing is because you can depend on food, spices, and recipes; they don't disappoint or hurt you like people do."

A lump formed in my throat that tasted like guilt. "I'm sorry. Patrick was right..."

Before I could continue, Aileen shook her head. "It's all right, Taylor. I guess what I'm trying to say is that standing up to you was the reemergence of my old confidence. I'm not quite there yet, but it's returning. In some ways you did me a big favor."

I wanted to say more, but if Aileen could let it go, so should I. Instead, I asked, "Where are the men?"

"Brian went back to Couloir for the night, and I told Patrick to go with him for dinner, so we could have a little space. It took some time to convince him, but he went."

While the tea steeped and the corn popped, I said, "I heard J say something about a piece of art in your bedroom. May I see it?"

"Sure. Follow me."

My spirits lifted as soon as I walked into her room. "Wow. Who decorated your room? It's gorgeous."

Aileen came in behind me. "I did. It's how I survived my last year in prison." She said with obvious pride in her voice.

I stiffened, unsure how to respond. Aileen *never* mentioned her incarceration. If she noticed my discomfort, she didn't acknowledge it.

"You know," she continued, "I thought once I got through the first year, the worst was over. But looking back, the last was far more difficult. I started counting the days until I'd get out, scared to death something would happen to extend my stay. It became clear I needed a project to stay sane but had no idea what that could be. Then I heard two of the girls talking in the dining hall about their dream houses. Since I didn't think I'd ever have enough money to buy a house, I decided to design the perfect bedroom." Pointing at the magnificent weaving, she added, "Using that as my centerpiece."

"You have quite a gift. This is the first time I've walked into a room and immediately felt…" I looked for the right word, "joy."

Aileen looked pleased. "That's how the room makes me feel. It was a lot of grueling work, but it turned out just as I had imagined."

"YOU did all this? The painting? The crown molding?"

She laughed. "Yes. And I painted the furniture, upholstered the chairs, and made the pillows. The only thing I didn't do myself was install the windows."

I couldn't take my eyes off the crown molding, as I asked, "Where did you learn carpentry? How to upholster furniture?"

"Prison."

Her candor was so disarming, it seemed the right time to ask a question that had been bugging me for a long time. "I don't mean to pry, but why did Brian buy you a house? Was it like a signing bonus or something?"

Aileen's laughter was only hampered by her cracked ribs. I stared at her in astonishment as she fought to regain composure. What was so funny? I didn't find any humor in our boss buying her a house. "I'm sorry. I didn't mean to be so personal. But I don't see what you find funny," I snapped.

Her body still vibrated with stifled laughter. "Why would you think Brian bought me the house?"

I was incredulous. She was going to try to deny it? "The whole management team knows. Right before you started at Couloir, Brian was looking at houses. He not only bought the house, but he also stocked it with everything from dishes to linens and had one of my housekeeping crews clean it."

She wiped her eyes with the back of her sleeve. "No wonder everyone resented me when I joined Couloir. Brian found the house at Patrick's request because Patrick was in Colorado. It was Patrick who bought the house for me." Her voice caught as she glanced at a picture of Patrick on her bedstand.

I was mortified. "I thought... we all thought... Brian never said... I can't believe we all assumed... I'm so embarrassed... I shouldn't have even asked the question."

"Oh Taylor, I'm glad you did. It explains so much." Aileen's eyes widened. "I also understand why you thought I was having a relationship with Brian. In your shoes, I would have too."

While I searched for the right words, Joe with impeccable timing walked in carrying his food bowl in his mouth.

I was fascinated watching Joe eat his food as Aileen poured our tea and set out the popcorn and cookies. I'd never seen a dog eat so delicately. It was crazy. He took one bite at a time. Finally, I asked. "Is this how Joe eats all of his meals?"

Aileen nodded, as she took her place at the table. "Joe has many unusual traits." He looked up from his dinner, and chuffed. "See what I mean?" He'd stopped eating and looked back and forth between the two of us. "He knows we're talking about him."

"Well, I don't want to interrupt his meal. Tell me, where did you find the weaving in your bedroom?"

"It was a gift from Cindy Reynolds. It was her first *completed* weaving. We'd been quite close before the arrest. As you can see, she's quite a talented artist. It used to hang it in my office at work."

"Cindy Reynolds? They let you take it with you when you… uh… left?"

"Apparently Cindy left it on Patrick's porch after I was arrested with a note saying she made it for me and wanted me to keep it. When Patrick told me he was going to throw it in the trash, I begged him to pack it with my belongings." She whispered to herself, "If things ever calm down, I need to get it repaired."

"Are you referring to the tiny little hole toward the middle? I was wondering whether that was part of the design or damage."

"Damage. There used to be a beautiful piece of blue glass with faint yellow lines running through it where the hole is. I understand Cindy blows and cuts her own glass now, so I'm hoping she'll duplicate the original." Wrinkles creased her forehead as she added, "It may be quite a while before I can ask her. As you know, I'm not very popular with her family."

We sat in comfortable silence, sipping tea, nibbling on our snacks, and Joe on the floor between us keeping watch. Aileen grimaced as she stood up, and I thought she was getting something in the kitchen until Joe sat up, his ears perked. She began to pace. I was about to ask her what was wrong, when she said, "This afternoon I heard Brian and Patrick talking when they thought I was asleep. They seem to think I'm the target, and you've just been in the wrong place at the wrong time. I'm embarrassed to say I hadn't really thought about it, but they're probably right. After all, who would want to hurt you? This is *my* fault; I am so sorry."

Aileen seemed to shrink in on herself. When I stood to comfort her, my sling caught on the side of the chair. A sudden jolt of pain pushed me back in my seat, stars flashing before my eyes. Aileen and Joe were immediately at my side. I took deep, slow breaths to get the pain under control, finally managing to say, "We don't know that. Besides, *you* have nothing to be sorry about. *You* didn't do this to us." I couldn't help but needlessly add, "I wish we knew who did before..."

Sobered by the thought another attempt could be made, we finished our tea and snacks in silence. "We can't let this jerk get to us," Aileen said. "I have a collection of chick flicks. Want to watch one?"

Patrick walked in during the last scene of *Me Before You.* He started to say something until two tear-stained faces turned to shush him. The only one happy to see Patrick was Joe, who quickly followed him into the kitchen. Credits over, emotionally exhausted, Aileen and I said good night and went to our bedrooms, leaving the couch—Patrick's bed—available when he was ready.

The repeated ringing of the doorbell pulled me out of a deep sleep. I heard Patrick swearing, as he moved from the couch to the front door, and Joe left his guard post to see what was happening. I reached for my robe as Patrick's exchange with the visitor grew loud and angry with Joe barking his support. Aileen and I almost collided in the small dark hall, giving each other confused looks. Then Patrick yelled, "I didn't order any God-damned pizzas, and I'm not paying for them."

Day 11
J, the consultant

Morning sun filled my bedroom, lifting my spirits. The snow gods were granting a temporary reprieve. A peek out the window confirmed no dark clouds lurking on the horizon, and dozens of crocuses in the yard were poking their heads through the snow. It was definitely a day to be outside. But first, coffee.

I startled mid-yawn as I entered the kitchen. Dressed to go cross-country skiing, Mary and Bob impatiently looked at me then down at the kitchen table where my parka, wool beanie, ski pants, and heavy socks lay in a jumble. What a great idea. I was about to tell them I needed thirty minutes to get some coffee and dress when I remembered today's schedule: a meeting with Brian, a trip to the seamstress for a wedding outfit and a visit to an art gallery. Reading the resignation on my face, they didn't wait for an apology. Both just shrugged as they disappeared hand in hand. I made myself a double cappuccino and sulked.

It wasn't until my second coffee that I turned my attention to the morning's meeting. Brian was not going to like my recommendation. He was angry and wanted answers from Sierra. I would counsel against any confrontation about Sierra's personal life. Employers were not entitled to information that wasn't relevant to an employee's job. And who Sierra dated did not directly impact her ability to do her job. To do so would be to violate her privacy and risk legal action. I was sure he would counter with breach of confidentiality, or loss of confidence, but both were almost impossible to prove. In Sierra's case she was already hostile toward Brian. She was the only person on the management team who was not a director, and she resented it. In addition, she made it clear Brian hired me to do what she believed was part of her job. It was a good move to tell him not to speak with Sierra until after we met. His tendency to lead with his emotions when he was angry could get him into trouble, which would resolve nothing.

I was finishing some avocado toast when he called. "J, I think I blew it."

My chest tightened. "Blew what, Brian? I thought you were working out this morning, then meeting with me before you took any action?"

"I'm *in* the health club. Sierra barged in while I was on a stationary bike. I told her we would speak this afternoon, but she insisted we talk at once. I told her technically I was not at work and was not going to discuss anything with her while in workout clothes. I asked her to meet me at one o'clock in my office."

Brian paused so long I thought we lost our connection. "Brian, are you still there?"

There was a sharp intake of breath followed by a long,

slow exhale. "Sierra said she was taking the day off to meet with her attorney."

It was my turn to breathe deeply. "In that case, it's time to put your attorney on alert. He may want to wait and see what Sierra does, or he may want to meet with you."

"She."

"I beg your pardon, she?" I took a sip of my coffee.

"My attorney is a woman. Lynette Germaine. She's in Bishop. Do you know her?"

I almost spit my coffee all over the dining table. "I do. I did some... er... work for her last year."

"Was that you?" Brian asked in surprise.

"Was what me?" I asked cautiously.

"Of course, it must have been," he mumbled to himself then addressed me. "Lyn told me she'd hired a consultant to help her discover who on her staff was trying to destroy her reputation."

Did he refer to Ms. Germaine as Lyn? "I've consulted with her," I said vaguely. "She's definitely a good person to have on your side. You should call and brief her as soon as possible."

"I'll call her right now then get back to you."

Leaving my half-eaten breakfast on the table, I ran for the shower. If Brian made contact with Lynette, she would most likely want to meet with us immediately.

I was covered head to toe with soap suds when I heard my phone buzz twice. I grabbed for it and almost dropped it on the tile floor. The first text read: *"Driving down to meet with Lyn, will update you later."* Slightly mortified by my assumption he would want me with him when he met with

Lyn, I almost missed the second text. It was from an area code and number I didn't recognize. A low growl escaped my lips as the text revealed itself to be a single picture. A selfie of Mary and Bob showing off the pristine conditions on the Lake George trail at Tamarack Ski Lodge. My wet hands tried to type in a cryptic reply when the text disappeared as if it had never been there. How did they do that? I glumly returned to the shower to rinse off the suds that were steadily pooling on the floor.

First on the errands list was my seamstress, a remarkable craftswoman who had been altering my clothes for years. As I was about to drive out to Crowley Lake, a small community about ten miles out of town, it seemed prudent to call and make sure Dianne was free to meet with me this morning. After two rings, her recorded message informed me she would be out of town for the month of May. This morning was just getting better and better. What was I going to do about a wedding dress? I searched through my contact list to see who might recommend another seamstress.

Just as I was about to give up, my eyes lit on Mrs. Simpson's name. It was a long shot, but she just seemed like the kind of person who might know a seamstress. I phoned her with little expectation she, or anyone for that matter, could help me.

I was surprised when she responded, "Actually, J, I do. I found Molly by accident. I had a summer dress I'd worn for years, and it looked like it. When I saw her shop, I took a gamble and asked her if she could replicate it. Her work was amazing. I even asked her to make a second one in a different color."

When I asked where the shop was, she said, "It's between the bookstore and the coffee house. It's a very, very small space, possibly a sublet of a storeroom turned into a shop. Go see her, I'm sure you won't be disappointed."

Mrs. Simpson was right. If she hadn't told me where the shop was, I would have missed it. A bell tinkled as I walked into the long narrow room, and a little girl of about five looked up from a small table where she was coloring. She stood, went to the back of the small room, and shouted through a curtain, "Mommy, there's a lady here."

I heard, "Ashley, please tell her I'll be right out."

She gave me a shy smile and returned to her coloring.

Looking around the small area, I silently agreed with Mrs. Simpson's observation. It looked like a storeroom someone had walled off and sublet. My appraisal was interrupted when a young woman who looked to be in her late twenties came through the curtain, holding a bolt of cloth. "I guess it doesn't look like much, but most of our work is done at..." her voice trailed off. We stared at one another. She looked vaguely familiar, but everyone in Mammoth did; it's a small community.

As I studied her, she tossed the cloth onto a small counter and hugged me. When she let go, she shook her head, grinning. "J, you don't remember me, do you?"

Mortified, I responded, "You look really familiar, but... no. I'm sorry."

By this time the little girl was standing next to her mother, watching us closely. Her mother bent down and said, "Honey, this is the lady who changed our life."

She sensed my discomfort. "J, I'm Molly. Molly Burton..."

And just like that it all came back. This was the young woman, a single mother, who had originally filed a sexual harassment complaint against her boss, a man who was considered an unimpeachable pillar of the community. I had conducted the investigation that resulted in revealing him as a serial harasser of his young female employees.

Molly was still talking. "The settlement gave me the opportunity to start my own business doing something I love. Now I can purchase my own health insurance instead of having to work in an office for someone else to get coverage. Mom started teaching me to sew when I was Ashley's age, and it's been my passion ever since." She stroked her daughter's hair. "We even have enough business so mom can quit her job at the hospital when she's ready, and work with me." There were tears in her eyes. "But I'm guessing you came here for a reason. What can *I do for you*?" Placing special emphasis on the last four words.

"I need a dress to be married in…" I faltered, finally understanding just how outrageous my request was. "… by early next week."

Instead of laughing at the absurdity of the request, she asked, "And what do you want your wedding dress to look like?"

"I don't know."

She didn't flinch. "Ashley, how would you like to come with us next door for a hot chocolate?"

Ashley's face lit up. "Hot chocolate?!" She ran to her table to get a paper and crayons.

"Let me grab my tablet, and we can design your dress over coffee."

"Really?" I asked in a whisper.

"Absolutely." A tear glittered in her eye. "It's my privilege."

Beverages in hand, Ashley busily coloring as she sipped her cocoa, I explained the wedding party would only include four people. We would have a celebration with our friends in the summer. My attire preference was something simple but memorable, tea length, cream not white with perhaps a touch of color, and it needed to be versatile enough for the ceremony to be inside or outside, depending on the weather.

Without commenting, Molly quickly began to draw on her electronic tablet while I drank my third cappuccino of the morning and watched. With her attention entirely focused on her design, I had a chance to really see her. She looked like a completely different person, from the scared and disillusioned young single mother I interviewed a few years ago. She looked confident, radiant, and… I searched for the right word. Before I could find it, Molly said, "Something like this?" And turned the tablet toward me.

I gasped. "It's… it's beautiful. How could you know? It's perfect." The dress had a mock turtleneck, long sleeves, and a form-fitting bodice that ended at the hips. My mother would have said the color was ecru, but I called it cream. The skirt, which hung to just below the knee, looked soft and full, hinting at a lot of movement. It was also cream-colored but had squiggles of forest green. Next to the dress was what looked like a small shawl or large scarf. It was forest green with cream-colored squiggles identical to those on the dress.

Ashley stopped what she was doing and went to her mother's side to see what we were looking at.

You really like it?" Molly asked tentatively. "The bodice

would be a super-light jersey, and the skirt, chiffon-blend.

"I love it. It's what I asked for: simple but memorable." Pointing to the scarf, I asked, "What made you think of a scarf?"

Molly's eyes grew animated. "You said you may be inside or outside. You also said you wanted a touch of color. If you go outside, you can use it as a shawl, or cover your hair Monte Carlo style. Inside you can wrap it around your neck. And it accentuates the color in the skirt."

"How did you know forest green is my favorite color?"

Molly laughed. "J, I know we've only seen one another a few times, but you always have forest green on."

Looking down at my attire, a cream-colored bulky turtleneck over forest green cords, I mumbled, "Maybe you're onto something." I couldn't take my eyes off the sketch. Then my excitement faltered. "It's stunning, Molly. But I need it in less than a week. Where are you going to find material with squiggles on it?"

"I have the materials for the bodice and skirt, and I can order the scarf material and have it overnighted." She paused, smiling at Ashley who was now sitting in her mother's lap. Her cheeks flushed, "I'll paint the squiggles on the skirt and scarf. Besides being expedient, it will ensure that no two squiggles look exactly alike."

"You can paint material?" I must have spoken loudly, because even the barista looked at me in disapproval.

"I do." Molly said with a grin. "In high school I started making all my own clothes. I would see something I liked on the internet and put my own spin on it. Often it was by adding color to an otherwise drab outfit. Since Mammoth doesn't have a fabric store, I would order basic fabrics online, and paint my designs on them."

I was speechless. How difficult it must have been for Molly to work in a clerical job for health benefits when she had all this talent.

Molly stood. "Ashley, please get your things." We need to go back to the shop and get J's measurements."

While she was taking my measurements, she asked, "Where are you getting married?"

"Couloir."

"Oh, I love it up there. You don't happen to know Taylor Hunt, do you? I think she's a manager up there."

"I do." I cringed a little inside, hoping she wouldn't ask me if I knew about the crash or the poisoning.

"When I first opened my little business, she came to me with a beautiful scarf that had belonged to her mother, who passed away when she was in college. She was desolate because she'd ripped it. The scarf was beyond repair, so I told her I could replicate it for her. It came out better than I had hoped. She was so excited." She pointed to a group of pictures of various garments hanging on the dressing room wall. The scarf was stunning. It was the colors of sunset.

"It's… it's stunning." I examined the picture closely. "Is this a little "M" in the corner?

Molly's cheeks flamed. "It may sound vain, I put an "M" on all my works. Usually, it's on the inside of a garment, but that's not possible with a scarf."

"Most artists sign their work. Given your talent, I think it's quite appropriate."

"Thanks. If you see Taylor, please say hello for me."

Less than an hour later as I was leaving Molly's storefront, I stopped at Ashley's table to say goodbye. When she murmured "Okay," without looking up, I squatted down to see what she was coloring with such concentration. Every page I could see was filled with crude pictures of tee shirts. No two were alike, and they were all quite colorful. It appeared there were going to be three generations working in the business in the near future.

High from my reunion with Molly, I headed to the industrial park to find the art studio. As I drove up and down the mostly deserted streets, I cursed myself for not finding out the name of the shop. Then I cursed myself again when I realized all I had to do was look the gallery up on my phone. I pulled to the side of the road to type *art galleries* into my phone, when I saw Tom coming out of the shop directly across the street. I couldn't help but wonder at the coincidence that brought us to the same road. Turning to see what shop he visited, I saw it was *Daydreams, Textile Art*. How odd.

All thoughts of Tom vanished when I opened the door. It was like walking into a different world. Enhanced by skylights, the walls were silver white; the shape of the large room galley-style. Weavings of all colors were spaced far enough apart so that instead of competing with one another, the viewer could experience the unique ambiance of each piece. I blinked several times, trying to take it all in, when a petite young woman, dressed in shades of soft gray, asked if she could help me. Before I could respond, another young woman, identical in stature and dress came from the back of the gallery and stood beside her.

"I understand why you named your studio *Daydreams.* I feel like I'm in one." Then added, "Are you two twins?"

Their laughter broke the spell. The woman who first approached me held out her hand. "I'm Cindy, the owner. This is my assistant, Luanne. We dress alike to add to the experience, but we're not twins, just good friends. Would you like to browse, or are you here for something specific?"

"Actually, I was hoping to find a wedding gift for my soon-to-be husband."

Cindy lit up. "You're getting married! How wonderful. Unless you already know what you want, I would suggest you look around and see if there is a piece you like. We can always customize the art to suit your taste. Would you like something to drink while you see what catches your eye? Perhaps a cappuccino?"

"No, thank you," I answered. "I've already had three today."

Cindy's eyes widened. "Well, then, perhaps I should let you know the restroom is at the back of the gallery. Just let me know if you have any questions."

I'd just made my choice when a cell phone chimed nearby, and a subdued, "Hello," broke the silence. The caller was yelling so loudly, I could hear what he was saying. It sounded like, "Mom's on a rampage... Dad... better get over here..." The owner ran to the back of the shop, returning with her coat and purse. She was crying, though by the look on her face I didn't know whether they were tears of anger or sorrow. As she headed for the door, she said, "I'm sorry, I have an emergency. Luanne can answer any of your questions." Then she was gone.

Luanne walked to the front window and watched her boss drive away. With a long sigh she said under her breath, "Now what's going on? Can't they just leave Cindy alone? She's already an emotional basket case. I don't think she can take much more." Turning, she gave a little shriek when she saw me staring at her. She tried to regain her composure. "I'm sorry. I guess I forgot you were here." Smoothly changing the subject, "Have you seen Cindy's work before?"

"Yes, I think I've seen two of her pieces."

Luanne gave me a quizzical look.

"I saw a beautiful piece at the home of a client. In fact, she's the one who told me about the gallery. And I think I saw one of her creations at the police department."

Luanne's face darkened, and she took a step backward. "Yes..." she said cautiously. "It was a special order by the Chief of Police. It's in the interrogation room."

"I saw it when I was doing some work for the chief," I assured her. "It's really quite beautiful."

She visibly relaxed.

"Does Cindy make all her own ceramic and glass beads?"

Luanne brightened. "She does. Why do you ask? Are you interested in something special?"

I led her over to the work I thought Ross would like. "I was hoping she could enhance this piece with a little more color." Adding sheepishly, "And I need to pick it up the day after tomorrow."

"You're in luck. Cindy doesn't have any special orders at the moment. Let's go back into the workshop and you can tell me what you'd like."

Moments later Luanne was telling me what a great choice I'd made and leading me out of the work area. I paused midway, looking at a number of bottles on a shelf over the workbench. Some of them were labeled "sodium sulfate." Luanne turned and followed my stare. I asked, "Isn't that..."

"Arsenic? Yes. It's used as a fining agent." I must have looked confused, because she added, "It helps raise the temperature of the glass, eliminating bubbles, making it more fluid, and easier to work with."

Work order completed and deposit made, Luanne handed me a business card. "If you have any questions or want to make a change, here's Cindy's information." She quickly escorted me to the front door like a woman who had something urgent to do.

Pausing in the doorway, I asked, "Do you know who the man was who was leaving as I arrived?"

"That was just Tom, Cindy's neighbor." She said brusquely, guiding me out the door. By the time I completed the few steps to my car, the closed sign was displayed, and I could see her talking on the phone. Looking down at the card she'd given me, I was startled. The card said *Cindy Reynolds.* And to my knowledge there is only one Reynolds family in Mammoth Lakes.

Arsenic, Tom, Cindy Reynolds. It was going to be hard not to jump to conclusions.

Aileen, the food & beverage director

Taylor and I were going stir-crazy. Our staffs seemed to need little to no guidance, especially mine. Every time I called to check in, I was told Missy had everything under control and I should rest. Taylor received similar responses from her supervisors. To make matters worse, whenever Brian and Patrick talked business, they stepped outside so they wouldn't *disturb us.* We decided it was high time to take back control of our lives.

Before leaving for Couloir Patrick asked if we needed anything, as he did every morning. I took a chance and asked him to pick us up sandwiches at Bleu. Both Taylor and I were surprised when he agreed, even though none of what we ordered was on our approved diet. After he made our Bleu-run and left for work, we stared longingly at the sandwiches, finally deciding that two sidelined invalids didn't have to wait until noon to lunch. I pulled out a bottle of Ferrari-Carano chardonnay I had chilling at the back of the refrigerator—which fortunately had a screw top, and took it with two wine glasses, our food, and some treats for Joe to my room. With only one good arm, it took me two trips. Knowing Patrick, Brian, and even Ian had a bad habit of dropping in unexpectedly to check in on us, we locked the door.

By our second glass of wine, we had decided to attend next Monday's management team meeting in person, with the intent of going back to work part-time. Neither of us were on prescription pain medications; we both looked beat up but were mobile; and the utility road should be clear enough of snow, so we didn't have to ride behind a snowmobile. By our third glass of wine, we wrote and sent an email to the rest of the management team announcing our plan and to circumvent Brian's and Patrick's inevitable objections. Then we wrapped up the leftover food; washed and put away the wine glasses; buried the empty wine bottle in the bottom of the recycle bin; turned off our phones; and went to our respective bedrooms to take a nap.

I awoke to sounds of an argument between Patrick and Brian. As usual, Patrick could be heard in every room of the house. "There is no way in hell Tom, or Sierra for that matter, is coming back to Couloir, especially if Aileen and Taylor follow through with this asinine idea to go back to work."

"My attorney says differently. Currently, there are no charges against either of them, and—"

"Well, it's just a matter of time. Besides, Tom is certainly guilty of making false accusations, insubordination, and stealing a thousand-dollar bottle of cognac."

As Patrick ranted on, I turned on my phone to text Taylor. Blinking dots indicated she was texting me. "*What do you think we should do? Your brother sounds pretty angry.*"

"I've only heard him yell like this when he thinks he's protecting me. I think we should let him wind down a little before we go out there. It shouldn't take too long."

"And when we do go out????"

"Brian needs to make the decisions about Tom and Sierra. We just need to make sure we don't back down about working part-time … but it will be awkward seeing Tom."

Within minutes we emerged from our respective bedrooms. I was taken aback when I spied the empty wine bottle on the kitchen counter—our empty wine bottle.

Brian looked amused as Patrick asked pointedly, "Is this the reason for that stupid email announcement you made today?"

I glanced at Taylor, giving her my *didn't-I-tell-you* look.

"Patrick, Taylor and I are not children, and we do not work for you." I held up my hand as Patrick started to interrupt. We had prepared for this, so I nodded at Taylor.

Addressing Brian, she said, "We will be back at work on Monday morning. We thought we could work half days at first. If our safety is the concern, we think we'll be safer at the hotel than here at the house alone. We are asking for your support."

Smiling, Brian answered, "If you agree to a few precautions, you have my support."

A furious Patrick gave Brian a dirty look then left to walk Joe. When he returned, Brian called us all into the living room.

Brian addressed Patrick. "I wanted you to be here when I explained my conditions for returning to work."

Still scowling, Patrick took a seat without a word. Joe

pranced over and sat by Taylor and me. Patrick gave him a dirty look.

Brian's expression was all business as he studied Taylor and me. "First, neither of you will drive. Patrick can drive you in the mornings. If for some reason he can't, I will come and get you. We will adjust our schedules so that one of us is available to take you home at noon. Until we know who is responsible for the attacks, Patrick and I are your only drivers." He paused. When no one said anything, he continued. "You will work Monday, Wednesday, and Friday mornings. I will not abide excuses or pleas for staying longer. You will both be working in the small glass conference room we reserve for guests. I do not want you hidden away in your small offices where someone could..." Brian seemed to be searching for the right words, "... drop in without being seen. The conference room means you will be visible. Tomorrow morning, I will have your computers and whatever you else you need moved into your work area." Again, he looked at the three of us, one at a time. "Finally, Joe Cocker will come with you, and stay with you." Joe raised his head and gave a quiet bark. "That means when one of you goes to the ladies room, all three of you will go." Joe dropped his head on the floor and covered his eyes with his forepaws.

Brian slouched back into his chair, looking satisfied. "Do you accept those conditions?"

Smiling, Taylor nodded at me to answer. "We accept, as long as you accept our conditions."

Both men startled. Patrick stood. "Your what?"

Ignoring his outburst, I continued. "Taylor and I made appointments for haircuts tomorrow. We both need more manageable styles if we are to maintain suitable grooming standards with our injuries. We were going to Uber, but if only you two can drive us, we will need transportation to and from the salon."

Brian laughed out loud. "Pretty sure of yourselves, I see. Any other conditions?"

"Yes. When you and my brother talk about what's happening at Couloir, we want to be part of the discussion. No more going outside to *discuss business*."

"Agreed. We brought dinner in from Couloir. I'll go heat it up, while you ladies set the table."

A sulky Patrick followed Brian into the kitchen. Taylor and I awkwardly bumped uninjured fists.

J, the consultant

Ross texted me not to hold dinner for him. The Canyon Lodge ski patrollers were having pizza and beer. It must have been a difficult day since that's usually when the patrol supervisors spring for pizza and beer. With only myself to worry about, I decided to have a glass of Dry Creek Meritage, and a charcuterie plate. I assembled a platter of Castelvetrano olives, almonds, Manchego, aged parmesan, prosciutto, cornichons, cantaloupe slices, whole grain Dijon mustard, and a baguette, which I brought into the living room with my wine.

I melted into my favorite wingback chair, letting the fire warm my feet stretched out on the hearth. It was the first moment of the day… perhaps the week, when I could just sit back and relax. No list of things to do nagging at me—at least for this evening. I was so laid back, I actually paused as I held my glass of wine so I could appreciate its rich ruby color in the firelight before taking a sip. The first taste was filled with ripe, rich fruit and spices. I sighed out loud.

As if on cue, my cell chirped.

Brian. I was tempted not to answer, but the situation at

Couloir was too dynamic. Anything could have happened in the last few hours. Besides, perhaps he would tell me how well he knew "Lyn" Germaine.

"Hello."

"Ah. I caught you at a bad time. Sounds like you were just about to relax when I interrupted—with a good glass of wine, I hope."

"Are you spying on me?" I asked, only half kidding.

Brian laughed. "No, but I know the sound of 'Oh shit, can't you just leave me alone for a few minutes?'"

"I'm sure you do, Brian. Especially lately. What's up?"

"Lyn says best to let Tom, and especially Sierra, continue working as if nothing has happened for the time being, unless an enforced company policy is violated, or, of course, one is arrested for a specific crime. She thinks Tom's actions, particularly with the wine closet audit, could provide a basis for discipline, but if he's a viable suspect for attempted murder, it's best not to pursue something so trivial at this time. Of course, since Tom is currently on a leave of absence for stress, he shouldn't pose an immediate problem, though I have asked Lyn to assess the risk of a stress-related legal action." Brian let out a long sigh. "It never ends."

I wasn't surprised about Lynette's hands-off strategy, though I didn't think stealing a thousand-dollar bottle of cognac was trivial. Actionable facts, not suspicion, were the only basis for employment or legal action. Other than the pilfered bottle of cognac, Tom's actions had been threatening—even provoking, but not enough for a suspension or arrest.

"As you can imagine, J, I'm going to need some guidance leading management team discussions until this entire situation is resolved. Are you in?"

A deliberate sip of the beautiful Dry Creek later, I said, "You have me until the wedding."

"I haven't forgotten your big day. If you can continue to help me over the next few days, the wedding and rooms are on me."

"A generous offer, but not necessary. I'm in."

Simultaneously, we said, "There's something I think you should know."

Awkward laughter.

"You first, Brian."

"I received a text from the front desk supervisor informing me that Fred Reynolds checked into Couloir this evening without a reservation, and indicated to the night clerk he might be staying for a while."

Stunned, my first response was an inarticulate "Wow," followed by, "That makes what I have to tell you even more intriguing." I told him about my visit to Daydreams, in particular that Fred's daughter, Cindy Reynolds, was the owner; Tom was Cindy's next-door neighbor and regularly visited the studio; and I spotted bottles of arsenic on my way out of the workshop, which was apparently used in glass making.

My revelations were met with silence. A full minute passed. "Brian, are you still there?"

"Sorry, J, it's a lot to process. Did you have a chance to talk to Cindy about Tom, or the arsenic?"

"Unfortunately, I learned about Tom and the arsenic from Cindy's assistant. Cindy received a phone call, became very emotional, and left for her parents' house."

"Interesting." After a long pause, he asked tentatively,

"Any chance you could go see her tomorrow—to casually feel her out about her relationship with Tom?"

Brian patiently waited while I tried to come up with a legitimate reason for going to Daydreams. Finally, I said, "Well, I ordered some custom changes to one of her creations. I could stop by to ask her what she thinks of my color selections, since she wasn't there when I made them. That is, if she's there tomorrow morning."

"Would you, please? I'm sure once I pass along your information to Ian, he's going to want to meet with us. You might learn something valuable."

Although I wasn't sure what new information I could pass on, I realized that I *would* like Cindy's thoughts about my color choices. "I'll be there when they open. And perhaps you should see if you can casually run into Fred. His presence at Couloir must be connected to Cindy's sudden departure for home. The little I heard of the phone call was something like 'Mom's on a rampage.'"

"Will do. Let's meet tomorrow afternoon."

As I set down the phone and picked up my glass of wine, I knew my relaxation time had ended.

Brian, the hotelier

J's tidbits were interesting, but we were still no closer to finding out who or why Aileen and Taylor were attacked. All we had were suspicions, and I was starting to question how viable they really were. After stewing for a while, I convinced myself it was stupid to hide in my office all night feeling helpless. It was time to go find Fred, and at this hour, facing his first night alone in a hotel, I thought I knew just were to find him. I smiled at the photo of my parents and said, "Here I go."

The lounge was crowded. I scanned the patrons sitting at the bar and was disappointed to find Fred was not among them. Turning my attention to the tables in the room, I finally saw him seated alone at a window table for two. His drink looked untouched; his focus was on the night sky.

"May I join you, Fred?"

Fred turned, melancholy masking his face. "I thought you might seek me out. Sure, have a seat." He went back to staring out the window.

A waiter brought me a drink before I was settled in the chair. God bless Matteo. Instead of small talk, I took a sip, let out a small sigh, and joined Fred looking for answers in the night. We would move at Fred's pace, not mine.

When Fred finally turned from the window, he saw two empty glasses. He caught the waiter's eye and held two fingers in the air. After we were served, he finally spoke.

"I suppose you're curious why I'm staying at your hotel… alone," he said after taking a sip of his drink.

I felt a surge of anger. Since Aileen had joined the Couloir team, the Reynoldses had done everything they could to humiliate and ostracize her. But I swallowed my bile and simply nodded.

As he began to talk, it became apparent he wasn't on just his second cocktail. "You know I've never understood it, not then and not now. Why does Maureen hate Aileen so much? When Aileen first came to work, Maureen was delighted." Hand to his forehead, he seemed to be concentrating on something. "In fact, now that I think about it, Maureen hired her." He looked incredulous. "And…" he held up his hand to emphasize his point, "… Maureen is the one who wanted me to train Aileen so she could work for us full time." He sat back in his chair, a shit-eating grin on his face.

I waited for him to continue, to no avail, so I prodded. "And Maureen hating Aileen is the reason you're staying at Couloir."

Fred was still smiling, "Precisely."

"I'm not sure I understand."

"It's really quite simple. I told Maureen her recent attack in the newspaper was out of line, and I was going to issue an apology. She told me to pack my bags. Here I am." His laugh induced a small belch, "And she'll never look for me here."

Hesitantly I asked, "How long are you thinking of staying?"

His mood had shifted from morose to almost giddy. "I may never go home. I have everything I could need or want here. Spectacular views, twenty-four-hour room service, a beautiful bar, and most importantly, peace and quiet." He closed his eyes and began to softly snore.

There was a fortunate lull in activity at the bar. I caught Matteo's eye and beckoned him over. Together we walked Fred back to his room, laying him on the bed. I took off his shoes and put a glass of water on his nightstand. We turned on the light in the bathroom and left.

Day 12
Brian, the hotelier

As I settled at my desk with my morning croissant and fresh orange juice, my attention drifted to the picture of my parents. Although several years had passed since their deaths, during times of stress the pain of missing them felt visceral. We'd been such a close family. Even as a child my mother and father included me in family plans and decisions. This inclusion helped me develop critical thinking skills and self-confidence. It also gave me an understanding of my parents most kids never get. Of course, this strong bond was a great impediment to forming any long-term romantic relationships. It was why I started building eco-hotels, my version of their dream, after they… My cell buzzed, breaking my reverie.

It was Fred. He said last night was a blur and wanted to know if he owed anyone an apology. I assured him he did not.

"And I suppose I owe you a thank you for getting me to my room last night?" The way he asked the question, I was pretty certain he remembered nothing of our conversation, or of the night, for that matter.

"All part of the service."

"Thanks, Brian. I guess you can tell I don't remember much after my second or third drink. Sorry. I've never been much of a drinker, and now I know why."

He hesitated, as if there was something on his mind. "Uh, do you have a small office I could use? I invited Maureen and our daughter Cindy to come up here to talk this afternoon. And I don't think asking them to my room will, er, set the right tone. And, of course, a public space is out of the question… though I'm not sure either of them will come."

"We have a few office suites for just that purpose. I'll have a key delivered to your room. It's yours for the day. If you need it longer, you let me know."

"Thanks, Brian. I mean it. Thank you. After the way my family has treated—" His voice cracked. "You know what I'm trying to say. Thank you."

My jaw was clenched, my shoulders and neck in knots. I needed to let go of my anger towards the Reynoldses, or at least Fred. He seemed genuinely contrite. But they had done so much damage since Aileen came to Couloir, it was hard to let go.

J, the consultant

The next morning, fortified by a double espresso, I entered Daydreams to find it eerily quiet and deserted. The website said they opened at ten, and it was half past the hour. I could smell coffee brewing, so I called out a greeting. No response. I walked to the workshop in the back, continuing to let the ladies know I was in the store. In the workshop I found my gift for Ross on a table awaiting enhancements, but neither Cindy nor Luanne was there. Just as I turned to leave, I thought I heard a whimper. Looking around and seeing no one, I decided it must be my imagination, and turned to go.

The sound was a little louder this time and coming from behind some shelving. That's where I found Cindy, sitting on the floor, holding her knees, rocking back and forth. She was murmuring between sobs. I crouched down to see if I could help her, and to hear what she was saying. It took a moment, but I finally realized she was repeating, "It's all my fault" over and over. I tried talking to her, but it was as if she didn't see me. She just kept rocking.

Unsure of what to do, but not wanting to leave her alone,

I sat down next to her, making soothing sounds as if she were a child. All my attention was focused on her, when someone roughly grabbed my arm, yelling, "What are *you* doing here?"

I was so startled I nearly fell trying to get to my feet. It was one of Cindy's brothers and he seemed outraged I was trying to help his sister. Before I could say anything, he pulled me to the back door. The last thing I heard as I was hurled into the back parking lot was Cindy saying, "She'll hate me."

Taylor, the guest services director

My phone chimed while Aileen and I were having a late breakfast. A picture of Charlie stared out from my iPhone. Why was the head of Maintenance calling me? "Hello, Charlie. I hope everything at Couloir is all right."

Aileen looked up expectantly.

"It's fine. You and Aileen must be doing a lot better than when I last saw you if you're coming back to work."

"Much better. In fact, we're getting haircuts today in preparation for our return. What's up? We're both listening."

I could hear the smile in Charlie's voice as I put him on speaker. "Hi, Aileen. We're all excited about seeing you two back here. Listen, the Boss asked me to move your offices into the guest conference room, and, well, you both have a lot of stuff. Like white boards with schedules, and personal stuff on your desks. Do you want everything? Or just your computers? It's a little confusing."

Aileen and I grinned at each other. We actually *were* going back to work.

Aileen spoke up. "Sorry about that, Charlie. I hadn't thought about what a mess our offices must be. How about if we have Patrick take us to Couloir this afternoon after our salon appointments? That would make it easier all the way around. And..." she beamed, "... both of us have been longing to be back. I know it's only been days, but it feels like months."

I jumped in. "Brilliant idea. Charlie, would that work with your schedule?"

"It would be a godsend." He hesitated. "Will... will the Boss and Patrick be okay with you coming up here?"

Aileen answered. "You leave that to us."

We could hear him muttering something to himself about an interesting afternoon as he disconnected.

"Charlie has a good point, Aileen. The guys are not going to be happy about this little change to the schedule."

"We just have to agree not to back down."

Four hours later we walked out of Blazing Shears. Aileen's long thick black hair had been cut into a short bob. Judy had done a great job. Aileen looked lighter and fresher, even with the fading bruises on her face. After seeing the freshness in her appearance, I told her she should have made the change a long time ago. My hair was more of a challenge. It wasn't thick, and it had a mind of its own. I kept reminding myself it was essential to maintain at least minimum grooming standards, so we needed wash and wear hairdos. When Judy asked if I would trust her, I said yes then asked her not to face me toward a mirror while she was working on my do. I didn't want to have second thoughts. Judy cut my long, out-of-control locks, and gave me a light perm. When I finally looked in the mirror my blond hair fell around my face in shaggy waves. I loved it.

Patrick was waiting for us. "Wow. You two look great. Who'd have known?" We gave him *faux* dirty looks and got into the car.

Once buckled in, he asked, "Anything else you need to do before we go home?"

"Yes, we have an appointment with Charlie at Couloir."

And the screaming began. Threats of calling Uber had no effect on him. Patrick was resolute we were not going to the hotel. So, while Aileen and Patrick yelled at one another, I texted Brian and explained the situation, reminding him Aileen and I were grown women with free will, and begging him to call Patrick. After a lot of back and forth, Patrick's phone rang just as we were turning onto Aileen's Street.

Patrick pulled over to answer the phone. He did not put it on speaker. His only words were an angry, "If you say so." He turned the car around, heading to Couloir. The silence was deafening.

J, the consultant

I knew something was wrong when I saw Mary and Bob rushing out of Couloir, Mary holding her hands over her ears. As I got closer, I heard a woman's shrill angry voice. Apprehensively, I poked my head through the doors. The reality was worse than I'd imagined. Some guests were fleeing the lobby, others sat on couches and chairs transfixed by the scene in the middle of the room. Maureen was screaming at Fred and Aileen. Fred was trying to comfort Cindy, who was crying uncontrollably. Taylor had her good arm around Aileen, while she glared at Maureen. And Brian was physically restraining Patrick from going after Maureen while trying to get everyone's attention.

When he spotted me, Brian pointed to the entrance to the private dining room at the back of the lobby. I nodded. Pushing my way to the center of the melee, I said, "Stop!" To my amazement, everyone did—including the fleeing guests. In a lower voice, I continued. "Airing your personal grievances against one another in a public place is—" I faltered.

Brian took over. "It's inappropriate." Addressing Maureen, he added, "You're causing a spectacle. Please follow me, so we can continue this discussion in private."

The Reynolds family looked dazed as they turned to find everyone in the room staring at them. Without a word they fell into line behind Brian, followed by Patrick, Aileen, Taylor, and me.

As soon as the dining room door closed, Maureen turned to Aileen, and spat: "Why did you come back? You, you whore. I gave you every opportunity and you thank me by stealing my money and my husband? And you have the nerve to return?"

Patrick stepped protectively between the madwoman and his sister. Again, Brian placed a firm hand on Patrick's shoulder, preventing him from moving any closer to Maureen.

Fred yelled at Maureen. "What the hell are you talking about?" But Maureen ignored him; she finally had the opportunity to confront Aileen and she wasn't going to let anything stop her.

Soft keening rose into the air, gradually growing in intensity and volume. Everyone stopped talking. Aileen was the first to see Cindy sitting on the floor in the corner of the room, arms wrapped around her knees, rocking back and forth, as she had done in her studio. Aileen bent down to comfort her. Maureen ran over and roughly pushed her aside, saying, "Stay away from her. She's my daughter."

Patrick advanced, "Don't you dare touch my sister." Brian grabbed Patrick. Fred dropped into one of the dining chairs, shaking his head as if he'd been sucker punched. Taylor moved as far away from the craziness as she could, shielding her damaged shoulder.

The moaning abruptly stopped as Cindy pushed her

mother away and stood up. "Stop it! Just stop it. It's my fault. I'm the reason mother and dad are fighting." She addressed Aileen as if she were the only person in the room. "I was jealous. When I was little, dad played with me all the time. He called me his princess. Then Phil and Mike came to live with us, and dad spent all his time with them. Somehow, I understood it was because they'd lost their parents, but it wasn't fair. As my brothers got older, I started going to the office with dad, and I was special again."

Fred approached his daughter, tears leaking down his face. Maureen got into his face. "Stop right there," she shouted. "It's all your fault. Can't you hear that?"

Cindy glared at her mother. "Please be quiet and sit down."

Maureen looked like she'd been slapped but complied.

"When you started working part-time, we had fun," Cindy continued talking to Aileen. "You let me help you. You treated me like a little sister. Then my parents offered you a full-time job, and things changed. Dad spent lots of time with you, showing you how he kept the books, introducing you to clients, teaching you the business. You and he became too busy to spend much time with me. I didn't understand. All I knew was that it was happening all over again. I couldn't bear to be nothing again, so I told mom you and daddy were doing funny things in his office with the door closed. And she believed me. After all, I was only thirteen."

Everyone turned to Maureen; a litany of emotions crossed her face, ending with resolve. "This does not change the fact that she stole a significant amount of money from us."

Cindy looked down at Maureen. "No, Mother. This is the time for the *whole* truth."

Maureen went white.

Fred looked confused. "What do you mean the whole truth?"

"Aileen didn't steal the money. I helped Mother do it."

Cindy's declaration sucked the air from the room. Reflexively, I opened a window as we all tried to process what we'd just heard.

The door opened and a smiling Missy strolled in, pushing a small cart with water bottles on it. "I thought you might like—"

Fred ignored the interruption. "That... that's impossible, Cindy. You were a little girl. Little girls don't know how to embezzle money. Besides, Aileen and I were the only ones who knew the password to access our accounts."

Missy froze mid-stride, mouth agape, eyes wide. Brian quietly signaled her to leave. She left the cart in the doorway and fled.

Tears streamed down Cindy's face. "That's where you're wrong, Dad. I made my first hanging to give to Aileen, and Mother put a camera in it. Then I convinced Aileen to hang it on the wall behind her desk so everyone would see it. But really it was so Mother could see what the password was."

Charlie poked his head in around the open door. "Ladies, my crew is waiting—" He looked at the angry faces and closed the door, mumbling, "I guess it's best to reschedule."

Brian held up his hands. "Fred, I think you need to call your attorney before anything else is said. Why don't you take your family to your room for some privacy?"

Zombie-like, Fred and Maureen started walking toward the door. Patrick stepped in front of Maureen. "So, when your nasty newspaper campaign didn't work, you tried to kill my sister?"

Maureen broke down, "No. No. I had nothing to do with her accidents."

"They weren't accidents!"

Brian grabbed Patrick. "Sit down and cool off. This is a matter for the police."

Cindy fell in behind her parents, then stopped and approached Aileen, tears streaming down her face. "I'm so ashamed and so sorry. I don't expect you ever to forgive me." She followed her parents out of the room.

As the door closed, Aileen whispered, "But I do forgive you."

Aileen, the food & beverage director

I closed my eyes and remembered. The police knocking on the door. My father gesturing over his shoulder when he was asked if I was home, then walking out the front door without a word. Patrick yelling at the police when they put me in handcuffs. Waking up the next morning in jail stiff, cold, and disoriented. The arraignment when I told myself not to worry, this was a big mistake that would soon be cleared up. Unable to make bail. My father refusing to be responsible for me, meaning I was in jail until my trial. The verdict that seemed to surprise only Patrick and me. My first week in prison, being taunted, poked, and victimized by a small band of inmates—long-haul divas. Learning to never complain regardless of what was done to me, or what disgusting assignment I was given. All the while screaming in my head I didn't belong there; I was innocent. Finally giving up any thoughts of vindication and serving my sentence one day at a time.

I also remembered Patrick's visits, letters, packages.

His unwavering belief in my innocence. Meeting me outside prison the day I was released in a rented limo with a bottle of Veuve Clicquot and a large Giovanni's masterpiece pizza. Flying to Colorado with him in business class. The first time seeing the condo he bought for us, and the room he furnished for me, including new clothes, a computer, and a smart phone. Discovering he'd vetted potential employers and set up job interviews. Then some years later after I told him I yearned to return to Mammoth, finding me the perfect position, and buying me my own house.

Someone touched me, breaking my reverie. I must have started because J immediately apologized. A quick look at my surroundings revealed I'd been lost in my past for only seconds, not the hours it felt like. Brian was still trying to calm Patrick down, and, Taylor, sitting in an armchair, looked stunned.

"I'm going out to call Ian and thought you might want me to bring you back something," J offered.

My face must have been blank because she continued with a slight smile. "You know, like a stiff drink?"

I declined with a thank you. As J left, Charlie, Sierra, Beth, and Missy entered.

"Is it true?" asked Beth. "Did Maureen really frame you, Aileen, then try to kill you?"

Sierra glared at Beth, while Brian looked disapprovingly at Missy, who had the good grace to look sheepish.

Still irritated, Brian asked everyone to sit. He explained what had happened. Halfway through his recitation, all eyes locked firmly on me. Brian concluded with, "None of the information I just shared may go out of this room. I'm not trying to be a hard ass, but if any of it is leaked, there will be consequences for the leakers."

I was still the center of attention when Missy asked, "Do you think Maureen tried to kill you and Taylor just happened to be there?" This time Missy got the dirty look from Sierra.

Brian started to respond when I interjected, "I don't think the Reynolds family had anything to do with the attacks. Cindy would have told us if they had."

When everyone started talking at once, Brian broke in. "Don't you all have jobs to do?"

Reluctantly, the four newcomers got to their feet. Brian reminded them again of the need for confidentiality.

Charlie, Beth, and Missy filed out, and Sierra approached Brian. "I need to let Phil and Mike know so they can be with their family." It was a statement, not a question.

Before Brian could object, I said, "Good idea."

Sierra left without another word.

For a moment Taylor, Patrick, Brian, and I just stared at one another, as if to say *what do we do now*? Until J walked in. "Ian is on his way. He left three instructions. Don't leave. Don't tell anyone what happened. And," she said, rolling her eyes, "order him a steak sandwich because he missed lunch."

Taylor and I smiled, but Brian and Patrick were all business. Addressing Patrick, Brian said, "You should have just enough time to drive the ladies home and return before Ian gets here."

"We're not leaving until I speak with Ian," I announced firmly.

Predictably, Patrick's response was loud, followed by Brian's more measured and calmer but equally dogmatic response.

Taylor and I sat patiently while they ordered and cajoled, but we refused to leave. Brian was the first to accept defeat, but Patrick wasn't through. "What do you have to speak to Ian about? Cindy just told us her mother framed you for embezzlement. Now it's time to set things right."

"Patrick, I just want to speak to Ian before Taylor and I leave," I said quietly.

As Patrick continued to rant, a sense of tranquility came over me. I didn't think about my decision, I'd just made it, and I *knew* it was the right thing to do. Taylor took the chair next to me and squeezed my hand. She looked curious, yet ready to support me.

Patrick continued his tirade. At one point I noticed Brian calling someone, but that didn't interrupt Patrick. He'd spent his entire life taking care of me; it was his job.

He finally stopped and dropped into a chair, seething. Ian arrived, followed by a cheery Missy who not only had a covered dish that could only be a steak sandwich, but also bottles of beer and wine, accompanied by a cheese and fruit platter. I caught her eye. "Thanks. Perhaps you should prepare something similar for the guests in the lobby. We put on quite a show earlier."

Missy gave me a slight smile. "Good idea. I'm on it, Boss. As soon as I finish this set-up."

Ian immediately picked up his sandwich and took a large bite. Mid-chew he asked, "So what's all the screaming about this time. You all should be celebrating."

"I don't want to press charges."

Everyone but Patrick turned to me.

Taylor, the guest services director

I was stunned. Aileen was framed for a crime she didn't commit and spent nearly five years in jail. Sentence served, retribution paid, she returned to Mammoth and was greeted with a campaign to get her fired. When that failed, her reputation was shredded in the newspaper. *Her* response to learning who caused all this grief was to refuse to press charges. Clearly, she was a far better person than I.

Then once again I remembered how I treated her and was mortified. When Aileen started working at Couloir, I only saw a convicted felon, not a competent, self-contained professional. When she demonstrated the breadth of her skills, overseeing several holiday parties and weddings, I decided she must be having an affair with Brian, and filed a harassment charge against her. As soon as the complaint was found spurious, I quit. Aileen's reaction was to insist Brian do whatever it took to get me back.

I didn't get it. Who wouldn't get angry? Who wouldn't want revenge after being so callously treated?

I was taken aback when I heard someone ask, "Taylor. Taylor, are you all right?"

Having no context for the question, I answered. "I'm fine. Why?"

Aileen took my hand. "Because you've been shaking your head and mumbling."

I looked around at the concern on everyone's faces except Ian's, whose attention was riveted on his sandwich. Even Sierra was watching me from the doorway.

I was about to offer a lame excuse but couldn't help myself. "Aileen, don't you ever get angry?"

She looked wistful. "I used to, but it never got me anything but disappointment and a headache."

Thinking of my own recent experiences with anger, "I get that. But Maureen hurt you badly. Shouldn't she have to pay?"

Aileen seemed to consider her response. "But she *has* paid a price. Her relationships with her husband and daughter are tenuous at best. If she's incarcerated, how is she going to repair her relations with them? That means Cindy and Fred will suffer too, more than they are now. Maureen has always been a community leader. She will need to mend many of those fences. She can't if she's not here. That means the community will suffer." Aileen paused and focused on Patrick. "I'm not being naïve or obsequious. I just believe enough people have suffered; enough damage has been done. It's time for all of us to accept what's happened and move forward."

Patrick gave an imperceptible nod, a hint of pride in his eyes.

The mood was broken by Ian. "Unfortunately, it's not your call, Aileen."

Ian had our attention. "That's not the way it works. You don't press charges. I file a police report. The District Attorney reviews it and decides whether to prosecute. I can't tell you what he'll do, but with the damage that has been done in this case, I expect he'll take the matter forward." Ian looked around the room for some reaction. Getting none, he went on. "Right now, all we have is the daughter's version of events, and she was a child at the time of the crime. What I'll be looking for is proof."

"What kind of proof? It's been over ten years," Patrick demanded.

"Oh, I don't know. The film from the camera, verification of a deposit made shortly after the theft, the textile concealing the camera—something tangible."

Everyone quietly contemplated how unlikely any proof remained after all these years.

I sat up straighter as it dawned on me. "Didn't you say the hanging in your bedroom used to be in your office, Aileen?"

Aileen nodded but didn't look happy.

"Does it still have the camera in it?" Ian asked hopefully.

Aileen shook her head.

"But there *is* a hole in the middle where the camera must have been hidden," I offered, avoiding Aileen's stare.

"It's a start. I'll stop by in the morning and pick it up. I'm interviewing each of the Reynoldses tomorrow." With the hint of a grin, he added. "Perhaps I'll substitute it for the art in the interrogation room, see how Maureen responds when she sees it."

"Well, they're both by the same artist," J whispered.

Brian looked at his watch. "It's getting late. Let me go see if there's an available table in the restaurant big enough to serve us all."

Missy immediately halted mid-task and walked toward the door, but Brian told her he would handle it.

While we waited, Aileen turned to me. "It's time for us to focus on the future. What's next on your life-goal list?"

It was a good question. "Well, I have a job I love in a town I never want to leave. I guess it would be to own my own home, instead of renting. Something like yours…"

Missy snorted.

"No," I said a bit too sharply. Taking it down a notch, "We were wrong. Brian didn't buy Aileen the house. Patrick did."

A stunned Patrick asked, "Who thought Brian bought Aileen her house?" When no one responded he said. "I bought the house for my sister because she needed a safe haven after all she'd been through."

"But Brian is the one…" Missy started.

"I was in Aspen, so I told Brian what I was looking for and how much I could spend. He did the rest."

Aileen looked impatient. "That's all water under the bridge." Returning to me, "Why don't you move out of your apartment and in with me. Then you could save the rent money for a down payment on your own place?"

"Good idea," chimed Patrick. "And then Aileen won't be living alone after I leave."

"Are you serious?" I half whispered to Aileen.

"Very."

"Then I think I'll take you up on your offer."

"What offer?" Brian queried as he entered.

Patrick answered. "I'll tell you about it after I get back. I need to drive Aileen and Taylor home, then I'll meet you in the dining room. This has been a long and dramatic first day back for both of them."

As Aileen and I looked for our coats, Brian invited everyone else to join him for dinner and a debrief. Charlie and Missy declined. There would only be four at dinner.

Aileen, the food & beverage director

"Patrick, do you mind dropping Taylor and me at Bleu? We're both feeling hyper. We really want a chance to relax out of the house. We can get an Uber home."

Uncharacteristically, Patrick answered, "I think it's a good idea. After today, you two deserve a night out. But I'll call Uber and leave the car for you. You can drive, can't you, Sis?"

"Absolutely." Taylor and I looked at one another wide-eyed and didn't say another word, fearful he'd reconsider, and an argument would ensue.

Before we knew it, we were sitting at a high table in Bleu, sipping Patz & Hall chardonnay, and studying the menu. Unexpectedly, we were presented with a new challenge. We hadn't eaten in public since the crash. Both of us could only use one arm. Taylor's right arm was swaddled in a sling, and she had not yet mastered the art of using a fork with her left hand. I, on the other hand, could eat with my right hand, but neither of us could use a fork and knife at the same time. Theresa, who must have had some kind of restaurateur's sixth sense, came to our rescue. Before we could explain, she studied us, then the menu, and offered to have sandwiches made. Soon we were happily chowing-down —a veggie stack for me; a pressed ham and brie for Taylor; a second glass of wine for both of us. Life couldn't get any better.

We had agreed on the way to the restaurant not to discuss the past; rather to keep focusing on the future. As the evening progressed, we talked about the logistics of Taylor's move. Since each bedroom had a sitting area and its own bathroom, we could have alone time when we wanted it. While our personalities were quite different, our values and temperaments were similar. We even decided to go in fifty-fifty on a sofa-bed for the living room so our guests—primarily Patrick—wouldn't have to sleep on the couch. Over cappuccinos we discussed what we wanted to plant in the garden when the weather warmed, compromising on equal parts vegetables and flowers.

Yawning in sync, we knew it was time to go home. I looked at my watch, surprised at the time. "We are way past our bedtime. I hope Patrick hasn't gone home yet." A glance around the room gave me a start. We were the only ones left in the restaurant except for Theresa who looked upset as she quickly approached the table.

"I'm so sorry we kept everyone waiting to go home, we…"

Theresa ignored my apology and thrust a phone into my hand, concern distorting her beautiful face. Tentatively I put it to my ear. "Hello…"

Patrick was crying. After a deep, wrenching breath he

said, “Thank God, you’re alright. Taylor IS with you, isn’t she?”

“Of course. What’s…?”

“Stay there until the police arrive. They’ll take care of you.”

Taylor leaned toward me, trying to listen.

“We… we’re fine. We don’t need the police. What’s wrong, Patrick? You’re scaring me.”

“The house is on fire.”

Brian, the hotelier

While we waited for Patrick to return from taking Aileen and Taylor home, we busied ourselves with our cell phones, except for J who was staring intently out the window. No one seemed to have the energy or words to converse. Even though Patrick took much longer than expected, we said little. The restaurant was at the height of dinner hour by the time we entered. Several guests stared openly as we made our way to a table at the back of the room. I assumed they were either in the lobby for Maureen's tirade or had heard about it. A buzz went through the room as some realized the chief of police was with us.

I refused the menu and ordered the special for everyone. No one complained. We were all anxious to debrief the day's revelations and hear from Ian how the investigation was going. As the waiter took our drink orders, I studied my guests. They looked as shell-shocked as I felt.

J was the first to speak once the waiter departed. "Before we start processing today's events, I was hoping Ian would share what's happening with the investigation."

There were nods around the table, so we waited for Ian

to finish the handful of warm cashews he had just put in his mouth. "Unfortunately, we have no new leads. The arsenic is the same brand we found in Cindy's studio..." He gave a slight nod to J, "... and in almost every other glass artisan's workplace in Mammoth. The only fingerprints on the bottle were Cindy's. We've canvassed Aileen's neighbors, but no one actually saw the basket being delivered to her house. The basket assembled by the perpetrator was used, not recently purchased, and the food items readily available at the grocery store. No prints on the basket or any of its contents."

Ian sighed and took a swig of his beer. "We did discover who made the prank calls to the gas company, fire department, and Dominos." We leaned forward expectantly.

Ian addressed Patrick. "Apparently you haven't been very friendly to the boys who live across the street from Aileen. It was payback for kicking them out of the front yard." Patrick emitted a growl. "Don't worry. Their parents have all the boys' free time planned for the next several months."

Patrick looked disgusted. "Let's get down to it. We all know Tom is responsible..."

Ian shook his head. "No, we don't. Everything we think we know is based on circumstance. I have no proof he's responsible. Besides, after spending hours interrogating him, I'm beginning to agree with Taylor and Aileen. Tom doesn't have the intelligence, cunning, or courage to pull off the two attacks. His claim Aileen was stealing booze from the wine vault is more his style."

Patrick started to object when J interrupted. "I agree. He's a blowhard, not a killer. Besides, if he did sabotage the sleigh, I don't think he would have driven the snowmobile. Not only would he be suspected of sabotaging the vehicle, he also might have seriously injured himself."

"Then it must be Maureen. You saw how venomous she is toward my sister." Patrick's voice rose as he spoke. Heads turned toward the table.

"Do we have to move this meeting to my office?" I asked through clenched teeth.

"Certainly not," cried Ian who glared at Patrick. "We haven't had dinner yet."

I kept my focus on Patrick. "Anger and accusations are not getting us anywhere." My head was pounding. I wasn't sure how much more emotion and intrigue I could handle this evening.

"I'm interviewing Maureen and Cindy individually tomorrow morning, and the rest of the family in the afternoon. I don't think Cindy had anything to do with the attacks, but I want to be thorough. She could just be a great actress. I also have two officers assigned to tracking their movements on the days of both attacks. I should have a better feel for their possible involvement by the end of the day. For now, I think we should broaden this discussion to other possible suspects."

It seemed like Ian wanted to say more, but he was distracted by the waiter approaching with warm bread and salads. Once served, Ian looked at his plate suspiciously. J, on the other hand, smiled in delight. "Roasted beet salad. This is a treat."

We started our salads in silence. Ian cautiously put a yellow beet with some candied walnuts in his mouth, chewed for a moment, nodded to himself but did not eat with his usual vigor. J was staring at her untouched plate.

"J...?" I asked tentatively.

"I think Ian is right. We keep focusing on the obvious suspects. Perhaps we should consider everyone at Couloir who regularly interacts with Aileen and Taylor. Try to determine if anyone else has a motive to harm one or both of them." She looked up expectantly.

"Why just at Couloir?" Patrick asked sharply.

Unfazed by Patrick's tone, J said, "Everything I've learned from and about Aileen and Taylor makes me believe their jobs are their lives. If that's accurate, then wouldn't it follow that whoever wants to hurt one or both is connected to Couloir?"

We started listing staff, beginning with the management team, and possible motives. The list was short and the motives weak. We were becoming overwhelmed with our lack of new insights. Ian glanced over my shoulder and perked up. Clearly, dinner was about to be served.

As the server placed a plate of red wine-braised short ribs over fresh egg noodles in front of him, he sighed in contentment. He barely waited for all four of us to be served before he picked up his fork, only to be interrupted by the untimely buzzing of his cell. Without letting go of the fork, he answered. "This is the chief. This better be an emergency." We could all hear sirens and muffled shouts coming over his phone, then his side of the conversation.

"Anyone injured?"

"Are you sure?"

He ended the call with, "I'm on my way."

Instead of standing to go, he leaned forward, his face flushed. "Patrick, where are Aileen and Taylor?"

"What's wrong?" Patrick leapt to his feet.

With calm authority, Ian said. "Sit down and answer my question. "Where are they?"

Patrick looked like he was going to explode but answered. "They wanted to have dinner at Bleu, so I left them there with the car." Tears filled his eyes. "*Why*?"

"Will you call Aileen, please." When Patrick just stared at Ian, he added. "Now."

Patrick punched Aileen's code into the phone and waited, fear distorting his features.

When it was clear Aileen was not answering, I tried calling Taylor. It went to voicemail.

I looked at Ian, shaking my head.

The chief of police—not Ian—leaned forward and began. "There's been…"

J interrupted. Holding her phone out to Patrick, she said, "They're still at Bleu. Theresa is bringing her phone over to them now."

Ian's voice cracked. "Thank God they went to Bleu." Turning to face Patrick, he said, "Your neighbor called in. Your house is on fire. She only found your dog, who is a little singed but okay. Tell the girls to stay put, I'm sending an officer to pick them up." He headed for the door, Patrick and me on his heels.

J, the consultant

I managed to catch up to Brian as he rushed out of the restaurant. "Will you let me know if there's something I can do. Or at least with an update." He nodded without looking back.

Returning to the table to get my purse and jacket, an anxious-looking Missy waited for me. "Was something wrong with the food?"

"No, they were unexpectedly called away."

Concern creased her forehead. "Did something happen?"

I was about to play dumb when it dawned on me that most of Mammoth probably already knew about the fire. Quietly I told Missy what had happened.

"Is… is everyone okay?"

"I think so, but I'm waiting for confirmation."

Missy grabbed the back of a chair to steady herself. "Do you think there's something I can do?"

"I suspect the best way to help is to keep everything here running smoothly."

She sighed, then picked up a large bag I hadn't noticed. "Take these with you. Two of the dinners." I began to object, but she added. "Otherwise, they will go to waste with the rest of the food." With the hint of a smile, she added, "I included some more of the roasted beet salad you like."

I accepted the offering and thanked her, leaving a twenty-dollar bill on the table for the waiter. When I reached the lobby, I ran into Sierra whose face was puffy from crying. "Is something wrong?"

It took her a minute to establish eye contact, then whispered something unintelligible.

"I'm sorry. What did you say?"

"That's a stupid question," she snapped and ran out of the room.

To my surprise, a solemn-looking Charlie waited at the foot of the stairs to drive me to the parking lot. In response to my curious look, he nodded toward the long line of guests waiting for transport down the hill. "Boss said you'd need a ride down to your car. He didn't want you to have to wait." I thanked him and inwardly marveled at how Brian could think of my comfort at such a time of crisis.

Neither of us spoke during the ride. When we reached my car, Charlie said, "Brian told me about Aileen's house, but he said everyone's okay."

I couldn't tell if it was a question or a statement, but the angst on his face suggested the former. "Fortunately, Aileen and Taylor went out to dinner, so they're fine. Last I heard a police officer was on the way to pick them up."

Charlie let out a long breath. "He was in such a rush, I guess I just wanted confirmation."

I stopped him as he got back onto the snowmobile. "Out of curiosity, do you, Missy, and Sierra always stay this late?"

"Missy will be here until the dinner rush is over. Sierra always seems to be lurking around." Looking bemused, he added. "I was waiting to take the Reynolds family down to their cars so they wouldn't be transported with other guests."

"Are they still here?"

"Just Fred and his daughter, and as far as I can tell, Fred has no plans to move back home. The missus and her sons left with the family attorney." With a shake of his head, he added. "It wasn't a dignified departure."

Driving home, I started to fret about something I'd heard or seen this evening, but my adrenaline-spiked awareness had diminished. I couldn't make my brain work. All I wanted was dinner and bed. Turning onto our street, I let out a long groan. There was strange car parked in the driveway. I considered texting Ross to say I was still working, then hiding out until the guest left, but that wasn't fair to Ross. Besides, I had no eating utensils in the car.

As I navigated past the strange vehicle into the garage, I saw it was a rental. A jolt of panic hit me when the possibility of an overnight guest crossed my mind. Ross was always telling visiting former ski patrollers they could stay with us when they came to town. Closing my eyes, I took a few calming breaths, then screamed when someone opened the passenger door and yelled "Surprise."

It was Kate. She slid into the passenger seat, and, as usual, her guileless joy chased away my fatigue and bad mood. Or at least, most of it.

"I know you're not getting married for a few days, but I couldn't wait any longer. You're really doing it, J. You and Ross are getting married. You need me! Do you already have your dress? Can I see it? What's the plan for flowers? Is it still just the four of us? Should I…?" Her voice trailed off as she sniffed the air. "What is that divine smell? You picked us up dinner. I told Ross not to tell you we were here, just that there was a surprise waiting for you, and to get home as soon as you could. You must have known it was Nathan and me. Did…"

Nathan started gently pulling Kate out of the passenger seat. "Kate, J must be exhausted. Why don't we let her get out of the car and into the nice warm house?" As he extricated Kate from the car, he said, "Hi, J. Hope you don't mind our early arrival. If Kate had her way, we would have arrived the day after you invited us to stand up for you and Ross."

At the top of the stairs, Ross hugged me, took my bag, and handed me a martini. Kate and Nathan followed, Nathan holding the meal-bag. When Ross saw I brought food, he said, "Oh good, J. You got my message. Since I didn't hear back from you, I was afraid you might have turned off your phone."

"What message?" I took a sip of my drink and headed to the living room to sit by the fire. Mary and Bob were there drinking the 2018 Opus One Proprietary Red I'd been saving for Ross's birthday. I gave Mary the evil eye, but she just held up her glass in a toast.

"You mean, you didn't get any of my messages? Then how did you know to bring dinner?"

"Missy, the Couloir chef, gave me two dinners after Ian, Brian, and Patrick left because Aileen's house is on fire." Closing my eyes, I took another long sip, knowing without looking I'd shocked Ross, Kate, and Nathan. "I'll explain after we eat dinner."

Kate set the table. Nathan poured the wine. Ross plated the food. I supervised from my perch by the fire. Fortunately, the two dinners proved more than enough for the four of us. Conversation was sparse as we devoured the food. All four of us ate as if we hadn't eaten in days.

Missy had even included dessert—raspberry-filled shortbread cookies with chocolate truffles—which we brought into the living room with our cappuccinos.

"So, what's going on, J?" asked a concerned Nathan while my phone simultaneously vibrated on the kitchen counter.

I held up my hand. "This could be the update Brian promised." After scanning the text, my body began to relax.

"Good news?" asked Ross.

Nodding, I read: "*Fire is out. No one hurt. Kitchen and dining room took the biggest hit. Initial assessment is that one of the laptops overheated, but this needs to be confirmed. Patrick, Aileen, Taylor, Joe, and I are on our way back to Couloir. Even if this time it is an accident, they'll be staying there until this matter gets resolved. Am arranging for twenty-four-hour security. Let's talk in the morning.*"

"That's a relief—product failure rather than another attack," said Kate.

"Not necessarily," Nathan said grimly. "Someone could have hacked into the computer's batteries, made the machine think it was in a safe temperature mode when it was already overheating, causing it to explode."

We looked at Nathan incredulously. He shrugged. "I heard about it at last year's American Bar Association conference."

My pulse began to race. "Taylor and Aileen were supposed to be home alone. Going out to dinner was a spur-of-the-moment decision. Ordinarily they would have been asleep by eight or so since they're still recovering from their injuries."

"And if you're hacking into someone's computer," Ross added, "you don't have to enter the house and deal with Joe."

"Joe?" Kate asked.

My mind was racing with the possibility of a third attack, so Ross answered. "A very smart, protective, large dog."

Kate's eyes widened. "Oh."

"J, I tried to explain the situation at Couloir while we were waiting for you, but did a poor job. I couldn't answer any of their questions. You may want to start at the beginning."

I began with Aileen's embezzlement conviction and the Reynolds's campaign to have her fired when she returned to town then the two attempts on Aileen's and Taylor's lives. Ending with Fred's move to Couloir, Maureen's outburst in the hotel lobby, and Cindy's confession.

Kate jumped to her feet, but Nathan was first to speak. "Do the police think the Reynoldses are the ones trying to kill Aileen and Taylor?"

"No, and neither do I. The embezzlement sham and the two assaults are being treated separately."

Kate was indignant. "I can't believe anyone would set up a young woman because of jealousy. What was Aileen's reaction to the confession? She must have been livid, after being tormented by the Reynoldses, vilified by the local press, spending years in jail then being forced to make restitution. Is she pressing charges? Was Maureen arrested?"

"The matter is under investigation, but Aileen doesn't want to press charges." When Nathan started to explain the charging process, I jumped in. "I know. The police chief explained it's not her call, but she *can* make an appeal to the court if the matter goes forward."

Kate fell back into her chair. "But they don't know for certain. Maureen, and possibly her children, *could* be responsible for the attempts on Aileen's life."

Nathan's eyebrows rose. "Maybe we're getting ahead of ourselves. Is the target Aileen? Taylor? Or both?"

Three heads turned to me. I shrugged. "We don't know."

"What do you *know*?" Nathan placing special emphasis on the last word.

"When you get right down to it, not much. We have lots of theories, but other than the actual details of the attacks, nothing."

"What are *your* working theories?"

"Only that it's someone who works at Couloir. More than likely, a member of the management team. Both attacks..."

Nathan cleared his throat then raised an eyebrow.

"Ok, all *three* attempts required knowledge of Taylor's and Aileen's movements. Aileen and Taylor were the only ones in the snowmobile cab when it crashed. They were home alone for a short period of time when the poisoned cookies were delivered. And, if Nathan's right about the computer being remotely triggered to overheat, he or she probably knew there was a large dog protecting the ladies in the house, and that Patrick was still at Couloir. What they couldn't know was Aileen and Taylor had spontaneously decided to go to Bleu for dinner before returning home this evening."

We stared at one another. It was like trying to play a card game with half a deck. It felt hopeless.

Ross stretched, and suggested it was time to turn in. "You and Kate have a big day tomorrow; you both need your rest."

"We do?" Oh no, what had I forgotten?

"Yes, Molly called me when she couldn't find you. She wants to do the final fitting for the dress tomorrow morning."

Kate turned to Nathan. "See, Hon, our timing was impeccable."

I was exhausted but couldn't turn my head off; too much had happened. The house was still. Ross snored softly beside me as I continued to stare at the ceiling. I finally gave into the inevitable, pulled on my sweats, and escaped to the kitchen. The house was illuminated by a full moon shining in through the windows and skylights, so I made a cup of tea without turning on the lights. I gave a little start, splashing hot water on my hand when I saw a dark figure quietly walk into the kitchen. I had to stifle the scream in my throat; my hand was on fire.

Nathan handed me a kitchen towel. "I'm sorry. I didn't mean to startle you."

"It isn't your fault. I'm just rattled and wasn't paying attention." I attempted a smile. "Would you like some peppermint tea?"

He nodded and moved to sit on the small couch at the far end of the kitchen. When he saw it was occupied, he acknowledged Mary and Bob with a nod and took a chair. They smiled back at him. "I couldn't sleep either. Thought I'd come upstairs so I wouldn't disturb Kate." He chuckled softly. "Though I don't think anything could wake her. I wish

I could fall asleep as easily as she does."

I handed him a mug of tea and slid onto the chair opposite him. "I'm afraid for Aileen and Taylor. So far, they've been incredibly lucky; they're injured but still alive. Can't help but think their luck won't last forever, and I have no idea who's behind the attacks. Unfortunately, neither do the police."

Nathan surprised me by pulling an iPad out of his robe pocket. "Why don't we list what you do know?"

With a grateful smile, I nodded. While he created a new document, I thought about the strange path to our friendship. He'd been Mary's attorney. The first time I met him was at Mary's house when he came to discuss her estate. He was compassionate, smart, unflappable, and of course his best attribute, a twin. As Kate, Nathan, and I settled Mary's affairs we discovered the plane crash that killed Bob and Mary had been no accident. During our efforts to uncover the murderer, Kate was seriously injured. Kate and Nathan fell in love and got married. And we learned Mary and Bob were not totally out of our lives.

A hand on my arm broke into my thoughts. "Let's start by listing possible suspects. You said you believed it was someone at Couloir, so let's focus our attention there."

"Sounds reasonable. Let's start with the management team. That includes Charlie—"

"Since I don't know any of these people, why don't you include the area they manage."

"Of course, Charlie's area is grounds and maintenance; Beth oversees IT; Sierra's in charge of human resources; and Tom is the controller. If we're not making any assumptions, we should add Brian, the owner and CEO."

"Great. How about other people that work closely with either of the ladies?"

"Hmmm, there's Matteo. He's the lead bartender, and reports to Aileen. Actually, he did file a sexual harassment claim against Aileen, but Brian thinks Sierra…"

"Let's just list names and positions for now, otherwise I think we'll get into the weeds."

My cheeks burned. I'm usually the one who keeps others on track. You're right. Missy is Aileen's executive chef. From what I've seen, Taylor has a number of supervisors who report to her, but I've never met or heard about any of them."

"Then let's focus on this group. If someone else comes up in our discussion, we can add them to the list. We will operate on the assumption the computer fire was intentional. So, for each of *our* suspects, we need to answer the universal three questions. Does he or she have a motive to execute the attacks? The knowledge or skills required to execute each incident? And the opportunity? Perhaps, we should—"

From the direction of the staircase came a loud whisper. "Nathan, are you up here?"

A smile crossed Nathan's face as he closed his tablet. "I'll format and send you the document. We should talk after you've filled in some of the holes."

And just like that, I was alone in the kitchen. Even Mary and Bob had disappeared.

Aileen, the food & beverage director

Brian brought Taylor, Joe, and me to one of Couloir's larger family suites—two bedrooms with ensuite bathrooms, a living room with a small kitchen, and balcony. I realized I'd never been in one of the hotel's suites—the rooms luxurious, the views spectacular. But we were so physically and emotionally exhausted that as soon as Patrick and Brian left, we went to our respective bedrooms and collapsed. I didn't even take off my clothes; just fell onto the bed and closed my eyes. Dreams came.

The jury foreman yells "guilty" then the courtroom erupts into flames. Maureen leads me out of the chaos all the while insisting I eat some of her cookies, that is, until Patrick shoots her. Feeling something sticky all over me, I shriek when I see I'm covered in Maureen's blood. Cindy tries to wash the blood off my face, as she repeats "I'm sorry" over and over. I want her to quit wiping my face, but she won't stop. Then someone calls my name.

My eyes slowly opened to see Joe licking my face as Taylor gently shook me, saying, "Aileen. Aileen. Wake up..."

"Please don't leave me alone, Taylor."

Without a word, she piled pillows against the headboard of my queen-size bed, and gently sat on the bed next to me. We both fell asleep crying while Joe paced the room, keeping watch.

Day 13

Aileen, the food & beverage director

A knock on the door startled us awake. Joe and I hurried to answer it, as Taylor slowly made her way to a standing position. A concerned-looking Missy entered pushing a cart laden with breakfast goodies, including four cappuccinos. She was followed by Brian and Patrick looking grim and anxious. Brian gave Missy a perfunctory smile and dismissed her. Even half asleep, I could tell he had hurt her feelings.

"That wasn't very nice. You could have been more gracious," said Taylor who had just entered the room.

"I don't feel very nice," barked Brian. He took a deep breath. "You're right, Taylor. I'll apologize when we're through here."

"I think that would be appropriate," I said. "Did you bring clothes from Taylor's condo?"

Brian didn't answer. I turned to Patrick. His jaw was clenched so tightly, I thought he might crack his teeth. Suddenly I was on alert. I could feel tears starting to leak from my eyes as I sank onto the couch. I didn't think I could take anymore. Taylor sat down next to me, and we waited.

Brian looked at Taylor. "Someone broke into your condo and trashed it. The police are there now."

I took Taylor's hand. "What do you mean 'trashed it'?"

Brian looked at a loss for words. Patrick spoke up. "Someone slashed everything. Your furniture, clothes, curtains. Nothing was spared."

Taylor went very still. When she could speak, she asked, "Everything?"

"It looks that way," answered Brian gently.

Tears slowly trickled down Taylor's face.

Brian collapsed on a chair, looking as beaten as I felt. Patrick took two glasses of ice water off the cart, handed them to Taylor and me then took a chair. No one moved or said a word.

After several minutes Taylor stood and let out a long sigh. "I guess that means I *am* a target, not just collateral." She headed to her bedroom. Her voice was shaky as she added, "I'll just go freshen up then let's have breakfast and discuss what we do now."

Taking her lead, I silently headed to my room. I heard Patrick say he would walk Joe as I shut my door.

Taylor and I picked at our food while the men cleaned their plates. I was reminded how differently men and women tend to handle stress. Our conversation was about everything but the fire and the break-in. Patrick said he would go into town to buy us some clothes and whatever toiletries we needed. Taylor said she would make a list. Brian stated we would not be leaving Couloir until an arrest was made. I pointed out that if we were correct in thinking the culprit worked at Couloir, staying here could be a problem. Brian said he hired twenty-four-hour security first thing this morning.

Just as we were running out of logistics to talk about, Ian bounded in. "Wow. Nice digs. Hope you left me something to eat. Between responding to the fire then the condo intrusion, I haven't eaten since..." He made a disgusted face, "... that beet salad last night."

He was so predictable I had to smile and felt the muscles in my neck loosen a little.

Once his plate was piled high with food, he began. "There was no finesse in this break in. The intruder broke a window to gain entrance. It appears he brought his own knife because none of the knives in the kitchen were missing or looked disturbed. We're not sure if anything was taken, but it doesn't appear likely. Whoever did this entered the condo and went berserk."

He swallowed the food in his mouth and addressed me and then Taylor. "Someone really hates you two. First, they try to burn down your house, then they go and destroy everything in your condo. You must have some idea of who it is."

Taylor stood shakily. "I need to excuse myself." She walked into her room and closed the door. To my horror, I burst into tears, and fled to my room.

Taylor texted me. "I think I'll stay in my room until they leave. I need a break."

I answered, "Going to go back to sleep then taking a long, hot shower. See you when it's quiet."

She responded with a thumbs-up emoji.

Rested, pink-skinned and clean, I stared at yesterday's

dirty clothes, hesitant to put them on. With no sound coming from the living room, I assumed Taylor and I were alone. I wrapped myself in the spa robe when there was a soft knock on the door. "Come on in, Taylor."

But it wasn't Taylor. It was Patrick. I ran to him, and he held me. Just like that we were kids again, and together we could overcome anything. Taylor came in, hesitating when she saw us crying together. Patrick threw back one of his arms and we had a desperately needed group hug.

After instructing us to go nowhere on the grounds unless all three of us—including Joe—were together, he promised to get us some clothes and toiletries. Almost as soon as the door closed behind him, Taylor said wistfully. "How lucky you are."

As we left the bedroom, we paused at a full-length mirror. Most of the bruises and scrapes on our faces were close to, but not completely, healed. Bizarrely we started to giggle. Besides the obvious slings we both sported, our faces were the motley colors of camouflage. Taylor quipped, "Aren't we a pathetic pair? But what did you suggest earlier? Oh yeah. Let's focus on the future not the past. I think it's a good idea. Perhaps we should also avoid mirrors."

The living room had been tidied, and the food cart was gone. A note on the counter said there were snacks and cold drinks in the kitchenette, and to call if we wanted anything more. I was hungry. Looking at my watch, I knew why. "It's after five! We slept a long time. Since we can't go anywhere in our robes, let's get room service."

We were trying to decide what to order when there was a knock on the door. Before I could open it, a key card was inserted in the lock and the door opened. Both of us unconsciously backed away, until we saw Joe prance into the room looking smug. Patrick followed carrying several bags. Once in, Joe went back to the door and nudged it closed.

"I hope these clothes work. Most of the stores were short on inventory since it's technically shoulder season." He dropped the bags on a couch and went to get a beer from the refrigerator. We sorted through the bags, knowing the difference in our sizes would make it easy to tell which garments were for whom. I looked at Taylor and raised my eyebrows. No underwear!

"Brian wanted to know whether you wanted to have something to eat in the suite, or the restaurant."

Simultaneously, we both said, "The suite." I added, "I don't think either of us is up for questions and sympathy just yet." Taylor nodded in agreement.

"Fine by me. I'll let Brian know, and he can order. We'll start with appetizers. Anything special you'd like?"

"No, just tell Brian we're both really hungry." Then we each picked up our clothes and left to dress.

Throwing open the bedroom door, I said, "Cashmere sweats, Patrick? I love them. I may never take them off." I laughed as Taylor's door opened and saw she was wearing the identical outfit, except mine were heather blue and Taylor's heather fawn. "Thank you."

Our timing was perfect. Patrick was ushering in the room service waiter, followed by Brian. He was carrying a large bouquet of flowers, and a wrapped package that he placed on the coffee table. "Ah, I see Patrick was successful." He winked at Patrick. "And the outfits match their eyes. Nice touch." I couldn't believe it, Patrick's cheeks flushed.

"The flowers are from Charlie, and Beth told me the package is from Michael. She wanted you two to know he only told her they were books, which he paid for himself. Beth is interested to know the titles. All three wanted to drop by, but I told them you needed some space. Hope you don't mind."

We emitted a grateful sigh.

Brian put the flowers in water, while Patrick tackled the package. I could see there were two identical books. He snickered as he handed them to us: *iWatches for Dummies.*

Brian left after appetizers; Patrick went to his room after dinner. Once they were gone, we turned off the lights; opened the nightshades; and watched twilight turn to night. It was a clear night. Stars began to light up the snow-covered peaks, as the full moon made her entrance. Taylor was the first to retire. Joe and I reveled in the vistas a while longer. The silence soothed my nerves and my soul. Taylor was right. I am a lucky woman. As always, Joe sensed my sentiment and chuffed his agreement.

Brian, the hotelier

It was hard to leave the suite. Taylor and Aileen were telling Patrick and me their plans to modernize the kitchen, since it took the brunt of the fire. They seemed to be recovering better than I. My nerves were shattered. Every time my phone buzzed, I expected the worst. Which didn't help since I still had a meeting with Ian tonight. Of course, it was for dinner. He's a character, but he's very good at his job. While waiting, I listened to voicemail. J phoned to tell me there is a strong possibility the fire at Aileen's was not an accident. She explained that a friend, here for the wedding, told her how a computer could be hacked and programmed to combust the battery. Something like that. But the end result was the computer's battery would overheat and burst into flames. If someone was capable of going to those lengths, he'd have to be really angry and tech-savvy.

I could hear Ian as he entered the restaurant. "Can you bring me a Coors, please."

Just by those few words, I could tell he was as discouraged as I was.

Once settled with his beer, I said, "J called and suggested

the overheated computer may not be an accident."

"I don't know how she gets her information. It's being investigated, but given the rapid string of attacks, I wouldn't be surprised if she's right."

"Let's order and then we'll get to it. Do you have a preference, or should I just get two specials?"

"How about something simple. Steak and fries?"

I had to smile. Beet salad really got to you?"

He made a face.

We ordered Caesar salads, New York steaks medium-rare, fries, and a bottle of Silver Oak cabernet. Then Ian started.

"I don't really have anything. We checked alibis for the time of the fire, but if it's a hacking job, that information is almost useless. As far as the vandalism of Taylor's condo, it's been several days since anyone was there, so it could have happened anytime since then. One neighbor did say she thought she heard someone ranting in or near Taylor's condo last night, but it also could have been partiers on their way home from a night out."

Ian put his hands over his face and let out a long sigh. "I guess I should have cancelled this dinner, but I was hoping you might have some ideas. I don't think I've ever been so frustrated in my career. I mean, clearly, whoever it is has a vendetta against Taylor. You should have seen her condo. Everything that could be slashed, was. Initially we spent most of our time focusing on Aileen's enemies, but now we know Taylor is the target. We don't know if Aileen is too or just very unlucky.

Our meal and wine were served as we contemplated our ignorance.

I had confirmation of how discouraged Ian was when I noticed there were uneaten fries on his plate and he declined dessert.

After he left, I went to the bar and was relieved to see it was quiet. I asked Matteo for a cappuccino.

"Do you want some cognac in it?"

I snapped, "No." Upset at myself for taking my frustration out on Matteo, I said, "Sorry. I'm just so frustrated. I don't understand what's happening. It's crazy. I need to find out who is responsible for this mayhem, and I am at a loss."

"I get it, Boss. We're all pretty shaken by all these attacks. I take it the police don't have any leads?"

"No. Ian is as baffled as I am."

Coffee finished and ready to retire, I remembered to ask Matteo, "You never told me how Sierra got you to file a complaint against Aileen."

He stared at the floor for almost a minute before saying, "She caught me smoking some weed in the garage after a double shift. Told me if I filed the complaint, she wouldn't write me up." He paused, regret plastered all over his face. "I love my job. It's what I'm good at. What can I say?"

I watched him retreat. "Hey, Matteo."

"Yeah, Boss?"

"I hope you won't, but if you ever get into another… ah… situation, come to me. Please."

His face went from self-reflection to self-flagellation, "I hope I'll never need to, but thanks, Boss. Really, thanks."

As I lay in bed, trying to turn off my head, I contemplated the chaos of the last several days. How could we still not know who was behind the attacks? There must have been signs I missed. I felt paralyzed and powerless, two emotions I seldom experienced. In the midst of this angst, I heard my father's words from years ago when my college girlfriend dumped me for my best friend. "There will be times in your life when you find you don't have all the answers, Brian. Plans fail, people disappoint you, or you disappoint yourself. Instead of wallowing in what you don't know or can't control, use it as a time of introspection. Learn and grow from these experiences." I remembered trying to look patient and grateful for his guidance without really listening to his advice. Now I thought I finally understood. As my eyelids grew heavy, my last thoughts were not about the current disaster, rather about my future. Instead of building more hotels, perhaps it was time to do a better job for those I had. Who knew, I might even make Couloir my home. Thanks, Dad.

Day 14
J, the consultant

Still half asleep, Ross and I stumbled into the kitchen to discover a spread of warm croissants, wild blueberry jam, sliced cantaloupe and strawberries, and a buoyant Kate. "Good morning. Please take a seat." She handed Ross a mug of coffee, "I believe you take your coffee black. J, your two-shot cappuccino will be ready in a minute."

Our bleary eyes widened when she added, "How do you like your eggs?"

After two large gulps of coffee, Ross asked incredulously, "Does Nathan get this treatment every morning?" I believe he thought he was being facetious.

Walking in at the end of Ross's question, he said, "I do, indeed." He kissed Kate on the back of the neck, asking, "Espresso?"

Kate giggled—I didn't think I'd ever heard Kate *giggle*—"Coming right up."

Eyes wide, Ross looked at me with an expectant question on his face.

I shook my head.

"Well, I tried."

As we finished breakfast, I said, "Received a rather discouraging text from Brian this morning. Everyone's stymied, including the police. He suggested we all take a break today." Looking at Nathan and Ross, "What are your plans today?"

"Getting a haircut this morning then I thought Nathan and I could go down to Bishop for a round of golf. It's supposed to get into the low to mid-seventies today. Does that work for you, Nathan?"

"Sounds like a great plan. Do they rent clubs?"

"I think so, but we'll bring J's clubs just in case."

"What's our plan?" Kate asked me.

"We have an errand to run this morning, then the final dress fitting. Thought we could have a late lunch up at Couloir so I can check on the arrangements."

Our first stop was to pick up Ross's gift at Daydreams. I reminded Kate that Cindy Reynolds was the owner and artist in case she was at the studio, but I didn't expect I would see her.

Kate was as gobsmacked as I had been the first time I entered Daydreams. "Oh, J, it's like entering a different universe. These works are breathtaking."

To my surprise Cindy walked into the gallery and greeted us. She appeared unaffected by the drama of the last few days. Over the years she must have become very skilled at masking her emotions. I introduced Kate, who chatted enough for all three of us.

On our way out, we praised Cindy's work and thanked her profusely. I left with Ross's gift, and Kate left with two artworks of her own.

Kate looked baffled as I parked in front of Molly's shop. "Where is it?"

"You're staring at it."

"I'm staring at a bookstore and a coffee house."

"Look where the two come together."

Kate scrunched up her face. "I think I see a narrow door. Will we both fit in there?"

Molly and Ashley greeted us as we walked in. After introducing them to Kate, Molly said, "I hope you brought the shoes you'll be wearing." I pulled a shoe bag from my capacious purse.

"The dress is in the back. Would you like help putting it on?"

Suddenly I felt nervous. "No, thanks," I replied ambiguously.

Kate and Molly exchanged a look as I went to the back of the shop.

The dress was stunning. I had feared the squiggles would dominate the dress. Instead, they were like little hints of color that gave the dress life. For some reason I became very emotional. I had to wait for the tears to stop before I put the dress on. I didn't want my tears to stain the material.

It must have taken longer than I thought because Kate yelled, "Are you all right, J? Need some help?"

In response I slipped on the shoes and walked into the front room. "What do you think?" Both Molly and I were staring at Kate.

"Oh, J." Her voice cracked. "You look so… so beautiful. I wish…" Her voice trailed off.

"I wish she was…" Just for a second, I saw Mary standing

behind Kate smiling at me then she was gone.

Ashley broke the spell. "Mommy, where did the other lady go?"

Fortunately, Molly's full attention was on the dress. She walked around me, appraising the fit. Pointing to my cream-colored satin mules, "The shoes are perfect. Jimmy Choo?"

Kate looked at my feet. "*You* bought Jimmy Choos?"

"Hey, it's a once in a lifetime event."

Molly bent down and touched the shoes. "Will you be wearing them with a lot of other outfits?"

"No, just this dress." I twirled around. "Why?"

"I could add some green to them to complement the outfit." Suddenly she stood up. "I forgot the scarf."

Kate gasped as Molly draped the scarf over my shoulders.

"What were you thinking of doing with the shoes?"

"The same green as the dress, but much more subtle."

"Let's do it!"

Once in the car, I asked Kate, "What do you think about me offering to lease a larger, more prominent space for Molly, so she can really get her business off the ground?"

Kate looked thoughtful. "Let me think about it. My first reaction is the offer would have to be worded delicately so you don't trivialize any of her success."

"Please do. We can talk about it before you leave."

Kate talked about the outfit until we were halfway up the mountain to Couloir. In one of the most dramatic changes of topic, she asked, "Do you think anyone will ever figure out who's been after Taylor and Aileen?"

Just like that, my mind shifted gears back to the attacks. "Right now, it doesn't seem like it, but if we don't, Aileen and Taylor will never really be safe. What's keeping me up at night is the fact that I either saw or heard something that didn't jibe, but I can't remember what it is. Maybe it will come to me today, but I doubt it."

"Perhaps you're trying too hard?"

"Probably," I said glumly.

Brian was leaving the restaurant as we entered. He looked concerned. "I thought I told you to take the day off. You must be really busy with your wedding plans."

"I took the day off." I introduced him to Kate, explaining she and her husband were standing up for us. "We just finished the final dress fitting and decided to come up here for a late lunch."

He turned and led us to the hostess desk. Pointing to one of the reserved-view tables, "I think that table would be perfect for these ladies. Please bring them a bottle of Bollinger Extra Brut, and whatever they would like for lunch. Give me the bill."

Before I could protest or even thank him, he was gone.

We both started with French onion soup, followed by Caesar salads with grilled shrimp. As we sipped the champagne and ate our salads, we nattered away like a couple of teenage girls. I glanced around the mostly empty room awed by its elegance. My eyes alighted on the table we'd been sitting at the night before last. It came to me.

Kate stopped mid-sentence. "What is it, J."

"I finally remember what's been bothering me. But now it doesn't seem like the game-changer I hoped it would be."

"Tell me about it."

"A few nights ago, Brian, Aileen's brother Patrick, the

police chief Ian, and I were eating dinner at that table. We'd been served our salads, when Ian received a phone call telling him Aileen's house was on fire. After making sure Aileen and Taylor were alright, the three men headed for the house, the dinners uneaten. I followed Brian and asked him to update me when he had more information, then returned to the table. It couldn't have taken me more than two minutes, and that's stretching it. When I returned for my coat and purse, Missy, the chef, had already bagged two of the dinners, including salad and dessert, which she handed to me. It just seemed improbable she could package all the food so quickly."

Kate leaned back in her chair. "I see what you mean. Improbable is not impossible, especially in a restaurant."

"Damn. I was so sure I was onto something."

I stared at my half-eaten salad, disappointment killing my appetite.

A voice said, "J, I was on my way home when I saw you and your friend having lunch. I have to go away for a few days but wanted to wish you all the best on your wedding day."

I looked up to see Missy smiling down at me. Wrapped up in a down coat, she was clearly ready for the trip down the hill to the garage. When I didn't respond, she frowned. "Sorry, Missy, I was a million miles away. Thank you for your wishes and your help planning the menu. This is Kate. She's standing up for me."

Her coat opened slightly as she bent down to shake Kate's hand. And there it was.

She turned and caught me staring. Her smile was warm

and open. Fingering the scarf, "It was a gift from my mother."

"It looks like sunset."

"It does, doesn't it." She beamed.

I was still while I watched her leave.

Kate looked at me confused while I tore through my purse, cursing myself for its size and disarray. I found the name in contacts and pushed call. Kate started to speak, but I held up my hand.

"Molly. Thank God you answered."

"No, no this isn't about the shoes."

"The scarf you replicated for Taylor. Was it one of a kind? Did you make another one like it for anyone else?"

"Thanks. Got to go. I'll explain later."

I punched in another number. "Come on, come on, answer."

"Taylor, this is J. You know the scarf Molly replicated for you?"

"Please, just bear with me. When was the last time you saw it?"

"Thanks. Promise to explain later. Is Brian there?" It's urgent."

"Brian. It's Missy, and she's on her way to the garage."

"As sure as I can be."

"She did? Whatever you do, don't let anyone eat any of them."

I could hear Brian yell, "*Stop*! Don't eat that."

"Get security to stop her. I'll call Ian."

"We'll be in the restaurant. We're not going anywhere."

Taylor, the guest services director

Aileen and I were dying of boredom. We couldn't listen to Brian and Patrick rehash the same theories over and over again. Aileen got Joe's leash. As she clipped it on, Joe looked as anxious to leave as we were. A walk around the grounds was in order. We opened the door to find Missy about to knock.

Smiling at Aileen, she said, "I just wanted to say thank you for sending me to the Annual Hotel Chef's Forum. I've always wanted to go to one, and this time it's in San Francisco."

Aileen smiled at her. "You deserve it, Missy. You've gone above and beyond during all this chaos. Thank you."

Her excitement evident, she added, "I met with staff and went over menus and assignments. The kitchen should run smoothly while I'm gone." She turned to go.

"Almost forgot. These are samples of the petit fours we're preparing for J's wedding celebration. I used your recipe. Hope you like them."

"Thanks. Knowing you, they'll be fabulous."

The door closed, and boredom instantly returned.

Joe chuffed. "We're taking Joe for a walk."

Patrick was eyeing the petit fours. I gave him my most serious look. "There better be at least two left when we return." Just a few steps from freedom, my phone chirped. It was a harried J.

"Yes, I know the scarf. It's..."

"It's always draped over the chair in my bedroom, there to remind..."

"Brian, it's J. She seems really anxious and in a rush."

Aileen looked curious and Joe looked impatient as I handed the phone to Brian.

"What can I do for you, J?"

"Are you sure?"

"Yes, she just dropped by some cakes."

Smiling for once, Patrick picked up one of the confections.

Brian listened, then yelled, "*Stop*! Don't eat that."

Patrick dropped it back onto the plate as if it were alive.

Motioning to Patrick's phone, "Security. I'm calling them now."

"Where will you be?"

Patrick had security on the line and handed the phone to Brian.

"Listen carefully, and do *exactly* what I say. Missy Stewart is on her way to the garage. Stall her any way you can without alarming her, but if she tries to get away, stop her. Use force if you must, but only if it's necessary. The police will be there shortly, and they'll take over. Oh, and, once you've detained her, stop all shuttles to and from the garage. Let me know as soon as the police arrive."

We were all frozen by shock. Missy? Missy's been trying to kill me? Just because I wouldn't let her stay in my condo?"

A long silence was broken by Joe who was whining softly to go out. Reluctantly, Patrick took him out.

The three of us sat on the couch stunned.

The next sound was Brian's phone. "Yes." He listened. "Resume them when all the police have left."

"Okay. You know where to send her. Thanks."

Brian let out a deep breath. "Missy is in custody. An officer will be arriving shortly to get the cakes."

There was a knock on the door. A tall policewoman whose name tag said Garcia entered, putting on latex gloves. "I'm here to pick up some cakes." Once bagged, she added, "The chief will be with you once he's finished interviewing Ms. Stewart. He requested that no one leave, including J Westmore." She looked around the room. "I hope she's still here."

Brian answered, "She's in the dining room. I'll ask her to come to the suite."

"Thank you. You should tell her she may be here well into the night if she needs to call anyone. Also, the chief requested a room where we can conduct interviews."

"Taylor, will you please call your staff and ask them to open up the adjoining suite and supply it with refreshments?"

"Anything else, Officer Garcia?"

Her shoulders slightly relaxed. "Please call me Elli. I think we're going to be spending a lot of time together this evening." She shook her head. "The chief said J discovered it was Missy. Is that true?"

"It is."

"How?"

"I'll be asking her that question as soon as she arrives."

A few minutes later, Brian opened the door for J and her friend. "We passed Elli in the hall. She said as soon as Ian has an initial interview with Missy, he'll be back. Sounds like it could be a long night."

We all just stared at one another. Finally, Brian asked, "How long have you suspected Missy?"

J looked at her watch. "Less than two hours."

Looking confused, I asked, "What did my mother's scarf have to do with Missy?"

"Kate and I were having lunch in the restaurant. Missy stopped by the table and told me she would be gone for a while and wished me a happy wedding day. I introduced her to Kate. When she leaned over to shake Kate's hand, her coat opened, and I saw the scarf. She said her mother had given it to her."

I was baffled. "But how did you know it was my mother's scarf?"

"Molly told me how she replicated the original for you when she was taking my measurements for my wedding dress. She has a picture of your scarf on the wall in the shop dressing room. It's beautiful."

For a moment I couldn't speak. "My mother gave me the scarf a few months before she died. She told me if anything ever happened to her, it would remind me she would always take care of me…" Grief and emotion took over, I had no more words.

Aileen placed an arm around me. "And she still is," she whispered softly.

J, the consultant

Officers Elli Garcia and Jon Cole were the first to arrive. Both rushed in with a purpose. They interviewed each of us individually in the adjoining suite, focusing on our recent interactions with Missy. I was the first interview. The officers took me through the five minutes I spoke with Missy and the stream of observations that led me to having her apprehended, over and over. It was brain-numbing.

At the conclusion of the last interview, carts were brought in with an assortment of sandwiches, fruits, sweets, drinks, and Ian. Without a word he grabbed a sandwich and walked into the adjoining suite, closing the door. When he returned, he barked, "A scarf? You figured out who was behind all the attacks because of a scarf?"

I shrugged. "Do you want me to walk you through it?"

"Officers Garcia and Cole already did."

Had I upstaged him? He sounded angry.

"Oh, and I hear you're getting married. That's news to me. Linda and I weren't invited. And, if I recall..." He paused dramatically, "You were my best man!"

Ah... That was the problem.

As I frantically looked for the right words, Brian, trying to stifle a smile, said, "There is no wedding celebration, Ian. Or not until this summer. None of us were invited."

Ian looked at me skeptically. "Is that true?"

I nodded.

"Well why didn't you say so?"

Before I could respond, Ian did a one-eighty. "You were right. Missy was responsible for all four attempts on Taylor's and Aileen's lives." Turning to Brian he said, "Now do you understand why I wanted J involved? She has some weird mojo."

Taylor spoke up. "Missy confessed? Really?"

"To everyone in hearing distance. At first her rant was incoherent. It took a while to sort out all the facts. Apparently, the first attack was aimed at you for kicking her out of your condo."

Taylor protested, "I didn't…"

Ian held up his hand to stop her. "It doesn't matter. She thinks you did. It wasn't pre-meditated. Sierra told her you, Aileen, and Tom were going to the high school. She saw the snowmobile pulling the sleigh unattended and decided to teach you a lesson."

"None of these attacks were aimed at Aileen?" Brian asked.

"I didn't say that, though Taylor was the primary target. She said she offered to stay with you to help with your recovery, and you turned her down. When she found out you were staying at Aileen's—the person she believes stole her job—she felt betrayed. So, she brought you two a basket of goodies."

"Then why was Tom driving up and down Aileen's street?" Patrick queried more to himself than to Ian."

"Interesting you ask. Missy was quite proud of the fact she told Tom he needed to go to Aileen's and apologize. She thought if he went to the house, someone might see him and think he brought the cookies. She was really upset the next day when he told her he couldn't get out of the car because he was afraid of Patrick."

"And Missy told you all of this? That's crazy."

"*She's* crazy."

"And the fire?" Brian asked. "Was it an accident or did she set it?"

"J's friend was right. She hacked into Taylor's computer, and..." Ian pulled a notepad out of his pocket. "I had to write it down because it sounded like science fiction to me. Quote, 'I hacked into the battery, and manipulated the values of the temperature to make the laptop think it was in safe temperature mode when it was actually overheating, causing it to explode.' Unquote. She may be bat-shit crazy, but she knows computers."

I suddenly remembered Beth telling me Missy helped with some of her outside jobs to earn extra money. I should have paid more attention.

Ian looked at Aileen and Taylor who both looked dazed. "She'd been watching the house for some time, and knew you two went to sleep early. The day of the Reynolds debacle, when she saw Patrick drive off with you, she heard he was going to drop you off at home and drive back to Couloir. Good thing you two decided to go to Bleu."

Taylor's voice trembled as she asked, "And the vandalism of my condo?"

"Missy said something about you moving in with Aileen to save on rent so eventually you could purchase your own house. Does that ring a bell? When she got to this part of the story, she began ranting again. The little I could understand, that's what pushed her over the edge to finish what she started."

Aileen asked. "Where is Missy now?"

"On her way to psychiatric lockdown to be evaluated. Toward the end of our interview, she devolved rapidly."

We sat in stunned silence.

Taylor and Aileen looked at one another. Both were crying. One of them asked in a whisper, "You mean it's all over?"

Ian squatted down in front of them. In a gentle voice he said, "Yes. All you need to do now is heal—both your bodies and psyches. I strongly recommend you both take advantage of our victims' counselling program." He stood, looked at all the waters and soft drinks on the drinks table and asked in his normal gruff voice, "What, no beer?"

Day 15
Aileen, the food & beverage director

Taylor and I had breakfast in the dining room like normal people. It was our first day back at work. We were both still stunned and more than a little traumatized after yesterday's revelations, but excited to be back. Since we were going to be living at Couloir until my house could be repaired, we didn't have to adhere to a half-day schedule. When one of us got tired, she could just go to the suite and take a nap.

After everyone left last night, we ordered a bottle of Rombauer chardonnay, and talked about the house. The kitchen needed to be rebuilt. Smoke had damaged the walls, carpets, and furniture, so they had to be replaced. I was disheartened to learn my homeowners insurance didn't cover arson. Brian and Patrick offered to give me the money, but they'd already done so much, I declined their offer. A go-fund-me appeal just didn't seem right. So, we tabled the expense issue, accepting it would be a slow process, and focused on the fun part—creating a vision of what we wanted.

Taylor said she liked my idea of designing her room around a single piece of art. For her that was, of course, her mother's scarf, which she wanted to have displayed in an acrylic box like my weaving. Before I went to bed, I sent an email to Cindy and asked if she would clean and repair my hanging and encase Taylor's scarf. She immediately replied affirmatively, sounding like the old Cindy. Giving me hope we could reestablish our friendship.

As we were finishing our coffee, Charlie stopped by the table. "Good to see the two of you back at work. You've been missed. Just wanted you to know the few things that were moved to the conference room have been taken back to your offices. If there's anything you need, just call me."

As he departed, Taylor said, "Did you notice not a word about Missy? I'm so relieved."

"Me too."

As we stood to leave, Fred Reynolds approached the table. "May I speak with you for a moment, Aileen?" The pain on his face broke my heart. This man had once been my mentor.

I nodded to Taylor that I was okay, and she left for her office.

"I… I… don't have the words to tell you how very sorry I am. The hell you must have gone through… I will never forgive myself…"

Out of the corner of my eye, I saw Patrick walk in. His face grew hot with anger as he stormed over. Before he could speak, I said, "Good morning, Patrick. Fred and I are having an important, private conversation. It's time to move forward. Please…" I begged him with my eyes, "…let us continue."

The color drained from Patrick's face. He looked really tired and nodded, saying only, "You're right, Sis. I'll just get breakfast and give you some space."

Turning to Fred, I said. "We have to move forward too. You need to start by forgiving yourself. I don't blame you for anything. Do you think we could be friends?"

"I do," he said softly. "Thank you. You grew up to be quite a woman." He stood.

"See you around?" I asked.

A hint of a smile crossed his face. "You will. I'm staying here for the time being."

He took an envelope out of his pocket and placed it on the table.

I queried him with my eyes.

"The restitution you paid us with interest."

"I can't…"

"You must. This isn't a gift, it's *your* money."

As I walked out of the restaurant, I stopped at Patrick's table. He was reading the newspaper on his phone. I kissed him on the forehead. This time I was the one with tears in my eyes. "Thank you for taking care of me."

His twin-grin from our childhood was back. "Always."

It felt like the first day of a new life. Which I guess it was. On the way to my office, I stopped at Taylor's. There were flowers everywhere. She grinned, "I think my staff actually missed me."

"That's evident."

I sat in the chair across from her desk. "How did it go with Fred?" she asked.

"Few words, lots of emotion on both sides, a promise to

be friends."

"Good."

I held up the envelope he gave me and opened it.

"What's that?"

I gasped. "For Fred, the restitution I paid them, with interest. For us, a remodeled home."

Day 16
J, the consultant

Kate, Nathan, Ross, and I followed the valet into Couloir. Kate explained which bags went with which reservation, while Ross and Nathan rolled their eyes. Neither could believe how many bags we'd brought for two nights. Ordinarily I would agree, but tomorrow Ross and I would become husband and wife. I wanted to look like a bride.

Kate had made us a dinner reservation. As we headed to our room, she instructed us to unpack and meet in the lobby. "Bring a warm jacket, we may want to go for a walk around the grounds after dinner." Clearly excited, she disappeared into her guest dwelling.

Fairy lights lined the path to our accommodations. Outside Couloir's main building were a number of small guest dwellings. Beyond those were a few guest cubes that appeared to be suspended from trees. All the buildings were sided with mirror-like panels that reflected the resort's surroundings. The effect was striking—not knowing where the buildings ended and nature began. Ross and I were staying in the honeymoon-cube, compliments of Couloir. The inside lights were set low as we entered, emphasizing the one-way mirror effect. We could see the lights of the town at the bottom of the mountain with the added benefit that no one could see in.

In the living room we found a bottle of Bollinger chilling, fruit, and chocolate-dipped strawberries.

Ross went for the strawberries, while I stowed the bags, and started to strip. Looking surprised, Ross asked, "What are you doing?"

"Dressing for dinner."

He rolled his eyes but said nothing. Good behavior for the day before one's wedding.

I pulled on a cream-colored cashmere turtleneck and a pair of warm black skinny pants. Wrapped my favorite forest green scarf around my neck and grabbed my puffy. Ross looked at me, then my discarded clothes, and shook his head. Though he said nothing, he made his point. What I'd put on wasn't that different from what I was wearing when we arrived. Walking back to the hotel I offered, "I admire your restraint." He almost smiled.

Fairly certain Kate had asked for a corner table, I was surprised when the maître d' led the four of us *through* the dining room out to one of the decks. The view of the town below and the rising moon were spectacular. A table for four was elegantly dressed, a low bouquet of white roses and orchids as its centerpiece. It was surrounded by heaters. Tears threatened as I took it all in.

"Surprise!" Kate said.

As I took my chair, I noticed a small bench between Kate and me. She saw me looking. "I said we needed it for our purses and coats, but I was hoping we might have guests."

"You thought of everything."

Two waiters approached the table—one with a bottle of Dom Perignon Brut, and the other with assorted canapes: smoked salmon, olive tapenade, prosciutto with chive cream cheese, and tomato with shaved parmesan and pesto. When the waiters left, I realized Mary was drinking champagne she poured into an emptied water glass and reaching for a canape, while Bob was opening up a bottle of Stag's Leap cabernet he'd found on a side table. All the while Kate retold the story of how the two of us had discovered who was responsible for all the recent attacks at Couloir.

The evening was a blur of friendship, superb food, fine wine, and a few tears. It felt like it was over in minutes, which in truth was close to four hours. Next thing I knew Ross was holding me, as we fell asleep. Our last night living in sin.

Day 17

J, the bride

I was dreaming Mary, Bob, and I were cross-country skiing in the Lakes Basin when I felt someone gently shaking me. "J. J. Wake up."

It took me a moment to transition. It was my wedding day. I opened my eyes, then confused, closed them again. It was pitch black outside.

I heard Ross grin. "J, wake up. I have a surprise for you."

"It's still night. Come back to bed."

"That's part of the surprise. Besides, it's morning." I put my pillow over my head. "Come on, J. I promise it's worth it."

Trying not to groan, I slowly sat up. "It may be morning, but the sun doesn't think so."

"Get up and put these on." I looked at the clothes he'd laid out for me. Long underwear, Patagonia ski pants, turtleneck, sweater, socks, gloves, beanie, and my ski jacket.

I was confused. "We're going skiing?"

"No. We're going to snowmobile up the mountain so we can see the sun rise on our wedding day. And, if you don't start dressing, we'll miss it."

As my brain started processing, I understood how much planning this must have taken. "Lovely. Give me five."

"Just don't make it ten."

We walked out of the cube to a dark but crystal-clear morning, where a snowmobile sat idling.

"How did you…?"

"I'll tell you over breakfast." And we were off.

Ross must have given dawn a bonus because the rising sun had never been so breathtaking. He held me as we watched and kissed me after the sun cleared the mountain peaks. For my part I cried.

"Let's go back. I'm starving," he said, breaking the spell.

As Ross piloted us down toward Couloir, my heart soared. It was the beginning of a perfect day. My bliss was shattered when I heard Ross scream, "*No! Hold on!*" as our vehicle left the ground.

Gas fumes seemed to suck the air from me. I couldn't open my eyes. For a brief moment I thought I was dreaming then remembered. I must have been thrown clear because I felt no pain. But Ross. Where was Ross? I struggled to get up, until strong hands lifted me. I managed to open my eyes. It was Mary. My voice cracked as I said, "Oh, Mary. Thank you. Once again, you've come to our rescue."

She looked so sad. "I'm sorry, J. Not this time."

Hearing her words almost knocked me over. I hadn't heard her voice since the plane crash. But I wouldn't, couldn't think about that. "Ross?"

She turned and pointed. Bob was helping Ross stand. Relief flooded me. Then Mary pointed past Bob and Ross to the mangled snowmobile and the two bodies that lay beneath.

Epilogue

Three days later Kate was finally cried out. She left the guest room and went upstairs to J's kitchen where Nathan was eating breakfast. Just seeing her come upstairs made Nathan rejoice. There was no way to adequately comfort someone who had lost her two best friends. He would just have to be there and wait. They'd spoken little since Brian told them about the accident. Words had been inadequate. But he stayed near and hoped it was enough.

Nathan was again heartened when Kate poured herself a cup of coffee, sat down next to him, absentmindedly picked up a piece of toast off his plate, and nibbled. "I think we need to get J and Ross's affairs in order and plan a memorial." Her voice cracked on the last word and Nathan took her hand. With a slight smile of affection, she said, "I'm okay. But I'm sorry, it will be a while before I can act normal. First Mary and Bob, now J and Ross." She didn't bother to wipe the tears spilling from her eyes.

He squeezed her hand, then surreptitiously pushed another piece of toast to her side of his plate. He thought it best to let her converse at her own pace, so he continued his support of attentive but quiet.

"I've been thinking about their memorial. Neither of them are…" She stifled a sob, "…were big on formalities. Perhaps an unstructured gathering with food and drinks."

"Sounds like a good idea. Where were you thinking about holding it? Here?"

"No," she snapped. She took a deep breath. "Sorry. I can't bear the idea of people walking around J's house."

He was about to say it was her house now but thought better of it. He didn't think she knew, and now was not the time to tell her. Instead, he waited.

"I was thinking Couloir. If the weather improves…" Looking outside she realized it was a bright, warm spring day. Slightly disoriented, she asked, "When did spring arrive?"

"A few days ago. If you look at the gardens, you'll see the daffodils and crocuses are coming up."

"If it's not booked, we could have it on the decks at Couloir. Though Brian may not want it there. He and his staff have been through so much already. And that was before the accident." Kate blew out air as if she'd just run a mile.

"Brian has already offered it as a venue for whatever you want to do. The whole staff seems anxious to help. He said if you're amenable, give him the parameters and he will take care of the rest." Nathan sensed working with Brian on the memorial would help Kate, at least for the time being.

"I don't know how we get the word out or how many there would be," she said, looking a little overwhelmed.

"That shouldn't be a problem. Once we have a date and time, I'll respond to all the emails we've received from people asking if there's anything they can do. You wouldn't believe the number of emails Couloir has received. They've been forwarding them to me as they arrive." Seeing her brighten, he took a chance, adding, "You should go downstairs and look at the front porch."

She cocked her head and stood. He had her interest. Nathan was about to suggest they open the garage door to look, but she opened the front door. Flowers, notes, and packages spilled into the mudroom.

She started to laugh and cry at the same time. Nathan knew she was on her way back.

Hoping the time was right he said, "J, Ross, and I met the day after we arrived to update and consolidate her trust and his will. In addition to several sizeable bequests to nonprofits, they left two individual bequests. One to Michele and her twins, and the other to someone named Molly Burton. I can't remember exactly what she said, but it had something to do with helping her with a new business. Do you have any idea who she is?"

Nathan finally saw Kate really smile. "I know exactly who she is. I think it will mean the world to her."

The day of the memorial was sunny, clear, and warm. Kate and Nathan had taken a room at Couloir for the nights before and after the memorial. As Kate had hoped, the gathering would be on the deck that wrapped around the hotel. Nothing about the venue hinted it was a memorial, except for three pictures: one of Ross in his ski patrol uniform, one of J with a chickadee perched on her finger, and one of J, Ross, Mary, and Bob. Kate and Nathan waited for people to arrive. She looked anxious, he left to get them each a glass of wine.

Aileen and Taylor walked around, making sure everything was in order, when they saw the pictures. They looked at one another, stunned. Approaching Kate, Aileen asked, "We were just looking at the pictures. Who is the couple with J and Ross?"

"That's J's twin and her husband."

"Will they be here today?"

Tears pushed into Kate's eyes. Taylor and Aileen looked at each other, concerned but puzzled.

Just as Aileen was starting to apologize, because Kate looked like she was closing down, Kate replied, "A few years ago, J, Mary, and Bob were flying back to Mammoth. The plane crashed. J was the only survivor."

Taylor and Aileen couldn't mask their shock.

Kate looked at the two young women closely. "You've seen them?"

Words escaped both of them. They nodded.

Tears threatened, but Kate forced them back. "You must be really special."

Nathan approached, handing a glass of wine to Kate. Something had happened. Kate was on the verge of crying. "What's up?" Taylor and Aileen expected Kate to say "nothing." Instead, she said, "They met Mary and Bob—recently."

Nathan looked at the two injured women with a kind of awe. "After this is all over, would you tell us about it?"

The women nodded, still too bewildered to speak.

And then they came. Young, old, dressed up, dressed down, crying, laughing. Friends from as far away as Marseille. They just kept arriving. Kate and Nathan were blown away. There were high school friends, ski patrollers, Mammoth

Mountain personnel, book club buddies, locals, clients, and people who were rescued by one or both of them. Kate had met or heard about many of them from J. It was overwhelming, comforting, and life affirming.

After the last few guests left, happy stories ringing in their ears, Kate and Nathan sought out Taylor and Aileen. They suggested a cappuccino in the bar. First the ladies wanted to know how Kate and Nathan knew Mary and J. They were surprised to learn Kate had been Mary's personal assistant and best friend, and Nathan her attorney long before either had met J. Kate had only intended to share a bit of her story, but found herself recounting the plane crash, discovery it had been murder, Kate and J's attempt to find and capture the killer, and the dramatic conclusion.

Slightly embarrassed by her lengthy monologue, "I'm sorry. We wanted to hear your stories, not bore you with ours."

Aileen laughed. "Trust me. That was not boring. I met them on a few occasions. The first time on the deck outside the lobby. I was having a rough day, saw them standing on the deck, coatless while it snowed, and I brought them blankets. What I remember is how full of self-pity I felt until they looked at me. Then I felt such peace." Aileen looked at Taylor.

"The only time I saw them was when I was in the hospital. Aileen and I were recovering from the effects of a poisoning, and I was panicking. They came to my bedside and comforted me. Much like Aileen said, I felt such peace."

Kate relaxed as she told the ladies a few stories about Mary and J. But soon it was clear all four of them were physically and emotionally exhausted.

As Kate and Nathan walked back to their room, Kate started crying. Nathan held her. "Too many memories?"

She shook her head.

He held her and waited as the convulsing sobs that wracked her body began to slow.

"We'll never see them again. They're back together. There's no reason to stay."

Nathan felt a loss bigger than any he'd ever experienced since losing his twin. Kate was probably right. He hadn't thought that far ahead.

Despondent, they went into their suite. Kate stopped at the bathroom to splash cold water on her face. Nathan took their coats and hung them in the closet. Burdened with a new sense of grief, they walked into the living room to find Mary and J arguing over the sweets in a gift basket, while Bob and Ross opened a bottle of zinfandel.

Life was about to get more interesting.

THE END

About the Author

As a child, Terry Gooch Ross became an avid reader of mysteries. Think Nancy Drew. Add in a little supernatural and she was in heaven. When her twin Mary lost her husband Bob then died suddenly, Terry's grief was overwhelming. She turned to the only way she could think of to deal with it—she temporarily altered reality by writing mysteries centered in Mammoth Lakes, her hometown of many years, where Mary and Bob frequently appear to help, protect, or simply hang out. She loves Ross, cross-country skiing, long walks, living in the mountains, and of course, Mary.

ALSO BY

TERRY GOOCH ROSS

A Twin Falls

When a soul mate dies, it doesn't necessarily mean she is gone. A *Twin Falls* is a story of mystery, fantasy, and friendship set in Mammoth Lakes, California. When one twin and husband are killed in a plane crash, the other, sole survivor of the crash, discovers the bond of twin-ship transcends death. With her sister's help, Janet Westmore solves the mystery of how her twin died, and foils the killer's second attempt at murder.

A Twin Pursuit

After solving the murders of her twin and brother in law, Janet Westmore retreats to her Mammoth Lakes home high in the Eastern Sierra mountains. Before she can slip back into a routine, a young homeless mother with twin babies arrives on her doorstep late one night in a blinding snowstorm - sent, of course, by Mary, her twin. And so our accidental sleuth sets forth on a snow-filled season of extortion, kidnapping, and attempted murder.

A Twin Pique

There's something about Janet Westmore that attracts mystery. Ever since her twin Mary and Mary's husband Bob were killed in a suspicious plane crash, people seem to show up on Janet's doorstep with regularity, bringing obscure riddles and conundrums. And Janet, who's called J, can't resist her amateur sleuthing. Good thing Mary and Bob still have her back.

www.ingramcontent.com/pod-product-compliance
Lightning Source LLC
LaVergne TN
LVHW011657050325
805087LV00011B/904

9781977258618